Hunting the Dragon

Hunting the Dragon

Waves of Darkness Book 8

Tamara A. Lowery

Steele Rose Publishing

Hunting the Dragon

By

Tamara A. Lowery

All rights reserved

Waves of Darkness series, Copyright 2011 Tamara A. Lowery

Hunting the Dragon, Copyright 2025 Tamara A. Lowery

Tamara A. Lowery DBA Steele Rose Publishing, 2024

Cover art, Copyright 202 Fatima Saddiqa

Interior art, Copyright 2021, 2024 Tamara A. Lowery

talowery.wordpress.com

Published in the United States of America

ISBN eBook 978-1-956849-61-5

ISBN print 978-1-956849-60-8

Table of Contents

Dedication

To:

Morgan, Jen, and Danielle

For:

Being brave enough to Become their true selves in the face of a society that is encouraged to fear, hate, and oppress them.

In Memoriam

Chattacon

1975 - 2025

Acknowledgements, Warnings, and Foreword

These. Books. Are. Not. For. Children.

I just wanted to be clear on that point. I don't write YA, which is such a BS name for an age-related genre, since the "young adults" are only adults in the sense that their bodies are capable of producing offspring. Mentally and chronologically, they are very much still children.

My pirates are not nice people; they are, after all, sea-going international criminals. Vampires, by definition, are serial killers. There is violence and sometimes graphic sex in this series. You have been warned.

That being said, **Hunting the Dragon** is the start of a new story arc in this series. The Sisters of Power arc wrapped up in **Maelstrom of Fate** with the defeat of Juma and Celie becoming the All-Mother. For those of you new to the series, feel free to jump to the Here Be Spoilers section in the back of this book to get a general idea of what has come before.

I also occasionally Tuckerize and/or red-shirt real life people in my stories. Tuckerization is the act of making someone a character. Red-shirting is a term borrowed from Star Trek fandom and involves not just making someone a character but killing said character off horribly. The sole red-shirt in this book has been red-shirted before in **Black Venom,** the fourth book in the series.

Matt Barnett was an annoying coworker, who is now a supervisor. He complained that I failed to give him a sex scene before killing him. So, I brought him back as a namesake uncle to his first character, gave him a sex scene, and killed him twice (for a grand total of three, if you count the book 4 incident). You'll have to read this book to find out how I managed a literary double homicide with a single victim.

Oh, and if I haven't offended you yet, give it time

Daughters

of the

Dragon

Once Upon a Tide ...

The woman stood on the western shore of a great sea. Ebony hair fell to her hips, so dark it swathed her in shadow save for blue glints of reflected moonlight. The glow of her pale skin put the full moon to shame.

Slowly, deliberately, she stepped into the gentle surf and waded out. A flash of light burst from the milky-white crystal suspended between her breasts the moment it touched the water.

She continued to wade forward until she vanished beneath the surface.

In the next moment, she stepped onto a sandy beach. Not a single drop of water marred her skin or hair. The reddish glow from beyond the dunes indicated a fire. She walked inland until she reached the glow's source.

A bearded man with skin almost as dark as her hair sat tending a small driftwood fire. On the opposite side of the blaze stood what appeared to be her reflection.

She continued to the fire and took a stance directly across from the woman who looked like her.

The man stood and smiled at her, but she saw the sorrow in his eyes. Glints of silver flecked the beard she last saw as blackest wool. She wanted to reach out and offer comfort but felt the compulsion which called her here now hold her motionless.

"Thank you for your concern, child. Welcome home."

"What troubles you, Elder? Why have you called me here? Why do I see my Sister instead of the All-Mother?"

At this last question, the other woman answered. "I no longer bear the mantle, my Sister."

Fear and anger roared through her, and she broke free of the Elder's compulsion enough to turn to face him. She saw him stagger at the psychic break and a streak of white appear in his hair. "Why have you stripped my Sister of her power?" she demanded.

"Celie, stop!" the other woman implored. "He hasn't fully recovered. You could kill him in his current state."

Celie closed her eyes and took a calming breath. When she opened them again, she noticed the Elder would not meet her gaze. He instead offered a look of gratitude to her sister.

"Gloribeau, what happened? Why? I don't understand." Her voice sounded like that of a lost child even to her own ears.

"She is not ready yet, Elder. The mantle of All-Mother will prove an even greater burden to her than it has been for me if we pass it to her now." Gloribeau looked at her twin with the same sorrow in her eyes as held in the Elder's. "I asked Zeke to remove the mantle from me to protect the All-Mother. My succubus-like nature makes it difficult for me to resist sharing my bed with powerful beings. There have been angels and demons seeking me out. When I share my bed, I share power. Against such lovers, I am not strong enough to retain all my power. The All-Mother cannot be allowed to be weakened or destroyed in that manner; else the world is doomed."

Zeke, the Elder, finally spoke. "I agree; Celie is not yet ready to take on the mantle, but one day she must. She is the only one who can." He sighed and stared into the fire.

Slowly, the crystalline image of a woman sharing the same features as the twins appeared in the flames. She reached out and caressed Gloribeau's face then turned to her other daughter. Gloribeau collapsed to the ground, sobbing.

"Your sister can never again bear my mantle or take my form. She willingly forfeited that privilege and duty in order to protect me. She will retain her native power just as you do. My magic will be divided into seven parts and distributed between both of you and five women of Zeke's choosing. When the time is right, the champion of your choosing shall gather the portions and deliver them to you. The heart shard you wear shall be the key your champion requires."

Celie bowed her head. "As you decree, All-Mother."

Celie knew the Elder's mind well enough to realize he would not only pick women with enough natural magic to safely wield the portions of the All-Mother's power but ones who wouldn't easily surrender it. She needed a champion equal to the task and powerful enough to survive whatever perilous challenges they set him. Not knowing how long it would be before she felt ready to accept her role as All-Mother, she planned to ensure her champion would survive beyond the natural lifespan of men and still retain his youthful vigor.

Only a few months later, she found the man she wanted in a small mountain village by a stream called Brandewyne in the local tongue.

A marauding tribe from the north made a foray on the village and killed most of the men. A young man returned to the village the next day from a successful hunt to find the marauders in the midst of debauchery.

Celie observed, hidden by her magic, as the hunter withdrew before his enemies saw him. He returned that night and moved furtively about, taking note of the location of each warrior. He then began his preparations for dealing with them.

The next day, the hunter strode boldly into the center of the village at first light and called out a challenge to the leader of the marauders. A burly, savage-looking man emerged from the former chief's hut, took one look at the young hunter, and said, "Looks like we missed one. Who will swat this buzzing fly for me? He interrupted a good fuck."

"Coward," the hunter sneered. "You had no problem slaughtering old men. Do you fear to face even one young man in honorable combat?"

The invader scowled as his men grew quiet and gazed in his direction. "You dare to call me a coward, boy? This one is mine!"

He hefted his war club and advanced.

The defender produced a bolo from his cloak and began to twirl it. His opponent raised his club directly in front of him to block the anticipated throw and continued to advance. He reached a small white pebble on the ground, and the defender released his weapon.

Rather than fly toward his target's head to wrap around the defensively raised club, the bolo struck his ankles and snarled his feet together. The marauder lost his balance and fell forward. A sharpened spike, hidden under a drift of leaves, caught him just under the chin.

The young hunter leapt forward and seized up the war club. He brought it down hard on the base of the marauder's skull.

He turned and noted where the rest of his enemies stood. As he'd planned the previous evening, none noticed the leaf piles in front of their huts or surrounding the central area where he stood; nor had they noticed the old, dead vines strewn about.

He crouched as if in anticipation of a group attack, thus luring a few more into the positions he wanted them in. He grasped one of the vines and studied their advance. With a quick tug on the vine, he pulled several small holding pegs out of the ground at each leaf pile.

Only a couple of the marauders avoided instant impalement as long, flexible rods with multiple spikes attached to them sprang up from their hiding places. Still, their night of debauchery slowed their responses. The hunter reached both men before either could reach their weapons. He used their erstwhile leader's war club to shatter their limbs, but he didn't go for the killing blow.

Instead, he went around and dispatched the impaled marauders. He organized the survivors of his village to remove the dead and the spike traps. During this, he ignored the two maimed men.

Once the village regained some semblance of order, he turned his attention to his remaining foes.

"You shall serve as a warning to any others of what I do to those who try to take what is mine," he decreed and turned to the women and old men who now looked to him as chieftain. "Strip them and drag one to the north path and the other to the south path. You and you, cut two young trees about twice the height of a man and trim them into sharpened poles."

At the north end of the village, the new chieftain ordered a hole dug to an arm's depth. Once the laborers finished, he instructed them to hold their crippled victim down with his head to the north and to spread his legs.

"Just kill me and be done with it, you bastard!"

He smiled down at the man. "I don't think so. Your death shall be slow and full of suffering."

Without further warning, he took the sharpened pole and began working it into the man's rectum. He went deliberately slow to keep his victim conscious for the ordeal.

The man screamed himself hoarse, intermittently cursing his tormentor and begging for a swift death. The young chieftain continued to stoically work the pole further in, twisting it whenever he met too much resistance.

Once he finally had it far enough in to provide an effective anchor, he instructed his followers in helping him stand victim and pole on end then dropped it into the hole.

The pole travelled further into the man's gut, and his screams filled the air until blood and darker fluids began to burble from his mouth, effectively strangling him. His flailing only made it worse, the pole traveling further up inside him to pierce into his organs.

The chieftain, knowing the prisoner would slowly suffocate as he bled out internally, led his people to the opposite end of the village and repeated the procedure on the other marauder.

Celie entered the chieftain's hut that night. She wore a simple shift of silky material previously unseen in that part of the world. She'd arranged her hair according to the local style, however.

The young hunter hid his startled reaction to the sight of the unfamiliar woman well. "You are not from my village."

"I am not. I came here because you have impressed me with your cleverness, your prowess in battle, and your ruthlessness."

He raised an eyebrow. "Are you offering yourself to me? What do you have to impress me with aside from your beauty"

She scooped the flame from his fire as if water from a pool. The living flame danced about on her palm until she poured it back into the larger blaze. Even as he rose and grasped her wrist to examine the undamaged skin of her palm, she said, "I'm sure I can produce something."

"*Vrajitoare!*" He shoved her away from him. She just smiled and waited for him to regain his composure.

He glowered, but she saw his body react to her. "How do I know I can trust you? You may just be some hag trying to steal my soul."

"I will change my appearance." Her clothing turned to animal skins, her complexion darkened to a rich bronze, and her hair took on a dry straw color and texture.

"You prove my point."

She held up a finger. "I wasn't finished. Take this stone in your hand. It is proof against my magic; then call in as many of your people as you like and ask them what they see. Will that be proof enough for you?"

"You say I will see through your tricks if I hold that stone?"

She nodded.

He took the milk-white crystal from her. "We shall s—." He peered hard at her then eased to the doorway and motioned for the first person wandering by to come in.

An old woman came in with a child in tow. "Yes, *domnul*?"

"Describe this woman."

While the old woman seemed confused by the command, the child answered right away. "She looks like the men from the north but much darker, and she dresses like us. She has ugly yellow hair."

"Is this what you see, *bunica*?"

The old woman nodded.

"You may go; be sure to reward the child for his honesty." He dismissed them and returned his attention to Celie.

"And what do you see when you look at me?" she asked with a knowing smile.

"You look as you did when I first saw you. What do you want with me?"

"You are cautious, but you are not afraid. Good. I need a champion. I have searched far for one."

"I have seen how powerful your magic is. Why do you need a champion? Who do you fear?"

She laughed. "I fear none, but I am not at my full power. A time is coming when I shall inherit my Mother's mantle. Soon her magic shall be divided and dispersed throughout the world to powerful women for safe keeping. I am forbidden to seek them out. I need a champion to find them and collect the magic for me."

He smirked as he returned to his bed furs. "What would I get in return?" He stripped his clothing off, making clear one of the things he expected.

A slight tremor of nervousness passed through her at the sight of his full arousal. Unlike her sister, Celie retained her virginity. Her hesitancy showed.

He raised an eyebrow and stood again. Slowly, he approached her. She remained still, watching him.

"You haven't answered me," he said softly.

She took a deep breath to calm her nerves. "I do not know how long the quest will take; therefore, I will grant you near immortality. Only the removal of your heart or head will kill you. The women who will become my Sisters in power will be jealous of their new powers and will not part with them easily; therefore, I will give you the strength of many men and the ability to fly like the birds."

He undid the clasps of her shift and watched the silky material slide to the ground and reveal her in all her glory.

"I like the sound of that." He grasped the back of her head and kissed her. With his other hand, he brushed the soft curls between her legs and probed her depths.

"You are virgin. Now I understand your sudden reluctance." He continued to stroke her.

She found it difficult to concentrate, but she had to warn him. "There is a price for this power. I — I can give it to you, but you must drink human blood to retain it and keep it s-str-strong!" Her voice trailed off into a scream as he slid three fingers inside her and split her maidenhead.

"That is a price I am willing to pay. I have always drunken the blood of my prey." As if to prove his claim, he laid her down on the furs and lapped up the virginal blood before he took her.

When dawn arrived, he rose with a feeling of vigor, such as he'd never known before. He found himself more than ready to pick up where he'd left off with the witch. She, however, stood fully dressed by the doorway.

He would have to do something about that.

She held up a hand, and he found himself immobilized. He noticed she once again wore the crystal which had protected him from her magic.

"I have shared power with you. My blood sated you for now, but soon you will feel the Hunger. As you feed, so shall your power grow. Those you feed on shall rise from death and be as you, but under your command."

"How exactly am I to feed?"

"You have the tools you need."

Only then did he realize his teeth felt odd. He found his canine teeth grown longer and sharp like those of a cat or wolf.

"What is your name, *vrajitoare*?"

"I am Celie. What is your name, my Victor of the Brandewyne?"

"I am called Vlad." He cocked his head to the side. "What does this word vik-tor mean; *domnul*?"

She shook her head. "No, it means *invigator*."

He grinned. "I like the sound of that. From now on I shall be known as Viktor."

She returned his smile. "When I return to you, Viktor, I shall give you this stone to safeguard you from my Sisters' wiles. For now, they have yet to be chosen by the Elder; so, your quest must wait. Spend this time exploring your new powers and learning to control them."

With that, she vanished before his eyes.

Viktor soon learned a thirst for blood wasn't the only hunger he'd acquired. His sexual appetite grew nearly insatiable. He also learned the power of his gaze. He had but to catch a woman's eye, and she would cater to his every whim.

Eventually, he grew bored of the women in his village and felt compelled to search abroad for new lovers.

He found one who quickly became his favorite in the slave market of a seaside village. Her raven hair and dark eyes reminded him of Celie. Her natural resistance to his gaze intrigued him further. The trader told him she'd been stolen away from a land far to the southeast. Her creamy bronze skin attested to the truth of the claim.

He had to have her.

Daring to try something new, he directed the power of his gaze on the slave trader. When he saw the slightly dazed look on the man's face, he knew it worked. "Give her to me and forget you ever saw either of us."

Without a word, the man removed the girl's shackles and handed the lead of her collar to him. He then turned away from them and shook his head in confusion. He yelled for one of his younger handlers and boxed the boy's ears for leaving hobbles on the ground to be tripped over.

Viktor removed the girl's bonds and collar as gently as she would let him. The whole while, she watched him warily with something between curiosity and hatred.

He smiled reassuringly at her and reached to caress her face. She bit his hand hard enough to draw blood. In that moment, he felt her will cave to his even more strongly than his gaze could accomplish.

"I mean you no harm. You don't have to fear me."

"Then release me, please!" Tears brimmed in her now terrified eyes, and he felt her will fighting against him in futility. He didn't recognize her language, yet he understood her and spoke it perfectly.

"Very well." He released his hold on her will.

She blinked and staggered a moment. "Who are you? What are you?"

"I am Viktor, and I'm no longer sure of what I am."

She cocked her head and studied him. "I sense the truth in your words. I will come with you."

"What is your name?"

"You are a strange man. All those who stole me, bought me, or sold me gave me new names. My true name is Lilith."

Viktor took his time with Lilith, earning her trust and even making her his wife. He did not take her until their wedding night.

Upon seeing him naked for the first time, she asked, "What is that marking on your back, Viktor? Is it some kind of animal? I've never seen anything quite like it."

"It is a dragon, my love. It is my totem and gives me strength in the hunt."

His answer seemed to satisfy her.

During their lovemaking, his Hunger took him. He'd neglected it for weeks while he wooed Lilith.

Before he realized what he was doing, he bit deep into the soft spot where neck met shoulder and fed. The euphoria of fresh blood flowing down his throat in great gulps paired with the sensation of filling her body with his erased any control he still held.

When he felt her body spasm around him, he continued on until she grew limp. Finally, he came with a roar of ecstasy.

Only after his senses returned did he see his bride, limp and pallid, below him. Her torn throat glistened with the barest trickle of blood. The contents of her bladder and bowels soiled their legs as well as the bed furs.

A grief stronger than he'd ever known tore through him.

☠

He cleaned her body and sat watch over it the rest of the night and into the next day. Per the custom of his village, he planned to bury her after the third day.

The second night, he felt a strange sensation and a familiar presence. A cold hand rested on his arm.

"Viktor, my love, what is wrong?"

"Lilith?" He remembered the witch's words finally. Anyone he fed on would rise from death and be as him.

"I am Hungry."

"I know, my love. Stay here. I will bring us food." He sensed she wanted to go with him but was powerless to disobey.

He went to the doorway of his hut and sent his power out until it encountered conscious minds. He'd fed to some extent on nearly every member of his village. It gave him total control over them. Soon two villagers answered his silent summons, their faces blank.

He sent one to stand near his bride and called the other to him. He fed first. Lilith took her cue from him and began to gorge on the blood of the other villager. She did not stop until her prey breathed no more.

Viktor soon surmised how quickly this situation could go bad. Remembering the witch's words once again, he ripped the heads off their victims to prevent them from rising and competing for food.

The morning brought the revelation that Lilith died with the dawn. In a state of panic, Viktor called to her, and she awoke. He felt how much weaker she'd become in just those few moments. To his mind, she seemed more like an empty vessel than his Lilith. No personality shone behind her eyes.

"Lilith, come back to me."

Finally, she returned to her body. "Viktor, what is happening?"

"I am not sure, my love. I think maybe you are dead but not dead. You died at sunrise. I called you back, and you awoke; but I had to call you again for your *inima* to return to your body."

She clung to him. "Please, do not leave me alone! I fear only your touch is keeping me alive."

"You may be right. Come with me to the Brandewyne. Maybe fresh water will help you."

The moment sunlight touched her skin, she screamed in agony and jerked free of his grasp. Her body collapsed in death once more just inside the hut. The hand he'd recently held now resembled a charred bird claw. He didn't understand why the daylight burned her flesh.

The next night, Lilith rose with the Hunger upon her. Viktor once again presented her with a fresh victim to drain.

This night, she led him to the furs after they disposed of the remains of their meals. During their passion, before he thought to stop her, she followed her instinct to feed.

She drained him to near unconsciousness before she returned to her senses. He felt like he was dying. He sensed a drastic shift in the balance of power. He found himself bound to her will just as he'd bound her to his. He also sensed she remained unaware of this development.

In his anger and fear he sent his people a compulsion to ensure she never realized it, a decision he later regretted.

Shortly before he lost consciousness, he felt his body begin to heal and realized he wouldn't die that night.

At dawn, villagers entered his hut and dragged Lilith's lifeless body into the sunlight. Flames consumed her leaving behind a pile of ash and two glistening fangs.

When Viktor awoke, he saw the results of what his villagers did at his behest.

Raw, primal rage consumed him.

He slaughtered every soul in the village, down to the last child, and impaled the corpses just as he had the two marauders. None would rise again. The mass feeding amplified his powers and senses to new heights. He detected the thread of power which connected him to Celie, and his rage found a new focus.

She failed to warn him he could die this way or would lose the daylight forever once he did. She'd cost him the woman he loved.

He reached out along the connection and roared at her. "I am Viktor of the Brandewyne no longer, *vrajitoare*! I am Dragon! I vow to do everything in my power to prevent you from ever becoming All-Mother. Your meddling cost me my bride!"

Far away, Celie trembled at the psychic attack— and for the first time she felt true fear.

Desperation grasped Celie's mind. She had to find some way of salvaging this unforeseen turn of events and repair the rift with her champion. She turned to her sacred fire and scryed to see the details of how and why he turned against her.

"I bring you a peace offering."

Dragon turned from his victim to face the witch he blamed for all his woes. "Begone, *vrajitoare*. You have nothing I desire unless you can restore my Lilith to me."

Celie bowed her head and allowed a single tear to slide down her cheek. "That is forever beyond my power, even were I the All-Mother. Her body was consumed by holy fire. I cannot undo that."

He returned to his meal and ignored her.

"Viktor."

He refused to respond.

"Vlad."

Again, he ignored her.

She approached him and touched his shoulder tentatively. She *had* to mend this breach of faith. "Dragon," she whispered.

He dropped his victim's drained body and turned to face her, his countenance impassive.

She met his gaze and noticed his eyes began to glow. This fascinated her. She caught the sense he wanted her to leave, and she almost felt willing to comply, briefly forgetting why she'd come here to begin with.

Celie smiled at him. "Your power has grown much faster than I expected. Your eyes are quite— captivating."

Some pain managed to make it past his pretended indifference. "Why do you continue to torment me?" he growled. "Is it not enough you cursed me to this unnatural existence?"

"It was not meant to be a curse, Dragon. I did not foresee the fate of your wife or her feeding on you. I came back to offer a mitigation of your condition."

"A mitigation?"

She nodded. "You are slowly dying. I cannot stop that now, but I can offer you a means of enduring the daylight when you rise as undead."

"You have my attention, *vrajitoare*."

She winced at the vitriol behind the appellation. "I can give you the ability to take on the form of any animal you feed from. With fur or feathers, you may move freely during the day. You will have to swallow some of the fur, feathers, or flesh along with the blood to achieve transformation."

"How will you give me this ability?" Clearly, he did not trust her words.

She produced a small box and held it out to him. "You still can eat solid food. This is called moly. Add it to your food twice a day until it is used up. Do not try to use it more often. In large amounts, it can make you sick or possibly kill you. "

He took the box, opened it, and sniffed the rough brown powder inside. "The fact you warned me against the potential for poisoning is the only reason I believe you."

"It is good you are skeptical of me. It shows you will use great caution when the time comes to seek out my Sisters."

The look he gave her, while not entirely hostile, made her nervous. His smile looked more appraising than forgiving. She tried to hide her apprehension as he moved closer to her. The fact he sniffed the air around her didn't help.

He gave a masculine growl of satisfaction at her gasp of surprise when he cupped her face in his hand.

She closed her eyes and leaned into the warmth of his touch, memories of their one night together flooding through her. She found she desperately wanted to repeat the experience.

He laughed. "I smell your need, *vrajitoare.*" This time, his words held his own lust rather than venom. He leaned down and kissed her, his hand moving to bury itself in her hair and grasp the back of her head.

She melted into the kiss, her guard momentarily dropped. She tasted blood and recognized the trap a moment too late.

Dragon placed his other hand on the witch's throat and did not release her from the kiss until he felt her swallow. Once he felt the connection to her will click into place, a revelation struck him. She possessed enough power to break free of this temporary bondage, yet she did not try.

He pulled back from the kiss and studied her face.

"I first chose Lilith because she looked so much like you, and she was strong. I could not control her so easily as the women of my village. I took my time earning her trust and love."

Celie remained silent, sorrow, or perhaps pity, glistening in her eyes.

"Making love to her was almost as delicious as my one night with you. It meant more to me, though. I loved her."

She reached up to caress his cheek. "I know you do not love me, Dragon, but I have longed for your touch since we parted."

"And I yours, *vrajitoare*. I know you do not love me, though. You sought to make me your tool."

She shook her head. "No, I sought to make you my champion."

His impatience with the game grew short.

"Strip."

He watched the mix of nervousness and anticipation on her face as she complied to the order. A growling groan of appreciation escaped his lips at the perfection of her body.

He intended to have some measure of revenge, and he intended to enjoy it thoroughly.

Before the witch could react, he took her to the ground, freed himself of his lower garments, and plunged forcefully into her softness. A wave of power rushed over him when she orgasmed from this one simple, if violent, act. In that moment, he realized she could break his hold on her at any time she wanted.

He needed to do something about that.

The wave of pleasure which took Celie stunned her. She hadn't expected her body to react with such intensity. Before she could regain her senses, Dragon began to thrust, slowly at first but with increasing speed and force. She writhed beneath him, unable to catch her breath or think clearly.

A second orgasm wrenched a scream from her.

She heard the man above her give a guttural growl then felt a sweet, sharp pain which made her vision grow white.

Celie and Dragon found themselves standing, facing each other in a featureless, soft glow.

She raised her hand to her throat and felt warm wetness. When she looked at it, blood coated her fingertips.

"You *bit* me?"

"By the gods! You are delicious! I want more." He reached for her.

She tried to step back. Her feet would not move. Still, he seemed to be in the same predicament and could not touch her.

The Elder appeared beside them.

"I put a stop to this foolishness before any more damage could be done. Celie, after seeing the fate of your sister, you should have known better."

"I hope to win him back as my champion, Elder."

"Ha!" Dragon let loose a bark of spiteful laughter. "You can *never* repay what I've lost because of you, *vrajitoare.*"

"You will not speak unless spoken to," the older man reprimanded.

Dragon's defiance showed plainly. He opened his mouth to retort. No sound emanated. He crouched as if to attack the older man and found himself frozen in position.

The Elder returned his attention to Celie. "I called you to this place outside of time to warn you of your miscalculations. You created a powerful predator without fully understanding his full nature or anticipating his malice. You cannot seduce him back to your service, child. In fact, you have compromised the possibility of ever taking the mantle of All-Mother."

"He is not the One Who Will Bring Change."

"How have I compromised, Elder?" she asked, clearly confused.

"Your careless eagerness: first, to find a champion as quickly as possible and well before you are ready to receive the Mother's blessing; second, your confusion of lust with loyalty."

He continued, "This being drank your blood. He now has the means to see your plans even as you form them. Luckily, you are powerful enough to resist any control he tries to wield over you."

Only then did she feel the force of Dragon's will. The compulsion to look at him, to touch him: it threatened to overwhelm her.

"Forgive me. I didn't understand."

Even she couldn't say for certain whether the plea was directed at the Elder or the vampire.

Dragon's eyes blazed with hatred.

In the next moment, he vanished.

"Celie, you can never be with him again. Each time you lose power to him. He is too new to accrue power of his own to give back."

She hung her head, finally aware of how her efforts to secure her future only served to imperil it. The Elder placed a gentle hand on her shoulder. She met his gaze with tear-brimmed eyes.

"There is still hope, child. The One will come to you. I have foreseen it. You must exercise patience and caution. Dragon will do his utmost to thwart you and your champions."

"Champions? I don't understand."

"You will choose others for this quest. All but one will fail. Be very selective, Celie. With each failure, you shall sacrifice power, and you will grow old."

With those words, mists swirled about her, and she found herself on an unfamiliar shore.

Chapter 1

Viktor turned to see Celie standing at the edge of the cemetery. He blinked to hide his surprise.

"I didn't hear you approach, Mother."

"Mother? Vik, are you saying that is old Mother Celie?" Hezekiah blurted.

The young woman with crystalline hair nodded and smiled. "Hello, Hezekiah Grimm. You knew me as Mother Celie; I now wear the mantle of the All-Mother. I am the embodiment of Hell's Breath Island."

She turned her attention to her foster son. "You are the One-Who-Will-Bring-Change; the true Viktor Brandewyne."

"I read the inscription; I know there was one before me thought to be the One. I didn't realize he bore the same name."

She waved her hand over the graves surrounding the black monument. The inscriptions became legible as the years of weathering faded away. Every stone bore the name, Viktor Brandewyne. The dates ranged back millennia.

"There have been scores before you. Each had some potential to fulfill the task of restoring me to a physical body. None ever made it past more than three of the Sisters before they met defeat."

"Which three?"

"It depended on what order they found them," she replied.

He just grunted. "At least now I understand why some of them refused to believe I was the One."

Hezekiah interrupted. "Forgive me, Celie; Vik said my daughter was 'born of the island.' Does that mean she'll become a Sister of Power?"

She shook her head. "No, she is going to be more powerful than any of them when the time comes. The time of the Sisters is finally coming to an end. Already their powers have started to wane; it was borrowed power, after all. Only Gloribeau will retain her full strength."

"If my suspicious are correct, their powers started to weaken before I was born," Vik said.

"Yes; that is why I took the gambles with you I did. I didn't train you to the job from your youth; I let you choose your own path with the occasional nudge, of course."

He smirked. He recognized now what he'd missed as a boy. All she'd had to do to keep him on the course she'd chosen for him was to expressly forbid him to do something. She knew his inherent rebellious nature and encouraged it without seeming to.

"I did more than that, Viktor," she said as if she'd heard his thoughts; she probably had, for all he knew. "I arranged for your initial encounter with Juma."

This news genuinely surprised him. He leaned back against the black granite marker and crossed his arms. "Do tell, Mother."

Zeke seemed to materialize from nowhere. "I helped her. I sent the sea witch to sing up the storm you sailed into." He held up his hand to forestall any interruption.

"She didn't know why I wanted her to, so don't go fussin' at th' girl."

"I wasn't going to," Vik said. "I'm just curious why you both wanted me to cross Juma's path— and at that time."

"To give you the tool you would need to succeed, and the edge you will need to fulfill your ultimate purpose," Celie replied.

"The curse?"

"The transformation; the curse part of it only provided incentive and motivation for you to complete your tasks. I reasoned the powers you've gained would agree with your nature. You are not the first vampire to be created the way you were, although Juma had no hand in making the other one."

"Who did?" Hezekiah asked.

"I did," she replied.

Vik noticed she looked embarrassed about it. He began to suspect where the conversation would eventually lead. He pushed away from the stone and took a step closer to her.

"Something went wrong, didn't it? What do I need to know about this vampire; and what do you need me to do once I find him or her?"

Relief crossed her features. "You always were quick to catch on, boy. I like that about you. However, this is a conversation best held indoors. Even on Hell's Breath, some things should not be spoken of openly."

"Celie?" Brianna blinked and peered at her as the group entered the cottage.

Vik and Hezekiah looked at each other surprised the woman recognized Mother Celie despite the drastic change to her appearance.

"Yes, child; I have become the All-Mother now."

Brianna smiled and embraced her. Celie whispered something to her, and she pulled back nodding, laughing, and crying all at the same time.

"Oh yes! Very much so! *Merci; merci!*" She hugged her again.

"The children will remain asleep until I have done this for you. No sound we make will disturb them," Celie proclaimed. "For now, we have important matters to discuss."

Viktor noticed Zeke remained reverently silent. The old wizard shot an adoring glance at Celie when he thought no one was looking. He wondered what the exact nature of their relationship had been or was. Zeke had always called Celie Mother; and she'd called Zeke Uncle; but Vik didn't know if those were just honorifics or true reflections of their connection.

If Celie noticed the looks, she didn't let on.

"Millennia ago, not long after Gloribeau was forced to relinquish the mantle of the All-Mother, but before the Sisters were ordained, I saw the need would arise," Celie spoke. "I already knew what powers were to be distributed, and I helped Zeke decide on the candidates to become Sisters. Juma was chosen to be the trusted courier to deliver each power one at a time."

Zeke spoke up. "My decision to strip Gloribeau of the powers for her own safety dictated that the courier would not be permitted to transport more than one at a time. The magicks had to remain divided. Celie and I both saw they would be reunited at some time, and she would take up the mantle of All-Mother."

"I was to be the last to receive my portion; necromancy, because I already had a talent for it from birth," Celie resumed. "I knew how all the other powers worked. Gloribeau and I, being twins, had a deep connection then; it has faded over the last few centuries. I was determined to recruit a champion to quest for the powers so I could unite them and claim my place."

She paused and lowered her gaze to the table with a heavy sigh. Zeke reached over and gave her arm a comforting squeeze. She smiled and looked directly at Viktor.

"Being young and foolishly impatient, I made the first vampire. He was much like you in cleverness and intelligence. I did not fully understand the nature of what I had created or what he was capable of."

He narrowed his eyes, trying to come to terms with Celie's admission of a mistake. Belladonna sent him a reminder of his similar admission to Carmella. He cringed mentally; he'd forgotten she was listening in on the conversation and mildly surprised Zeke hadn't blocked her.

"I have been guilty of the same with Carmella."

She gave him a grateful smile for his understanding. "I know the siren reminded you of that; but thank you for being mature enough to admit it."

"Why did you make the vampire specifically?"

"I wanted to make sure he would have the ability to face and survive all the Sisters. Unfortunately, another attribute he shared with you was his appetite for women. Before long, he turned one of his lovers."

"Granted, I'd expected something like that to happen," she continued. "I didn't expect the extreme difference in nature between my creation and his, though. There had never been a vampire made by another vampire before."

Viktor stroked his beard and said, "So, in essence, she was the first true vampire. She had the same limitations all vampires but your original and I have; correct?"

"Viktor, at this time you are the only vampire with little or no limitations or weaknesses. His new Childe had to obey him, of course; but he kept her as a lover and did not keep up his control in a moment of passion. She bit and infected him. The change came about gradually over about a month; but he eventually became as all other vampires are now."

"He did not like that he found himself under her command because of this, and he destroyed her before she could fully realize the power had shifted. He also blamed me for his predicament."

"He intercepted Juma," Zeke interjected. "She had already delivered powers to the other Sisters. He used his ability to influence to convince her to keep the necromancy for herself rather than deliver it to Celie and make her more powerful. In his spite, he wanted to make sure she never gained all the powers of the Sisters to become the All-Mother."

"But you cured me; surely you could've cured him," Vik said.

She shook her head. "I could have before his Childe turned him, but not after that without possessing all the powers of the All-Mother. Once his body died and he became true vampire, he went beyond my ability to lift the curse. The best I could do was to give him his transformative ability, much like the one you and Jim possess."

"I did that in an effort to win him back to my cause," she continued. "I thought if I gave him a means to once again move about in daylight, he would relent and seek out the other Sisters."

"He proved me wrong."

"So, he just decided to remain bloody uncooperative?" Hezekiah asked.

"Worse," Zeke said. "Over the millennia, he arranged for the weakening of at least two of the Sisters. He recruited the demon which seduced Gloribeau and stole a good portion of her magic; more recently, he arranged for Venoma to cross paths with that slave trading magician. Dorada, Clarissa, Circe, and Rosalia were all responsible for their own weakening."

Viktor posed another question. "Were any of my predecessors made vampire?"

"No; once I saw how it turned out with the first one, I determined the risks seemed too high. Part of me believes my reluctance led to their failures. By the time you arrived, I'd lost the skill to do it; hence arranging for you to cross paths with Juma, whose power had grown as mine had diminished."

She turned her gaze directly at him, and he became lost in its depths. He saw and understood much he knew she would never say. He was the only one she'd raised from infancy; all the others had been chosen as older boys or young men. She'd believed the All-Mother had sent his mother to her as a last, desperate hope of regaining a corporeal form. She'd carefully observed his development and guided it to make him the man he'd become. She'd almost sacrificed her last chance and not set him on an intercept course with Juma, not out of fear of unleashing another monster upon the world but out of love for him. In that, Zeke intervened at Hell's Breath's behest.

He also saw what she wanted him to do.

"What is his name; and how do I find him?"

Hezekiah and Brianna both scowled with shocked concern.

"Vik, you can't mean you want to hunt this creature down."

"Oh, I do, Mr. Grimm. He is enemy to the All-Mother, to me." He fixed his friend with a chilling stare and added, "and to you and your family."

"What?" Brianna exclaimed. "Why? We have never even encountered him."

Hezekiah grasped the gravity of the situation quickly. "He's the one who sent that vampire bitch we bottled up."

"Aye." Vik looked at Celie and Zeke for confirmation. "Celie made him, and they shared some faint connection. If I'm not off course, he always sent out hunters every time you sent out a champion, didn't he?"

She nodded. "He did. Occasionally they found and destroyed my Viktor before he could even locate one Sister. He did not come after you until I set you to find the Sisters. He saw my love for you and my reluctance to set you on this course as a sign of admitted defeat. I saw his rage and his dispatch of his eldest surviving Childe to hunt you down and destroy you. She was sent, because you were the only Viktor equipped with the means to truly stand a chance of being successful."

"He is vindictive beyond reason. He knows you defeated her somehow but did not kill her. When he learns how— and he will learn how— he will stop at nothing to wreak vengeance on those responsible for her defeat and imprisonment." She looked at Brianna. "If he does not kill Hezekiah before he learns he is the only one who can release his Childe from her imprisonment, he will go after you and the children to try to force her release. He will recognize Celeste as my heir and will seek to kill her or worse."

"Or worse?"

Hezekiah supplied the detail. "He'll turn her vampire in an attempt to control the All-Mother."

Zeke nodded.

"That is why the island brought you here and blocked my memory of you," Celie said. "The Dragon cannot set foot here. Hell's Breath is my holy ground."

"The Dragon; so that is why Carpathia was called a Daughter of the Dragon," Vik said. "Is that his only name?"

"He has many names and changes them every century or so to avoid detection by human hunters." Her mouth quirked up in a sardonic smile. "That has been one of my gambits in our age-old battle. It vexes him to no end that I set the first hunters after his kind and taught them the weaknesses of vampires. To be hunted by your own prey can be a troubling thing."

Viktor chuckled. "Aye; pirate hunters have learned that the hard way when they've encountered me. I take it you do not know what name he uses now."

"No; he does not personally say his names very often, especially if he suspects I am listening or watching. He made that mistake only once and learned quickly from it."

She placed a hand on Viktor's and gave him an apologetic look. "Had I been able to get word to you at the time, I could have advised you to learn from the captain of Carpathia's ship where his orders came from."

Zeke looked down at the table for a moment, which drew everyone's attention. When he looked up, he said, "The Dragon will send other hunters, but she was his best. He will want to investigate her disappearance personally. You must ready yourself for him. To do so, you will need to study vampire lore and hunting techniques. I believe you know where the closest resources are for that."

Vik nodded.

"New Orleans."

Chapter 2

Celie stood. "If you gentlemen will excuse us, I need to speak with Brianna privately."

Grimm shot his wife a worried look.

Brianna smiled and patted his arm reassuringly. "Do not worry, husband. I think I know what this is about. I'll tell you later. You and the Captain need to discuss your plans, anyway. Now shoo."

Vik chuckled at his friend's stubborn expression. "You won't win with either of them, Hezekiah. We might as well stretch our legs a bit."

Reluctantly, Grimm rose and joined him at the door. "You coming too, old man?" He looked around for Zeke, but the old wizard was no longer present.

With a shrug, the two pirates left the cottage.

"I never saw Zeke leave," Brianna commented.

Celie snorted. "He vanished before I told those two to leave. He's going to get them a little more sorted out about what they need to do."

"*Merci boucoup*, for this gift, Mother."

She smiled at the younger woman. "I have seen how good a mother you are, child. It is now within my power to fully heal your womb, if that is truly your wish."

"Oh, *oui,* it is!" Brianna nearly wept with joy. "I adore my children, but I want more so very much."

"Very well, child," Celie laughed. "I will also give you a special gift. You shall have the choice of whether or when to conceive. I do suggest waiting a few years between, if for no other reason than to give each child the attention they will need."

Brie sobered a little at the advice. "I hadn't thought of that, Mother. Thank you for your wisdom. I am reminded of some women from my village who bore children nearly every year. They lost several as infants, too."

She patted her hand and smiled comfortingly. "Brace yourself. This will hurt at first."

Without further warning, she placed a hand over Brie's womb and fed power into her. Sharp pain doubled the young woman over her hand. She held her up, refusing to allow her to crumple as she so obviously wanted to.

The pain proved intense enough to take her breath and prevent her from screaming. Brie clutched her arms and gritted her teeth. Childbirth didn't hurt this much.

Just as suddenly as it came, the pain vanished. Warmth flooded through her from the waist down. She felt her opening relax, and hot liquid flow out in a sigh of relief. Looking down, she saw blood soaking her skirts.

"Mother!"

"Easy child. You are under My protection. No one other than the two of us are aware of this mense. Even Viktor cannot smell the blood." Celie, the All-Mother, waved her hand, and the blood vanished as if it had never been. "The damaged tissue left your body with that flood. In one month's time, your full fertility will return."

Brianna digested the implications of this statement. "Hezekiah will be at sea with the Captain by that time."

"Unfortunately, yes."

"I shall treasure the time with the twins until opportunity arrives to give them siblings."

Celie smiled at her. "You were chosen wisely, Brianna Grimm. You do Me proud."

"You boys pull up a rock. Viktor, you didn't happen to bring any tobacco with you?" Zeke addressed them.

The vampire blinked in surprise. He felt around in his shirt and pulled out a large pouch of pipe tobacco. "I forgot I'd brought this for you, Uncle." He looked over at Hezekiah. "There's enough for both of you, although I never thought to find you here, Mr. Grimm."

To his further surprise, his friend waved off the offer. "I haven't had any since I've been here, however long that's been. Time seems to move differently on Hell's Breath. I don't really miss it, and I don't have a pipe, anyway."

Even Zeke raised an eyebrow at this information. "You are the first man I've met willing to give up smoke freely offered, Hezekiah Grimm."

The pirate smiled wryly. "Tobacco is much easier to give up than opium was." He sighed wistfully. "Although, I would give my left nut for a bottle of gin."

Viktor laughed and shook his head. "Your and Jon-Jon's fondness for that rancid bilge water."

"Honey mead is all well and good, but I miss the bracing bite of gin."

"I'll fetch you some bottles before I set sail."

His former first mate scowled at him. "Oh, I'm coming with you, Vik. This bastard you plan to hunt threatens my family. I'll not sit by in bucolic bliss while you risk all. It would unman me. How could I ever think myself worthy of my wife's bed?"

He held up his hands. "Peace, Hezekiah! I'll not say you nay. I just didn't feel I had the right to ask you. I have missed you, old friend."

"So long as that's settled. Besides, someone has to keep you and that firebrand siren from killing each other or the crew."

"She missed you too. We shared a bottle of gin to mourn your loss."

Grimm's eyes bulged. "Vik, I thought we agreed to never give her strong drink again. She nearly buggered poor Brumble to death last time!"

"She snatched the bottle away before I could stop her. Don't worry. She hates it as much as I do. Took one mouthful and promptly spat it against the bulkhead."

"Well, that's a small favor. I take it you finished the bottle?"

"Aye. I dreaded the thought of giving Brie the news." He grew silent for a while, remembering how horrible he'd felt during that bleak time.

Grimm smile. "She can be— difficult when she's upset, something I work hard to avoid."

"I forget," Vik added in an effort to change the subject. "When I was looking for her, I wound up shutting Percy Worthing down— permanently."

"What about the girls?"

"Cut 'em loose. They can do better than that sorry bastard."

Zeke nodded his approval. "You have gained mercy and wisdom, boy. However, do not let go of your ruthlessness entirely. You will need it in the trials ahead. The contained vampiress is but the leader of several. They will not be forgiving of what you did to their eldest sister. They know they are not as powerful as she is. That will make them more dangerous."

"You mean they won't make Carpathia's mistake of underestimating me. Her defeat will make them set arrogance aside and see me as the threat I am," he replied.

"It may. It may also make them try to be more clever around you. Some will be curious as to how such a young vampire could defeat their eldest sister."

He thought about this for a while. "Part of Carpathia's downfall was her desire to use me to get free from her master and take his place. I have to wonder if some of the others have the same desire for freedom."

"I'm not sure I follow your tack, Vik," Grimm interjected.

"Think about it, Hezekiah. I know we stayed out of it, but the colonies have been fighting for freedom from British rule and taxation. Thia wanted free of Dragon. It's like a fever spreading from place to place. Let one do it, and others see it *can* be done. What if I can turn some of his Daughters against him and get them to help me track him down?"

Zeke scratched his cheek and stared into his fire after giving it a good poke. "If you can encounter them separately, you might have a little luck with some of them. Don't try it if there's two or more of them together. They won't trust the others not to report them to their master.

Best just to kill 'em, if you can. As that wild girl can tell you, they are beyond dangerous when they hunt as a group."

"Belle's branding; I remember that."

Zeke looked at him. "I know you ain't stupid or careless, boy. Just remember, they've been predators a lot longer than you've been alive. I fear you may lose much you call important before this is done with."

"I will do what I must to make sure Mother is safe, Elder."

"I know you will." He stirred the fire some more then turned his attention to Grimm. "Celie's finished her business with your wife. Best you go pack and make your goodbyes to your family."

Chapter 3

Lazarus dozed in feline form on a coil of rope. With the Captain gone ashore on Hell's Breath, he knew nothing would threaten the ship or crew.

He appreciated that his animal forms allowed him to function in full daylight. He'd truly come to enjoy basking in the warm afternoon sunlight, something he'd never survive in his human form, since he was vampire.

Voices, plural, roused him. Who could Vik be bringing back to the ship? Surely not the old man.

Then he caught the scent, both familiar and unexpected.

His hackles raised, his back bowed, and his tail fluffed to twice its normal girth. He began yowling loudly in shock.

Viktor alit on the quarter deck near the caterwauling black cat. He set Grimm on his feet and stared at the creature with minor irritation and some amusement.

"Damn it, Jim. Announce it to the whole world? Stop that infernal noise."

The cat immediately silenced but remained fluffed up.

Hezekiah chuckled. "I've missed you too, Rigger." He looked around at all the crewmen staring at him. "You'd think you lot of lazy barnacles had seen a ghost. GET BACK TO WORK!”

Viktor grinned at the sudden increase of activity on deck. “Mr. Jon, fetch a couple of bottles of gin and meet us in my cabin. Mr. Grimm informs me he’s a bit thirsty after his prolonged absence.”

“Aye, Cap’n!”

☠

“Belle will be joining us soon. She decided to cut her hunt short,” Viktor announced.

Jon-Jon went to the liquor cabinet and retrieved four glasses. He’d already deposited the two bottles of gin on the table. “Which do you want, Cap’n?”

“Straight rum for now. Put one of those glasses back. Belle is not permitted rum, and she doesn’t like gin any more than I do.”

“Aye, Cap’n.” The ink-covered giant of a man put the one glass back in the cabin. “Out of curiosity, why is she not allowed to have rum?”

“Remember how she was when we came back from the Singing Mermaid in Tenerife?”

Jon-Jon blanched. “Aye, I thought she was gonna bugger me right there on the deck.”

“She would have if I hadn’t stopped her. As you probably remember, I sent Brumble to her, since he was the only crewman I figured she might not eat afterwards.”

“I remember that,” Hezekiah interjected. “Poor bugger couldn’t walk for a few days afterwards.”

“A testament to my skills,” the siren in question said as she entered the cabin. Viktor noticed with gratitude that she'd stopped by her cabin to dress first. "Welcome back, Mr. Grimm. I'm glad to see you weren't eaten."

"Thank ye, Belle. I share the sentiment; believe me."

"Pet, we need swift passage to New Orleans."

She gave him a look of extreme distaste. "Jeorge."

"While I hope to keep him as an ally, he is not the reason I am going there," he let her know. "I need to get in touch with Mr. Westin. He has valuable information."

"Information about what?" He heard the outright skepticism in her voice.

"Hunting vampires."

Silently, she asked through their link, *"Are you mad? You know how dangerous the Daughters can be. Granted, you are unusually powerful for one so young, but they have the advantage of numbers."*

"Thank you for the respect of keeping your message private, pet. On this, you may speak openly at the present."

"If you go hunting the Dragon, the Daughters *will* be sent after you. Of course, they probably would anyway once word of Carpathia's fate gets back to him. I still think you should've killed Wormsloe."

"I understand your concern, pet. Setting Wormy free, however, will work to my advantage. It will draw my prey out. Zeke already cautioned me about the Daughters if they hunt in a group. I will kill them before I let them attack *en masse*. If I encounter any individually, and if possible, I hope to turn them against him."

She just blinked at him and crossed her arms. "That you even think that's possible."

He smirked at her. "Not only possible but probable, Belle. Remember, Thia hoped to use me to free herself from her master and take his place. I've seen how jealously Jeorge guards his own power. I'm willing to bet the loss of their leader has kindled some of their ambitions. That may open them to manipulation."

The siren opened her mouth, closed it again, and repeated the process while adding a head tilt.

Grimm chuckled at the comical display. "I believe the Captain is learning how to play politics."

"Matter of survival, Mr. Grimm. I still loathe the process and have little patience for it. I merely do what I must," Viktor responded.

"Actually, that's not a bad idea. Even if none prove helpful or cooperative, it will sow dissent and distrust among their ranks. If enough wish to claim Carpathia's position among them, they may act recklessly rather than in their usual calculated methods of hunting," Belle said.

"Since I have met your approval, pet," he said with a sardonic smile, "I need you to sing up a wind to speed us on our way. I would like to stay ahead of the hunters rather than be caught unprepared."

She stuck her tongue out at him and headed topside to fulfill his request.

"I know you will have to deal with Jeorge when we get to New Orleans," Belle said later, alone with Viktor in his cabin.

"Aye. He will need to be aware of the storm coming. Only a fool would think this won't touch him eventually. Carpathia figured out I make port there semi-regularly,

I'm sure Dragon will have no trouble learning the same. My own daughters may have to go to another territory. It would be a poor repayment of his hospitality to draw further wrath down on him."

The siren kept her thoughts shielded from him. She personally didn't care what happened to the king vampire of New Orleans. She did know Viktor seemed to like him, however.

He gave her a knowing smirk. "I know you believe we'd be better off if Jeorge and his entire kiss were eliminated. Still, he has offered me no reason to kill him, directly or by proxy."

"Fine."

She jumped a little when she felt his hands from behind cupping her breasts. As long as they'd been together, it still unnerved her a little at how fast he could move.

"You're trying to distract me."

"Mm-hmm," he murmured into her hair. "Is it working?"

His breath felt warm against her ear, and his lips nibbled playfully along the upper edge. She closed her eyes and shivered.

"Yes."

They didn't talk much for quite a while after that.

Chapter 4

Ethan Wormsloe felt like he'd swallowed pure bilge. He dreaded his upcoming audience with his master so much he toyed briefly with the idea of just sailing back out of port and never looking back.

He knew better than that. Absolutely no doubt rested in his mind that the creature he knew as the Dragon would hunt him down should he fail to report. The summons to return came less than a month after he arrived in a European port from his latest stint in the western hemisphere.

Now he found himself sailing up the Danube River from Salinas, bound for the river port of Galati. He would learn there whether to continue upriver or to travel to his fate by land.

Only one other being could instill this kind of dread in his heart. He'd held a healthy respect/fear of Bloody Vik Brandee since they'd first crossed paths as boys in the salt marshes of Savannah. Now he knew the pirate to be vampire, as well, he counted himself lucky to have come out alive from their last encounter.

He did not like the fact he was caught between these two devils or that they seemed bound on a collision course.

Maybe he'd get lucky, and the Dragon would be angry enough to kill him outright. He doubted it; but he could hope.

Dragon cared not that some might see his anxiousness to get news from his emissary as weakness. Any foolish enough to think that only made themselves easy prey.

Carpathia fell silent several months prior. He knew she still existed. As her Sire, he would've felt her death. What he hoped to learn from Captain Wormsloe was why his eldest Childe failed her sacred duty. He'd sensed the seeds of rebellion early on in her hunt. Had she betrayed him?

More and more, he felt sure she had turned against him and now somehow was shielded from his mind, as impossible as that seemed. How else could he explain how the All-Mother walked the earth in Celie's form?

Oh, if only he could sink his fangs into that bitch. Perhaps he could even free himself from her ancient curse.

First though, he would make her latest Viktor Brandewyne pay for his interference.

As soon as the hateful daystar sank beyond the mountains, Dragon took on the form of his namesake and totem and sped down the slopes toward the river port. His spies told him of Wormsloe's return aboard a different vessel than he'd left on years ago.

Soon, all his questions would be answered— one way or another.

Wormsloe heard the great beast's roar as it approached. He might get his death wish after all.

Fate was not so kind.

The Dragon, once again in human guise, stood on the dock staring up at him. Well he felt the weight of that gaze. He knew he could refuse the creature admittance aboard his vessel. He also knew Dragon would just destroy the craft and question him anyway.

He sighed. *"Better to get it over with,"* he thought.

"Lord Dragon, I invite you aboard my vessel, the *Altamaha*," He gave the formal invitation. A mere second later, the ancient vampire stood uncomfortably close to him on the deck.

"Carpathia's failure."

"In my cabin, my lord? This crew knows nothing of my charge."

"Very well."

"She fell to Brandewyne," Wormsloe supplied as soon as the cabin door shut.

"If she fell, why did I not feel her die? I believe she betrayed me."

"No, my lord, to my knowledge she did not betray you. He somehow tricked her into a bottle now sealed by silver and magic. It is a prison she can never be freed from; I'm told."

Dragon narrowed his eyes and sniffed disconcertingly at the air. Even after all these years in his service, Wormsloe still couldn't get used to some of his more bestial mannerisms.

"You believe what you are telling me. How did you learn of this?"

"Here it comes." He sighed and prepared for his probable death. "The bastard told me himself. He said a spell was placed on the bottle so only the one who sealed it could open it. He told me his former first mate, Hezekiah Grimm, had sealed it but was now dead."

Dragon stood motionless for so long he almost seemed to disappear. Only hard concentration allowed Wormsloe to remain focused on him.

"You are sure of this?"

"Aye, I don't think he killed the man to ensure the Lady's prison, though. He seemed genuinely distraught over the loss. He also seemed relieved I remembered he sailed with the man and hinted that something or someone had erased that memory from many minds."

"That smacks of that *vrajitoare's* interference." Dragon gave a harsh laugh. "Even her favorite isn't safe from her machinations and cruel manipulations. That is very useful information, captain."

Wormsloe fought the urge to shake his head. He never knew how a vampire would take news. They just didn't think the same way people did. For now, it looked like he would survive this audience.

"I see you have a new, larger ship. You seek perhaps a nautical advantage over this Brandewyne?"

"Hardly. He has a dreadnaught of a warship. The guns on one side are enough to shiver this craft to mere splinters with a single volley. No, the *Altamaha* was a slave ship when I took her to feed the Lady's pet."

Dragon circled behind him and placed hands on his shoulders. He felt the implicit warning in the vampire's nearly painful grip.

"Where is Westin, by the way?" Fetid breath brushed his ear and cheek.

"Destroyed by Brandee's Childe. They came upon the slave ship shortly after I did and took the cargo. Turned out the young vampire was Westin's son seeking revenge for his mother's murder."

"Hmph, so Brandewyne truly is vampire, and clever enough to turn the young hunter." Dragon stepped back and tapped his chin in thought.

"Oh, he's vampire, no doubt; but he's unlike any I've ever encountered. He goes where he will without invitation, claims he can still eat real food, and doesn't burst into flames in the sunlight. Says he was cursed not turned." Wormsloe rubbed his neck in relief. "The Childe wasn't young Westin, though. It was Jim Rigger, apparently the younger son long thought dead. The one Westin abandoned. Rigger and Brandee have sailed together since they first took to piracy. Very likely he was Brandee's first meal. It would explain why the Reaper had been made first mate."

"Yes, it makes sense," Dragon agreed. "I imagine it would be hard for a vampire to fulfill the duties of first mate when he can only function at night."

A strange smile crossed the vampire's face. Wormsloe didn't know quite what to make of it; but he found it unsettling.

"I will share a secret with you, captain. I was once as Brandewyne is now. It seems he did not fall into the same trap as I did. Perhaps the bitch even gave him the warning she never gave me."

"Who?"

"Celie."

Could the Dragon be talking about the same woman he thought he was? Surely not. Dragon was ancient.

"The Thunderbolt Witch? I know she's old, but she's not a vampire."

"No, she is a necromancer, and now she is the All-Mother, something I've been trying to prevent for millennia. She was never human, that one. She made me what I am today or at least started the process. My beloved Lilith finished it unwittingly."

"She's his foster mother; raised him from a whelp."

"Yes, I know. She raised him specifically to gather power for her. She thinks she's safe from my vengeance now; but she shared power with me once. I've tasted her virgin blood. I intend to kill her once I've dealt with her champion."

He turned and looked at the cabin door. "This is a larger ship than the *Lorelei*. She demands a larger crew, I imagine. I hear their heartbeats."

"Aye, my lord. The Lady allowed me no time to properly maintain the *Lorelei*. Brandee took the live cargo for his own larder, but left both crews and me alive. We scuttled the smaller ship and took the sounder *Altamaha*."

Dragon stared at him with darkly glowing eyes. "Surrender your crew to me."

"As you command, my lord," Wormsloe heard himself say.

Dragon had his unwilling minion call crew members into the captain's cabin five at a time. He considered taking them one by one, but he didn't want to waste most of the night on this feeding. Taking five minds at once required minimal energy. It also kept the victims quiet, thus not alerting the rest of the crew.

To keep from exhausting Wormsloe, he had each new batch of victims behead the bodies of the previous batch.

A few short hours later, he felt he'd amassed enough energy to safely execute his plan without draining all his reserves.

He relished the look of terrified awe on Wormsloe's face as he let his power burst forth and flow to the far reaches of the earth. The waves of magic reached out until he touched the minds of each of his elite hunters, the Daughters of the Dragon.

Their images shimmered in the air before him.

"Hear me, my Daughters. Carpathia, my eldest and your leader, has fallen and is imprisoned. This man who dares call himself Viktor Brandewyne," he summoned an image of his nemesis garnered from Carpathia's memories when last he'd had contact with her, "is responsible for this crime and others. Hunt him down, but do not underestimate him. He is vampire, but he was not made as you were. He is still among the living, the result of a magical curse rather than a vampire's gentle kiss. Capture him and hold him for my personal justice if you can; turn him if possible; destroy him quickly only if you must."

"He has advantages over you. Daylight and holy objects hold no power over him. I am also told he travels freely where he will without need of an invitation to enter a dwelling. That he is clever goes without saying, as he defeated Carpathia."

"You have your orders."

He cut the connection and reached out to several of his lesser vampires close by. He summoned them to the ship and bade them scatter the corpses of his meal throughout the mountains. The wolves would dispose of the evidence of the mass murder.

☠

"I want you to set sail within the month. You will report back any news of Brandewyne you come across."

Wormsloe just looked at him. While he had good reason to fear the creature, he had moments like this in which he didn't care whether he lived or died.

"Need I remind you, my lord, you drank my entire crew?"

"As a matter of fact, I believe you should have fed them better. I might've been able to call my Daughters on half as many men's worth of blood had they been healthier." Dragon chided him with the air of an indulgent parent. "I intend to send one of my underlings along to facilitate hiring a new crew and to make for quick communication with me."

Wormsloe crossed his arms. "I'd just as soon you didn't. Vampires have a bad effect on crews during long voyages. Usually, the voyage lasts longer than the crew. The Lady and her pet cost me more time recruiting new crewmen than I would've cared to spend."

"You have a point, captain." The vampire puzzled over the problem for a while. Eventually something seemed to occur to him. "You say Brandewyne encountered you shortly after you took the slave ship."

"Aye."

"Yet, while he took the cargo, he did not take the crew."

"No." He blinked as sudden realization dawned. "He didn't. Even if he can eat real food, I know he has at least one Childe in his crew, possibly more, going by some of the stories we heard. Yet, he didn't have need of additional crew."

Dragon smiled patiently. "Did you hear any stories of how he manned such a large ship without devouring the crew?"

He narrowed his eyes at the vampire. "Yes, and I suspect you learned something of it from the Lady, as well."

"I did, but I want to hear it from you."

"Alcohol. I remember hearing he mixes it into harvested barrels of blood to keep it from clotting and to stretch the supply."

Dragon paced the cabin with his hands behind his back. "I wish to see if this trick will work for a true vampire. I shall have the one I plan to send with you try this— mixed drink. We cannot stomach alcohol and usually vomit it up immediately."

He turned and snapped his fingers. A knock at the cabin door came soon after. Wormsloe opened it to see a familiar face.

"Hello Ethan."

"Jared? What is this?" He turned an angry glare at Dragon.

"You agreed to serve me if I would cure your brother of his wasting disease. He is cured," he stated matter-of-fact.

"I didn't mean turn him!"

The bastard had the nerve to grin. "You never said not to turn him. You should know, captain, the devil is in the details."

"It's not so bad, Ethan," Jared Wormsloe said with a shrug. "I haven't suffered since my rebirth, and I've finally gained the self-discipline needed for the Master to trust me with important tasks. Besides, now we can get our revenge on that damn half-breed who stranded us out in the marshes after he stole our crabs and boat."

"You have to admire his enthusiasm, captain. Now, if you will provide a glass, drink, and a small portion of blood, we can be about this experiment before the night grows old."

Wormsloe growled in irritation but complied. It wasn't like any of the crew was left to act as a donor.

He placed a crystal tumbler and decanter on the table and drew his knife. He removed the stopper from the decanter of port, but Dragon stopped him from pouring.

"Blood first. We will add the drink in a small portion and increase from there to find the proper blend."

"Fine." He glared and took a swig from the decanter before picking the knife back up. He hissed as he drew the blade down his forearm, cutting deeper than he'd intended.

Dragon grasped his arm and guided the blood flow into the glass. Wormsloe realized he couldn't stop the vampire from letting him bleed out if he wanted to.

Just as he began to feel light-headed, the vampire lifted his arm to slow the blood flow and used super speed to bind the wound tightly.

Dragon then lifted him as if he weighed no more than a newborn and placed him on his bunk.

"Sleep, captain. You have served me well."

Wormsloe woke shortly before dawn. He saw no sign of Dragon. Jared sat at the table watching him.

"I wish you'd picked something other than port. You know I never cared much for the stuff."

"Sorry, Jare; it was the first bottle I came to. Did it work?" He sat up carefully, still a little dizzy. His arm ached. A glance at the bandage showed less sign of bleeding than he'd expected.

Jared answered his questions, both asked and unasked. "I can manage on a mixture of only one quarter blood. I won't like it, but it satisfies the Hunger enough to keep it under control. The Master fetched a doctor to stitch and cauterize the wound. You cut too deep."

"I just keep my knife too sharp. What time is it?"

"Nearly dawn. We can start hiring a crew tomorrow."

"The holds still smell a little, but they will be dark enough for you. I'll see about adapting better accommodations once we've got a carpenter aboard."

Jared gave him a grateful smile. "After sunrise, I won't notice the smell. Besides, there've been times when I 'slept' in sewers. The funk of unwashed Africans will smell like roses in comparison."

With blinding speed, the vampire who'd once been his brother vanished below decks.

Chapter 5

Dragon sat in his chambers, the excess power of his recent feed still thrumming in his veins. He could easily summon all his Daughters again.

Part of his conversation with Wormsloe sparked an old ache. He remembered the pure euphoria of coupling with Celie all those ages ago. Though he hated her, he wanted her so very much.

He also remembered how much she had wanted him when she came to him to make her apologies.

Their psychic connection had never been erased. It was how he always knew when she'd dispatched a new Viktor Brandewyne to gather her power. It galled him that the most recent one had finally succeeded in making her the All-Mother.

Oh, he would pay dearly for that.

An evil and thoroughly wicked idea occurred to him. He'd felt her rejuvenation when she took in her full power. Now that she no longer wore the form of a crone, perhaps her appetites had returned to her, as well.

He reached out along the thread of magic which connected them, careful not to alarm her. Gently, quietly, he eased into her thoughts and projected his lusty desires, keeping his malice buried deep and hidden.

Celie lay nude in a private glen on Hell's Breath Island. She'd had the Island manifest this hideaway for her personal meditation. A small streamlet flowed by her right hand. The confluence of water, earth, and the grass beneath her helped her center with her relatively new powers. Starlight and the waning gibbous moon shone down on her.

She sighed and closed her eyes.

Deep in her own psyche, she felt hands not her own tracing her body. While part of her found this alarming, it felt sensuous and relaxing. It brought back faint sensory memories, like she'd felt this before. She remembered liking it.

The warning in the back of her mind turned to a mental scream when she felt lips on her breasts and the teasing pressure of teeth on her nipples. She also felt pressure on her body pinning her to the ground. She opened her eyes and looked down to watch her aureoles pucker and her nipples harden and swell, growing darker as blood filled them. She wondered who was doing this to her.

The sensation of lips began to move first to her breastbone then slowly down her stomach. The weight pinning her lifted. Invisible hands slid down her arms to hold her wrists as something nudged her thighs apart and up. Something soft and wet began to methodically explore her folds, causing her to throw her head back with a gasp of unexpected pleasure. She felt her body tighten and power build up in warm waves, ready to burst out.

She heard a masculine chuckle she hadn't heard in countless millennia.

Dragon.

"No!" she cried out, fighting the impending orgasm and winning. She would not give him access to the power of the All-Mother.

"Yes," she heard in her mind.

The sensations changed to that of several fingers forcing into her opening and thrusting with inhuman speed. What had started as seduction quickly turned to rape.

"I. Said. NO," she growled through gritted teeth.

By sheer power, she cast his presence away from her.

In an instant, Zeke manifested and cast a cloth of silver over her form. This banished Dragon from her presence and Hell's Breath Island.

"Bitch!"

He'd been so close to siphoning some of her power. He wanted it so much he could taste it. She was magnificent! He'd never sensed such life force before.

He vowed he would hunt her down and take her physically. Surely, she couldn't repel him as easily in body. She was still only a woman.

Then, he would make her pay for all his suffering and for rejecting him. Oh, he would make her pay dearly, for all eternity.

"Thank you for your aid, Elder." As she spoke, the cloth of silver transformed into a shimmering shift. A thin, transparent, cowl-like veil now covered her head. Moonlight glinted off her crystalline hair through it. Only her arms and feet remained bare.

"It is my sacred duty, All-Mother," he replied. "We know he cannot set foot on the island without invitation. The silver will prevent him from opening the old bond you share with him again."

"Thankfully, my sexual appetite is not as strong as Gloribeau's. I shall not let myself fall prey to desire. Now I must inform my son of this attack."

A vision of the All-Mother sheathed in silver manifested in Viktor's cabin.

"Mother?"

She nodded. *"Dragon reached out through our ancient bond. He tried to seduce me and drain my power. He almost succeeded, but I cast him out. The Elder provided me with silver to prevent any further attempts at that ruse."*

"That he could reach you at all on Hell's Breath is troubling."

"As long as I maintain my guard, he no longer can."

"I will find and destroy him as quickly as I can, Mother."

"I know, my son. I love you, Viktor."

With that, she vanished.

Chapter 6

A pregnant young woman pulled her shawl tighter around her shoulders. Surely, she knew how dangerous wandering the Quarter at night could be. Yet some task or errand drew her out.

Not that it mattered to the watcher on the rooftops. The scent of her blood, rich with the burgeoning life in her womb wafted up like sweetest ambrosia to the hunting vampire. She'd taken pregnant street whores before, but this woman looked and smelled much healthier than any of that lot.

The vampire salivated at the thought of savoring her prey like a fine wine.

Britt Westin waited in a nearby alley pretending to be drunk and half asleep, his hat pulled low over his eyes. He knew a vampire was nearby. The creatures had a distinctive odor if one knew what to be alert for, vaguely metallic blended with an almost reptilian musk.

Slowly, he brought his hand up to his shirt front, which he kept slightly open, and pretended to scratch his chest. In actuality, he grasped the golden crucifix he wore, ready to pull it out.

He saw the pregnant woman pass the mouth of the alley, and it troubled him deeply.

A faint rustle of cloth and whistle of wind let him know the predator approached. Apparently, it didn't want to startle its prey and decided to play human.

Soon, he heard voices.

"Pardon, madam, I seem to be lost. Could you help me?"

"Where were you trying to go?"

He got up and moved quickly to the alley's mouth. He had to make sure the creature didn't touch the woman.

He saw the vampire, a female, stand very close to the woman, almost close enough to kiss her. Hopefully, he could get to them before he drew its attention.

"I am looking for someplace to get a good meal." The vampire reached for the woman.

His stomach clenched in dread as he realized he couldn't reach them in time. He broke into a run.

The vampire stopped mid-reach and remained as motionless as a statue. The woman stepped back, hand at throat.

"Quick, Britt, the silver cords before it recovers!" the woman hissed.

"Damn, Sam, what did you do to it, and why are you out here in your condition anyway?" He reached into his pouch and pulled out a thin rope woven through with several silver wires even as he chided his wife. "I've never seen one do that before, and I've been hunting them for years."

He proceeded to bind the creature at wrists, ankles, and throat, effectively hog-tying it.

"Nothing, my love. I hadn't even gotten my crucifix out yet. I don't know what's wrong with it." Her brows drew together in a scowl. "As for why I'm here, we already knew that this one favors pregnant prey, just from the rumors which led us to hunt this part of the Quarter. I'm the best bait. That we captured it proves that."

The vampire spoke, drawing their attention, but still didn't seem aware of their presence or its predicament. "I hear and obey, great Dragon. I shall watch for this Viktor Brandewyne and alert the nearest Daughters if I learn anything of him."

They looked to see what the vampire was staring at. They got the impression of a shadowy form with several others facing it just as their captive did. More clearly, they saw the shimmering image of the pirate the creature named.

The vision faded, and the captured vampire immediately became aware of what they'd done. It tried in vain to break its bonds and shrieked when the silver wires burned its flesh.

Britt and Samantha pulled out their crucifixes, careful to shield their eyes first. They knew to expect the blinding twin flashes of light.

It proved enough to render the vampire unconscious.

Luckily, the house they'd rented was near enough they could secure the creature before any *gendarmes* came to investigate the scream.

Two other vampires watched the capture from a safe distance. Though under orders not to interfere, they made note of where the humans took their prisoner.

They left to report to their lord.

"You will release me!" The female vampire stood just behind the bars of her prison. She'd learned quickly not to touch the metal. Her captors had the foresight to paint them with a silver slurry.

"So you can be free to murder again? I think not," the man said. "The best you can hope for is a swift end to your existence. If you prove uncooperative, I will open the shutters and allow the sunrise to end you in agony."

"Do you know who my Sire is? You will pay for this, human."

"As a matter of fact, I do not know who your sire is. Why don't you tell me? I can hunt him or her down and rid this world of their evil."

She let loose a mad cackle. "A human destroy the great Dragon? I am in the presence of either a madman or a suicidal fool."

He smiled complacently at her but did not approach the bars or meet her gaze. "I have heard those accusations before. Who is this 'Dragon' and why should I fear them?"

"He is the First. All vampires come from Him. Only a few of us have the honor of being His Children. We are elite, stronger, faster, more clever than common vampires."

He snorted in derision. "For one so arrogant, you were caught easily enough."

She snarled at him for daring to point out her shortcoming. Enraged, she tried to reach between the bars. A scream escaped her lips as her flesh sizzled against the silver coated metal.

"That sounded like it hurt quite a bit," the human said in mock sympathy. "I can ease your suffering."

"I will tear your heart out and drain it before your dying eyes, you bastard. Then I'll fuck your pregnant whore with a stick and drink the miscarriage before I kill her."

He seemed unfazed by the threat save for a hardening around the eyes. "You will answer my questions, then I will put you out of your misery."

"Hah!"

"What does this Dragon want with Viktor Brandewyne?"

She hadn't expected a question along those lines and answered before she thought not to. "He defeated the Lady Carpathia. Dragon wants revenge for the disgrace of His eldest Childe."

The man paled at the mention of the Lady's name. "Dragon sired Her?"

She smiled wickedly, catching the scent of his fear and hatred. She tried hard to capture his gaze while he was stunned, but he wouldn't look in her direction.

She used her most seductive tone of voice. "Yes, as I said, He is the First."

Still, he remained focused on the far wall rather than her cell. She looked where he did and saw a simple pull cord.

A sudden sluggishness in her mind and movements alerted her that the dawn drew near.

He walked to the pull cord and gave a quick tug. A shutter in the ceiling of her stone-lined cell rolled back to reveal more silver-infused bars over a skylight. She screamed when the first rays crested the edge of the hole. Her daytime death stole over her, and she fell silent.

By noon, nothing remained of her but ashes and fangs.

"Britt, are you well?" Sam noticed how shaken her husband seemed. She hadn't wanted to let him confront the creature alone, but fatigue due to the child she carried gave her no choice.

He strode silently to her and kissed her soundly then held her close. He did not answer.

"Britt?"

"I don't want you playing bait anymore."

She stiffened in his arms. "We've already discussed this."

He stepped back, and the look on his face stopped her argument. "Sam, I want to stop hunting, at least until after our child is born. A child deserves both parents. Neither of us had that growing up. I came too close to losing both of you last night. If that creature's maker hadn't demanded her attention, I wouldn't have reached you fast enough to stop her."

She sighed. "We did underestimate her. Perhaps you're right. We should stop hunting vampires, especially given we both have brothers who are vampires."

"That's been bothering you, too?"

She nodded and hugged herself. "I know they aren't alive anymore. I know they have to kill to survive. But, if you really think about it, people, living people, often won't hesitate to kill other people for much poorer reasons than just to ensure their continued existence. Can we really fault them for following their instincts?"

Britt rubbed the bridge of his nose. "I must admit, my convictions about the creatures have changed greatly since we encountered Captain Brandewyne and found our brothers. Hell, learning Jim survived to adulthood and that my father lied to me all those years just to salve his conscience was a shock. Then to have my once-living brother risk his own destruction to save us when his captain lost control of his urges; I truly don't know how I feel about vampires anymore."

"What did you do with the one we caught last night? I heard screaming."

"I let the dawn take her. She threatened you and our child." She heard the complete lack of remorse in his voice. The haunted look he gave her made her wish she could wipe all bad memories from his mind.

He remained silent for a while. She nestled against his shoulder to offer what comfort she could. She'd begun to doze when his voice startled her.

"We need to find some way to get word to them."

"What?"

"That vampire was sired by the same one who made Carpathia. She called him the great Dragon and said he was the first vampire. Given how old and powerful She was, I don't doubt this Dragon is the original vampire. He wants revenge on Captain Brandewyne for imprisoning Carpathia. You saw the vision the same as I did. He's sending out hunters." He held her at arm's length and gazed at her earnestly. "I owe my brother our lives and freedom. We have to find some way to warn him of what's coming."

"You're right. Perhaps we should see if Captain Bainbridge can get word to them," she agreed. "Still, keep in mind I hunted Brandee for years before we finally crossed paths. We may not reach them in time."

"That's what troubles me."

Chapter 7

Melanie rose to find her sister already up. She felt odd whenever she called Carmella her sister, even though it felt right; she'd been an only child before Viktor sired her into her new life. A smile traced her lips at the thought of how scandalized her human father would be to learn she called a mulatto prostitute her sister and meant it. He still served as the Lord Mayor of New Orleans.

Both women turned their faces to the door. They felt the summons from their lord, Jeorge. He awaited their report, having been otherwise occupied the previous night.

It didn't take them long to reach his audience chamber. They made obeisance before the nearly ancient vampire fated to eternally wear the form of a 16-year-old boy.

"Rise, my faithful servants. What news have you?"

"The hunters took Valara late last night. We marked the house they took her to. The woman is with child and acted as bait, proving they received and understood the clues you allowed out," Melanie told him.

"So, she was easier to catch than I thought she would be, for all her arrogant bluster of superiority and refusal to give me her blood oath," he surmised. "Still, she should cause us no more trouble."

"It was a close thing, my lord," Carmella interjected. "She would have murdered the woman if not for the vision."

"Vision?"

"*Oui*," Melanie confirmed. "We were not close enough to overhear much, but I believe her sire communicated with her at a most inopportune time for her. It allowed the hunters to take her while she was focused on his message."

"That is one of the dangers of that type of communication; but you said vision. I take it you could see this vision?"

They both nodded. Carmella continued the narrative. "Several women appeared in varying garb. They and Valara faced a male who seemed to emanate a crushing amount of power. Then an image of my Sire appeared but seemed to be an image only. Neither of us felt his presence."

"Could you hear anything of what was said?"

"I could only make out a few words, and only just barely," Melanie said. "It was as if something tried to muffle things, much like speaking low rather than whispering to avoid eavesdroppers. I mainly heard Valara mention 'Dragon,' 'Daughters,' and 'Viktor Brandewyne'."

Jeorge's face grew immobile. "Carmella, return to the house they took Valara to and learn what you can of her fate. I am trusting you to exercise your new-found control and remain undetected. If you are taken, I may not be able to help you. I have heard and read of this *Monsieur* Westin's reputation as a hunter. The risks are great. I have also encountered his bride before. She passed through a few years ago hunting your sire, Captain Brandewyne."

"*Oui*, my lord, she is sister to my brother Thomas. I shall be most careful." She bowed and left.

Jeorge turned his attention to Melanie. "My child, feed well then return to me. I wish to send a message to the Captain."

"*Oui*, my lord."

"Ah, Jeorge, my friend," Viktor said through his Childe, "why do I get the feeling my troubles have become known to you already? I had planned to let you know I was on my way to New Orleans tomorrow. I'm about three days out now."

"So, you have resolved your previous problems? I suspected so when your eldest Childe began to make vast improvements in her self-control. She is more tightly bound to you than you know, *mon ami*. Shortly after you left her here, we had to lock her up for a time. She very nearly turned revenant."

"I do apologize for that. The witch who cursed me and imprisoned her for so many years was getting her final blow from beyond the grave. I very nearly died. Was Carmella the only one to suffer?"

"Yes, my lord," Melanie replied for herself. "I never had any problems with my control, although I did sense your distress."

"Yes, Melanie is the reason I did not have Carmella destroyed. She advocated for her sister and informed me of what you were enduring," Jeorge added. "I had her feed well this evening, so she would have the strength to initiate this contact. We have learned, by chance, that the great Dragon has dispatched all of His Daughters to hunt you down. I fear he has learned of the Lady's fate."

"I'm not surprised. That is part of the reason I'm headed there now. I'm hoping your library has resources which will help me against them and to find him."

"I would caution you against hunting Him, but I know my words cannot dissuade you."

"Trust me, my friend, I am well aware I'll need everything I can get to defeat him. We are more alike, he and I, than you might realize. I know the secret of his origin, for it is almost the same as mine."

"I will have Jean begin compiling what you'll need. He has greatly improved the organization of my library. I thank you for sending him my way."

"You are most welcome, my friend. I will see you soon."

Viktor broke the connection. Jeorge caught Melanie before she could drop to the floor and placed her on a nearby chaise.

Chapter 8

Belladonna leaned against the bulkhead, arms crossed, and glared at Viktor. He sat back from the log entry he'd just scribed and gazed back at her, his expression bordering on bored.

"What?"

"I don't like it."

Damn, but he found her sullenness tiresome. "Be specific, pet." He knew the appellation infuriated her. He used it on purpose on this occasion.

"I don't trust Jeorge. How do you know where his allegiance lies? You know he's a power monger; else he wouldn't have been around as long as he has. What's to keep him from trying to play you and Dragon against each other?"

The fact she didn't rise to the bait told him her concerns were genuine and not just a display of petulance. "I am not without contingencies where Jeorge is concerned, Belle. I have no desire for control of his city or kiss. I don't want to be tied to a single port. I could take them from him, however."

"All the more incentive for him to make the gamble in the hope you'll destroy each other."

He chuckled. "Oh, I trust him to do whatever he deems to be in his best interest in this coming war. For now, he favors me over Dragon. I've a feeling he spent some time under Dragon's direct dominion in his early years. Jeorge fears him, but he does not fancy falling back under his control; just as he didn't like playing host to Thia. For that matter, Melanie told me he deliberately sent out clues which let Westin eliminate a Childe of Dragon's who'd been forced on him. This one was not one of the Daughters, though."

She shook her head. "I will grant you that, but I think you are too trusting."

He laughed outright. "Oh pet! I did not survive all these years, first as a pirate then as vampire by being too trusting of anyone, yourself included. If anyone is too trusting in this situation, it is Jeorge. My daughters are in his keeping, after all."

"Which allows him to spy on you; information he could pass on to Dragon."

"He sees only what I wish him to see, pet. I, however, see everything they do. Even Carmella can no longer shield from me, now I know she was while under Juma's control."

"What are you saying?"

"Jeorge may not trust Carmella, but he will in time; and she is very adept at reading men. He trusts Melanie implicitly even though he knows I don't let her see everything. She was already well-versed in political maneuvering when I brought her over. She grew up in that world. She shows absolute fealty to him, because I want her to. She has grown in his favor and is close to becoming one of his lieutenants because of her political acumen. Both my daughters hide their secrets from him without raising his suspicions."

"You are playing him?"

"I'm hedging my bets, pet."

"I'm not your pet."

He merely smirked.

Carmella flew to the roof of the Westins' house, an ability she'd only recently acquired and that only her sister knew she had. She hovered bare inches above the shingles, careful to make no noise so she wouldn't alert the humans inside. The barred, east-facing skylight drew her attention.

The moon emerged from the clouds briefly and glimmered on the suspiciously silver color of the metal bars. She avoided touching them. The roll shutter was retracted, leaving the skylight open, but she saw the same silver substance on the edge of it.

When she peered into the stone-lined room below, she saw more bars forming a cage or cell. The oily scent of burnt flesh wafted up to her. In the middle of the cell, she saw a pile of dust— or ash. Two sharp, elongated teeth gleamed in the pile briefly.

Clouds once again obscured the moon and threw the cell into darkness.

She knew Valara's fate.

She alit a few streets away, careful to remain unseen, and headed back to Jeorge on foot. Just as her sister kept secret her ability to fly, she kept the fact Melanie shared this advanced ability secret, as well. Only they and their sire knew about it. Viktor already let them know not to reveal how quickly their powers were growing to Jeorge or anyone else in his kiss. He might see it as a threat.

Of course, Carmella had another secret only Viktor knew. She could resist the daytime death, something a vampire her age should find impossible. She had been a vampire for not quite a decade.

That she could even keep a secret from her lord, with whom she'd entered into a blood oath, spoke of how powerful she'd grown.

☠

"Hello Belle." Jim Rigger managed to catch the irritated siren just outside the captain's cabin and pinned her against the bulkhead. "Care for some sport?" He rubbed against her suggestively.

She smiled sweetly, grasped his testes and slowly began to extend her talons. The vampire quickly distanced himself before the razor-sharp tips could pierce flesh.

"Maybe some other time," he said with a rakish grin.

She snorted and passed down the corridor.

Jim gave a cursory knock before he entered the cabin. "She's in a mood."

Viktor set two glasses on the table and pulled the cork on a bottle of rum mixed with human blood. He poured and passed a glass to his friend. "One of these nights she's going to make a woman out of you, Jim. She's always in a mood when I visit New Orleans."

"Well, it hasn't exactly been the most pleasant port to visit as far as her experiences with it. She's come uncomfortably close to dying there."

"True, but we aren't going into Glory's bayous. She doesn't like me having anything to do with Jeorge."

"I imagine she's not too happy about all the women you have in that port, either," Jim said with a snicker.

"That too," Vik agreed. "She's a territorial creature."

Jim took a swig of his drink. "You know what the problem is, Vik. The two of your personalities are too much alike."

"You may have a point there." He took a sip and set his glass down. "Fetch three more glasses and a bottle of straight brandy, would you?"

Jim nodded and got up to get the requested items from the liquor cabinet.

"Enter," Vik called out in anticipation of the knock.

The cabin door opened to admit first mate Hezekiah Grimm, navigator Zachary Brumble, and Thomas Brumble, part of Viktor's small cadre of vampires.

"Pull up a chair, gentlemen."

Jim poured brandy for Grimm and Zach and a bloody rum for Thomas, making sure to top his and the captain's glasses in the process.

"We're making good headway, Captain," Grimm informed him. "Mr. Jon has the helm. He'll keep her on course."

"Very good, Mr. Grimm." Without preamble, Vik switched to a more casual tone. "Jim, Zach, Thomas, I thought I'd let you know you'll have a little family reunion once we reach port. Mr. and Madame Westin have taken up residence in New Orleans."

Jim winced. "Bet that's going to make things awkward with Jeorge."

"Surely they aren't still hunting vampires," Zach protested.

"Oh, they are. Although, I think your sister's condition is about to put a stop to that for a while. She had a close call last night, according to my watchers," Vik corrected him.

"I'll kill him; putting her in harm's way like that!" Zach growled.

Thomas headed off his brother's ire. "You know as well as I do nobody makes Sam do anything she doesn't want to or keeps her from doing what she wants. I imagine he's tried to stop her from helping him hunt."

"She's definitely more woman than most men could handle," Jim agreed. The comment earned him a glare from Zach.

"That is enough, all of you." Viktor's tone left no doubt about the command.

"Family squabbling; one of the reasons I first went to sea," Grimm murmured.

Vik drummed his fingers once on the table to gain everyone's silence and attention. When he had it, he said, "I plan to pay them a visit, both to ensure they and Jeorge don't run afoul of each other, and to find out if Mr. Westin has any knowledge to impart regarding the Daughters of the Dragon." He fixed Zach with a pointed stare. "If you cannot give me your word you will be civil, Mr. Brumble, not only will you not be permitted to go ashore, you will be left in Belladonna's custody."

"And she's going to be in a foul mood the entire time we're in port," Jim added.

Zach paled. "You have my word, Captain."

"If you don't mind, I'll stay aboard, Vik. Not that much for me to do ashore here now I have Brianna waiting for me. Besides, Jon-Jon owes me an outstanding gambling debt. I intend to have his store of gin, if he can't win it back."

"That will have to wait, Hezekiah. I do want you to stay with the ship. I plan to accomplish much here, but quickly. Until I get a better read on the Daughters, I don't intend to spend much time in any one port."

"That being said," he continued, "I plan to have Mr. Jon and a small crew accompany Mr. Trundle to the food markets. We need fresh supplies and victuals. New Orleans offers several items other ports don't."

Grimm chuckled. "I'll make sure he picks the most reliable men. Over half the crew would volunteer for that duty and end up 'lost' along the way. I'll be sure to give 'em a generous helping of the special rum before they go ashore, too." He referred to the rum (or whatever drink proved most plentiful at the time) tainted with a few drops of Viktor's blood and used to keep the pirate crew compliant. Vik rarely needed it anymore except for new conscripts. None of the crew suspected it gave him control over their will; they viewed it as a treat and special reward.

"Thank you, Hezekiah. That will help speed things along. Now if only I could ensure Jeorge won't drag things out."

"Given how he felt about Carpathia, the threat of a visit from any of the other Daughters will probably give him incentive to keep it short and quiet and get you out of his city," Jim surmised.

"Aye, provided it doesn't make him so hasty as to rush me out before I get what I came for."

Two hours after sunrise, Carmella rose. First, she ensured Melanie still 'slept.' So far, her sister had not developed this particular ability. Satisfied, she set about swathing her limbs in layers of white linen. She'd found white fabric reflected the sunlight away from her skin. Dark fabrics tended to absorb the light and make it more uncomfortable to move about. Over this, she put on a shift, bodice, petticoats, outer skirt and jacket, and finished the ensemble with a hooded traveling cloak and gloves. She made sure the cloak's hood draped in a way to shield her face completely from the sun's rays.

Thus armored against the sunlight, she ventured from the vampire nest and headed for the Latin Quarter.

Knocking woke Samantha. She hadn't adjusted fully to a normal sleep schedule yet. She blinked at the brightness of the room and went to the window to close the interior shutters. Blearily, she wondered about the fact she'd been able to sleep at all in such a bright room.

The baby kicked and she simultaneously smiled and grimaced. Her bladder begged for release.

She toyed briefly with either waking Britt to answer the door or just ignoring it and hoping whoever it was would go away.

The knocking sounded again with an almost urgent cadence to it. She decided to go answer it. Her bladder would just have to wait, or she could use it as an excuse to remove herself from any unpleasant or annoying conversation.

She unlatched the door but kept a loaded pistol behind her back. The sunlight precluded any vampire attacks, but there was always the possibility of humans with ill intent. Whoever it was had to be a stranger. Captain Bainbridge wasn't due back for another week, and they didn't know anyone in the city.

"May I help you?" She had to shield her eyes from the glare of sunlight on white linen.

"You are Samantha Westin?" The female voice carried an islander Creole accent, slightly different from the Louisiana variation. She couldn't make out the woman's face.

"Yes. I'm afraid you have me at a disadvantage." Her eyes finally adjusted enough to see the woman huddled in on herself somewhat and her arms seemed to be wrapped in bandages. Given the relative warmth, this struck her as odd.

"My name is Carmella. May I please come in? I have a message from *Capitan* Brandee."

Sam immediately reasoned this strange woman was a local prostitute; sailors, and pirates in particular, favored such companions. The bandages and cloak must be a make-shift disguise.

"Of course, come in. It is frightfully bright out today."

"*Oui. Merci, madame.*" The woman hurried inside as if something hunted her.

Before Sam knew what was going on, Carmella flew about the room closing every shutter tightly, throwing the room into instant gloom. Sam's mind screamed "vampire," but she couldn't reconcile the thought with the bright daylight outside.

Too late, the supposed disguise made sense.

"Sam, what's going on? Who is that? Why are you pointing a gun at them?" Britt asked from the inner doorway, still in his night shirt.

"Vampire."

"Impossible; it's full daylight out." He stopped and frowned. "Why is it dark in here?"

"Vampire," she repeated, her pistol never wavering from its target.

Slowly, the linen-swathed figure raised her gloved hands and pushed back the cloak's hood. Glossy black curls framed a creamy, pale tan face with chocolate brown eyes.

"My name is Carmella. I am *Capitan* Brandee's eldest Childe. I mean you no harm. I bring you a message from my Sire."

"You lie!" Britt hissed. "My brother is his eldest."

Carmella shook her head. "Jim Rigger still lived when the *Capitan* made me. He did not yet know or understand what Juma had transformed him into. He killed me to satisfy a Hunger he had no control over. Juma kept me her slave until *Capitan* Brandee finally returned and defeated her."

"My crucifix isn't glowing, Britt. She's telling the truth," Sam said and lowered her weapon. She tried to hide the tremble of fatigue in her arm. One could only hold a gun steady for so long without firing it.

Britt scrubbed at his face. He looked down at himself and blushed. "Good lord! I do apologize for my state of undress, Samantha."

She couldn't suppress a giggle. "I've seen it before, my love," she said and patted her pregnancy for emphasis.

"But I shouldn't appear like this in front of another woman. The fact she is a vampire, and I don't dare leave you alone with her is the only reason I am not trying to save my modesty."

At this, Carmella grinned, showing fangs in the process. "I was a whore in life. I too have seen such before." She raised an eyebrow and added, "From what I see, you are much like your brother in that respect. Your wife is a very lucky woman."

Sam blushed. She'd lost her virginity to Jim Rigger, and Carmella's comment brought that memory back quite viscerally. She decided to change the subject.

"How is it possible you are awake at this time of day? I saw how you managed to travel in the sunlight, but according to what I've been taught you haven't been vampire long enough to fight off your daytime death on your own."

"Sam's right. Normally a vampire doesn't gain that ability until after at least a century," Britt concurred. "My brother is the only other vampire this young I've ever encountered who could do so. I don't count your sire, since I've seen more than enough evidence that he is not undead."

"I believe it has to do with being his eldest, and with Juma's necromancy. At first, she forced this on me by her will. Eventually, I learned I could wake during the day on my own."

Sam tilted her head to the side and crossed her arms above her belly. "That actually sounds plausible; but I am no expert on vampires by anyone's reckoning."

"Don't underestimate yourself, Sam. You are one of the most intelligent women I've ever met. You've learned what I've had to teach far faster than I did," Britt protested.

"Smart, loving, and well endowed; I'd keep this one if I were you," Carmella quipped.

"I intend to." She didn't try to hide the love in her voice.

Britt got the conversation back on track. "You said you have a message from Captain Brandewyne."

"*Oui*; he will arrive in port the day after tomorrow and plans to pay you a visit. He wishes to learn about hunting vampires and to find out what you learned from Valara about the Daughters of the Dragon. He also wishes to work out a peace between you and my lord."

Sam frowned in confusion. "He wants to learn how to hunt vampires, but he wants us to make a treaty with the head of the local kiss?"

"*Oui*. He wishes it for both my sister's and my protection from retribution as well as yours." Carmella grew apprehensive. "It grows late. I must return and sleep, or my Hunger will be hard to control when I rise tonight. I cannot afford to lose control ever again. My lord may destroy me rather than just imprison me."

She drew her hood low over her face. They felt a strong breeze, and she was gone.

The door swung in her wake.

Chapter 9

Viktor and Grimm stood overseeing the mooring of the *Incubus*. As a precaution, Viktor opted to set anchor in Lake Pontchartrain even though New Orleans' harbor was deep enough to allow the dreadnaught to tie up at the docks. That and having Mr. Jon's shopping detail take all but two of the boats would ensure the rest of the crew remained aboard.

Stores of the special rum were too low to dose the entire crew, something soon to be rectified. Viktor made sure several barrels of rum were on the shopping list.

"Still several hours until nightfall," Grimm observed.

"Aye. I plan to pay Angelique a visit first."

"Do you have time?"

Vik smiled, but a sad tiredness seemed to dwell in his gaze. "Sport is not my goal. I plan to ensure she cannot be used against me."

"I thought you'd worked out a deal with Jeorge for her protection."

"Despite what Belle thinks, I actually don't trust him to be reliable in that respect. He would be no match for the Dragon or the Daughters. No, my link with Angel must be severed."

He saw his sorrow mirrored in his first mate's eyes. "Is she the reason you didn't want to go ashore, Hezekiah? I know she's tempted countless men before you to betray their wives."

"I've some fond memories of dalliances with Angel, Vik, I won't deny it. I honestly have no desire for any woman other than Brianna." He shook his head with a rueful chuckle. "Never thought I'd see the day I'd turn eunuch for any woman."

"Nor I, my friend. You couldn't have picked a finer one to make that sacrifice for, though." He gave his friend's shoulder a squeeze. "I have to admit, I'm confused by your reaction to my decision about Angelique, now."

Grimm stared at the quarterdeck below them. "She was a fine whore and a likable woman. Still, I know you only intend to do what you must. I understand and respect that."

Viktor blinked at him as realization set in. "You thought I intended to kill her?" He laughed. "Oh no; that isn't my plan at all. Granted, I understand how you could reach that conclusion given this is me, but no."

"Sure sounded like that was your plan. What is, then?"

"I plan to send her to a priest to be cleansed. I know it will be excruciatingly painful for me, but I'm going to release her."

"I would advise against that," Belladonna said as she climbed up to the aft castle.

Viktor leaned back against the railing, his eyebrows raised. "You surprise me, Belle."

"If you release her from your thrall, you'll be removing the only real protection she has against the Daughters of the Dragon."

"How so?"

Her expression told him she thought he should already know the answer. "You really need to start paying attention to your own powers and how they work. You are an unique being, Viktor. You are the only living vampire. Yes, Dragon started the same way as you, but he hasn't been alive for several millennia now. Your magic works slightly differently from other vampires. You are correct that Jeorge can't protect her; but your power can."

"I still don't understand how."

She sighed and hopped up to sit on the rail next to him. "Perhaps it would be better to show you. Sometimes words are clumsy tools."

She opened her mental shields and reached out along the bond she'd shared with the vampire ever since she'd literally bitten a chunk out of him. He opened his shields and allowed her in.

Images and memories jumbled together in his mind almost too quickly to process. For a few moments, he wasn't sure which were his and which were the siren's. Finally, the images settled on one moment from his memory. He knew it for his because she hadn't been present when the events depicted occurred.

Yet, he saw his memory through the filter of Belladonna's perception and understanding of magic.

He saw himself with Carpathia and Jeorge when she destroyed his friend Guillaume and Jeorge's Childe, Memnette. Belle's perception allowed him to see the aura of power each vampire emanated. He saw Jeorge's aura diminish with Memnette's demise, just as he saw Thia's glow ever brighter from absorbing the life force of the two lesser vampires.

As he ordered Melanie to flee, he saw both her aura and his own encompassing hers.

Finally, he saw his confrontation with Carpathia. Her aura reached out hungrily for his despite her promise not to use her powers against him. At last, he saw what he thought Belle wanted him to understand. His power outshone Carpathia's even though she was supposed to be the second most powerful vampire in the world.

His power would've protected Melanie regardless of his physical presence. Carpathia was of Dragon's direct bloodline, and all other vampires descended from Dragon in some way or other. All but his, that was.

A curse made Viktor vampire. No vampire brought him over. Neither he nor any vampire he made were subject to the Dragon's power.

"I see what you mean, pet. Rather than release Angelique, I should turn her to ensure her safety."

She gave him a look which told him she thought him a bit slow. He scowled in frustration; and she made an attempt to soothe his ego.

"While that is a viable option, I'll admit, I don't think that would be the wisest course of action either."

He thought about it for a moment. "Ah, I take your point, pet. Jeorge probably wouldn't appreciate me creating another vampire for him to train. He already regrets taking in Carmella. So, what do you suggest?"

"I see you've forgotten another, indirect, encounter with Carpathia."

"Oh? Oh, you're right! I completely forgot about Turlington. She possessed him while he was human. I should be able to do the same, since I'm stronger; but it wouldn't be practical to do so on a continuous basis. Wouldn't be fair to Angel to make her a prisoner in her own body, either."

"Who are you, and what have you done with the captain?" she quipped.

Grimm snickered and said, "He is the Mother's son."

Vik nearly forgot the man stood next to them. The mental transference between vampire and siren had proved intense enough to make the present fade from view.

"Just as your Children enjoy the protection of your power, so do those you've marked as potential Children. If you fed on them, they fall under your protection." She confirmed his suspicions.

"That eases my mind more than you can know, pet."

"Hello pet." Viktor greeted the proprietor of the juju shop in the Quarter as he came through the door. He stopped about a foot into the room, acutely aware of the powerful ward protecting the shop as well as the brothel occupying the upper floors. He felt sure he could break through it but refrained from doing so out of respect for the woman who cast it and for the Sister of Power she served.

"Captain Brandewyne, you don't know how glad I am to see you," Celine Thibideaux said and lowered the ward to grant him entry.

He sauntered to her and kissed her hand with a mischievous smile. "Now that is the kind of welcome I like to receive, Madame Thibideaux. Unfortunately, I haven't the time for sport this visit."

"Damn. Can you at least go up and console Angelique? She's been plagued with nightmares about you and is convinced you think she's grown too old and intend to cast her aside." Celine crossed her arms and rolled her eyes at the last comment.

Viktor sighed and shook his head. "She does love her theatrics. In truth, I had planned to release her from my power and send her to a priest for cleansing. Her protection from what is coming, not her age, played a factor."

"Gloribeau warned me about a week ago to strengthen my shields and wards, but she didn't say why." She scrutinized him closely. "Angel's nightmares and your presence confirm the need. Your words, however, tell me you've changed your mind about that plan."

"Aye, Belladonna convinced me Angel has greater protection in my power rather than free of it. I don't know how Glory knows about the coming danger, but I'm grateful for her warning to you."

"Viktor! Don't cast me aside; I beg you!"

He looked over at the blonde woman standing in the doorway to the back room and stairs. Given how sheer the fabric she'd draped herself in was, she might as well be naked. She wore jewels in her hair, and dark kohl rimmed her gray eyes.

"As I said, she loves her theatrics," he muttered under his breath. "Angel, pet, you'll be pleased to know I've decided to keep you. Now go put real clothes on."

"But aren't you coming upstairs?"

"Haven't the time. I've much business to attend to and want to be out of this port before my newest hunters learn I've even been here."

Angelique pouted, but he ignored it and turned to leave. "Keep those wards strong, Celine."

"I intend to, Captain. I'd just like to know what they are supposed to be protecting us from," the Creole madame replied.

An anguished cry cut his answer short. "It's true! You think I'm too old."

He stopped where he stood, his back still to her, clenching his fists and jaw.

The next moment, he crossed the room and clutched her to him. He kissed her hard while he pushed the sheer cloth aside to thrust two fingers inside her. With speed no human could match, he moved his fingers in and out as well as teased her nub with his thumb. She screamed, and her body bucked with the unexpected orgasm this caused.

He withdrew, lowered her gently to the floor, and wiped her juices from his hand with a rag Celine passed to him.

"Sorry pet, but I really don't have time for anything further," he said and turned toward Celine. "The other Daughters of the Dragon have been sent to hunt me. Thia was the strongest, and I defeated her. Bear in mind, though, that is no reason to underestimate any of the others should they track me here."

"Understood. I wish you well."

"My thanks. Give my love to Gloribeau."

"You are suicidal, Viktor Brandewyne. She would eat you alive."

"She already has on one occasion, and I returned the favor."

She laughed at his parting shot and turned to tend to her stupefied business partner.

☠

Viktor flew to the rooftops of the Quarter and travelled via that route to the home of Britt and Samantha Westin. He dropped to street level in a nearby alley and made his way to the front door. His navigator, Zach Brumble, soon joined him.

"Captain? I thought you were going to Madame Thibideaux's."

"My business there was brief," he said in a tone which conveyed the subject was closed. Brumble knew better than to question him further. He turned and knocked on the door.

Britt answered the door with his crucifix visible. Viktor raised an eyebrow at the ineffective jewelry.

"Hello, Mr. Westin. Surely you remember that does not work against me."

"Captain Brandewyne, Mr. Brumble," Britt acknowledged them. "I remember, sir. This is to allow me to protect my wife should your Childe return."

"I see. I give you my word, sir, she will never intrude upon you nor threaten you. I forbid it. I only sent her in order to facilitate my visit. May we come in?"

"I don't trust you enough to invite you into my home, Captain."

Viktor's Hunger and temper threatened to rise to the surface. He took a deep breath and smiled. If his smile was less than friendly, it couldn't be helped. "I will remind you; I don't need your permission or invitation. I merely asked out of courtesy."

"Britt, my love, we already decided to offer our help" Sam said from just behind her husband.

The vampire hunter growled under his breath but stepped aside and motioned for the two pirates to come in. He pointedly did not extend a verbal invitation to either of them.

Viktor preceded his navigator then stood aside to let the man embrace his sister. He didn't miss the glare Zach directed at Britt.

Apparently, it wasn't lost on its target, either. As Britt started forward, Viktor placed a hand on his shoulder. He leaned in and spoke low enough for the siblings not to overhear. "Leave it be, Mr. Westin. He thinks you endangered his sister with your vampire hunting."

"Kindly unhand me, sir. I would never put her in harm's way," Britt hissed.

"I believe you, sir," Vik said and removed the restraining hand. "Keeping her out of trouble is likely the difficulty. I really did come here to learn about hunting vampires and if you know anything about the Daughters of the Dragon."

"Ow! Sam!" The crack of a slap and Zach's sudden cry drew their attention.

"You idiot! He tried to make me stay home, not join him in the hunt! And you call yourself my brother. Clearly you don't remember our childhood well. You, of all people, should know no man can make me do something I don't want to; not even your bloody captain, I dare say!"

"I believe she has him straightened out now, Mr. Westin," Vik said with a grin. "She'd make a fine quartermaster."

"I'm not interested in the job," Sam told him.

He bowed before her and lifted her hand to his lips. He raised his eyes to her face as he did so and observed a slight hitch in her breathing. He heard her heartbeat speed a little, as well.

He stood straight again and allowed her to pull her hand from his, giving her a wickedly playful smile in the process. "Of course, pet. I would never try to make you do anything you didn't want to."

She gratified him with a blush.

He did not pursue her when she moved to stand next to her husband. He knew from her scent and reactions, both conscious and not, it wouldn't take much to seduce her if he'd a mind to.

Time for that later, he reminded himself. For now, he had business to attend to.

"My daughter tells me you recently captured and destroyed one of Dragon's get."

"We weren't able to learn very much from her save that Dragon is the original vampire and has dispatched his Daughters to hunt you. She was— uncooperative," Britt replied. "She threatened Samantha. I had to destroy her."

"Had to?" Viktor crossed his arms and tilted his head to the side. "Carmella told me about your holding cell. You could have held her easily with no danger to your wife."

Britt shook his head. "I couldn't be sure of that. I have had a vampire escape that room once. I'm not sure how. Luckily, he didn't return to murder us. This one would have. We'd hunted her for about a week at Sam's insistence."

Zach looked at his sister as if she'd gone mad. He even said as much. "Sam, are you insane? You are with child! How could you take such risks?"

Unflinching, she replied, "It was for my safety I insisted we eliminate her. This particular vampire had been preying on pregnant women almost exclusively."

"Before I opened the shutter to let the morning sun take her, she threatened to," Britt began then looked at his wife and paled.

She placed a hand on his arm and nodded. "It's better for me to hear it than leave it to my imagination."

"She said she would violate you with a stick and drink the miscarriage before she killed you. I'm sorry, love; I wanted to spare you that image."

Viktor's eyes flashed emerald fire, and his face hardened. He bowed and said, "My apologies, Mr. Westin. I would have done the same. May I see your holding cage? Perhaps I can spot how one vampire managed to escape. We can leave Madame Westin and Mr. Brumble to visit with each other."

Britt nodded and led the way.

Tamara R. Lowery

Chapter 10

Viktor inspected the cell carefully, to the point of going in it and pulling the barred door closed behind him. He tactfully ignored his host's nervous gulp when he touched the silver coating the bars with no ill effect.

The cell contained no furniture of any kind. Obviously, Westin had more concern for not providing anything which might be used as leverage for breaking bars or removing the door than he was for his prisoners' comfort. A quick inspection of the door and its hinges showed how difficult if not futile any attempt to dislodge it would've proven anyway. Silvered cotter pins secured the hinge pins in position.

He levitated to the still open skylight next. Just as Carmella had shown him, the bars sat too close together to pass more than a hand between them.

"Would you close this, please? I'd like a better look at the rolling shutter. Quite an ingenious device, that."

Britt obliged and cranked the skylight shut. Viktor admired the overlapping interlock pattern to the slats which allowed the shutter to roll onto its cylinder. He also saw how effectively they blocked the sunlight. He wondered if some substance could be applied, much like the method Westin used to apply the silver coating, which could make it waterproof.

Apparently, rain leakage presented a problem with these particular shutters. He noticed the drain in the flagstone-paved floor when he alit.

He next looked at the mortar between the stones of the floor and the wall. Some of it looked quite crumbly.

"Did you add this room on?"

Britt shook his head. "I added the bars and the skylight's shutter. There had been a glass paned window in it before. The landlord said the room was built as an aboveground wine cellar, but the previous tenant added the skylight to use it as an atelier."

"I see. I need to know about your escapee."

He rubbed his chin, trying to recall the details, it seemed. "He looked like an older lad just on the cusp of adulthood. His hair was dark with a slight reddish tint to it. He spoke French and English with equal ease and tried to come across as personable. Sam said he seemed vaguely familiar to her, too, now that I recall."

Viktor began to chuckle. This earned him a perplexed look from his host. "I believe I know the vampire you speak of. If I am correct, I know how he escaped. He is ancient enough to use the means I have in mind. Did he give you a name?"

"No. How did he get out?"

"I see three possible routes he could have taken. You should get some more silver slurry and paint all the joins of the roof boards, any knot holes, repair the mortar used for the wall and floor, and regularly pour holy water down the floor drain. I see water partway down the pipe, so I know it never fully empties."

Britt gave him an incredulous look. "How could anything get out by any of those routes? He couldn't even fit between the bars."

"He could if they weren't already silvered. He is old enough to take the form of mist."

The man sat down hard on a nearby chair outside the cell. "I'd heard stories of that ability. I always thought it part of the misinformation they deliberately spread, like the lie they cast no reflection."

Vik exited the cell and shut it behind him. "As I said, he is ancient enough to do that. No true vampire under five to ten centuries should be capable of the feat. Jim and I are the only young vampires who've demonstrated the ability. My cadre and my daughters cannot. Were his clothes still in the cell?"

"Yes, they were. I take it clothing doesn't make the transition to vapor."

"It does not. If you still have the garments, I can verify my suspicion about who he was."

"Of course!" He got up and rummaged in a nearby cupboard. He returned with a finely tailored suit only a few decades out of fashion.

Viktor smirked. "He does like to play the dandy at times. You should feel honored, Mr. Westin. Those clothes and the scent they carry tell me you've played host to the ruler of the New Orleans and Louisiana kiss of vampires."

"In truth? How could such a powerful vampire be captured so easily? It was one of the least difficult hunts I've conducted."

"Because he allowed you to. He probably even orchestrated the whole affair; though to what end, I have yet to learn. I shall ask when I see him tonight." He stroked his beard and mused, "It wouldn't surprise me if he directed you toward your latest prey in some manner. By your account, she was the type of vampire he prefers not to have in his territory; far too indiscriminate of a predator and liable to attract unwanted attention."

Britt scowled skeptically. "If that was the case, why wouldn't he have disciplined her directly?"

Vik sighed. "I may loathe politics, vampire politics in particular, but I understand the reasoning which drives them. Her direct bloodline from Dragon made it impolitic for him to deal with her directly. Your actions make it appear her habits engendered her destruction, and he is left absolved of any perceived wrongdoing."

"Oh."

"Indeed."

They spent the next few hours discussing vampire hunting, its methods, and what little Britt and Sam had gleaned about the Daughters.

"Dusk is in about half an hour," Vik observed as they lingered over the dinner Sam served them. "I have an appointment to keep. If all goes well, I hope to leave port on the morning tide."

"May Zach stay here tonight, or must he return to the ship?" Sam asked.

"Entirely up to him," Vik replied. "Thomas and Jim would like to visit and pay their respects." He saw their hesitation. "I can ensure they feed before leaving the ship. I've a good store of bloody whiskey aboard. I do not allow any of my cadre to feed in this port out of respect for Jeorge."

"Jeorge?" Sam asked.

"Aye. He was your escapee and is the head of all the vampires in this territory."

She stiffened, and her scent changed. He caught a mixture of fear, wonder— and anger. "It was him!"

"Sam?" Britt shot his wife a look of concern.

"Back when I was still hunting for the Captain and my brothers, Captain Bainbridge and I stopped in this port. There was a kerfuffle over my being a Brumble, I was still passing as a man then. The mayor's daughter had gone missing, and he thought Thomas had taken her."

"My apologies, pet. I'm afraid that was my fault," Vik said.

She shot him a glare. "Oh, I know you took her. She is a vampire here now, isn't she?"

"She is, but how did you know?"

"Jeorge was curious about you and my hunt. He took me, stripped me," she clenched her dinner knife like a weapon, "and called her in to compare bite radii to see if the fang marks I bore were from you or one of your get."

"I was powerless to resist him. I couldn't even move! That was both humiliating and infuriating. Then, he tried to make me forget the encounter ever happened. I knew he looked familiar!"

Britt grew angry on her behalf. "If I'd known, love —.""

Vik cut him short. "You would possibly be dead now if you'd known and tried to seek revenge, Mr. Westin." He waved a hand at Samantha. "You know how strong-willed she is, and she only now, years later, broke fully free of his compulsion to forget. Remember, I said he allowed himself to be captured. Your skills had nothing to do with it."

"I'm willing to bet neither of you has rescinded the invitation you extended him by bringing him into your home. At the moment, I don't think you need to fear him.

If he'd truly wished you harm, he'd have returned and eliminated any threat you might present to him by now."

Sam placed a protective hand on her belly. Britt got himself under control and rose to stand behind his wife. He hugged her around the shoulders and stroked her hair, as she leaned against him.

Viktor saw the distress this caused in Zach, as well.

"We need to move; tomorrow, if possible," Britt said.

Even though he'd released them from his power and allowed a priest to cleanse them, Viktor still considered them under his protection.

"I will make an arrangement with Jeorge for your protection when I speak with him tonight."

"What about the Daughters of the Dragon?" Britt asked. "Can he protect us from them? Your connections in this port almost guarantee some of them will come here."

"He cannot," he admitted. "While I intend to hunt them down, I cannot promise they won't come here." He stared at the table and sighed. "There is one hope of protection I can offer you which doesn't involve relocation. Madame Westin is too far along to put through that kind of strain at present."

"What?" Sam looked at him with unshed tears and desperation in her eyes.

"You won't like it, and I am loathe to suggest it."

"Why?" Suspicion colored Britt's voice.

Sam caught on quicker. "You mean give up our freedom to you; freedom you regret granting us. Tell me, Captain Brandewyne, did you arrange all this?"

"The only thing I regret about granting your freedom is the physical pain your cleansing caused to Jim and myself."

A heavy silence filled the room.

Finally, Viktor broke it. "I will not press the matter. I go now to tend my business." He stood and gave them a half bow. "You have my word; I will abide by your decision."

With that, he left.

"Captain Brandewyne, welcome. I understand your need for haste. Jean awaits you in the library with the best references he could find on such short notice," Jeorge said by way of greeting.

"Thank you, my friend. I imagine you want me away from your territory as quickly as possible, given the latest developments," Vik replied.

"Not to be rude, but I fear you know me too well. Your presence presents an unique danger to my kiss."

"Yes; They have been sent." He deliberately walked at human speed, forcing the older vampire to hold back. "I have to wonder, Jeorge, have there been many new vampires of His direct bloodline in your territory recently?"

Jeorge stopped. "*Oui*. It cannot be helped. This was the Lady's last known location before she vanished." He sighed and looked around before speaking again. "It troubles me how He has sent some of his more indiscreet Children to me."

"I take it none of them are powerful enough to be Daughters."

"Hardly. These have been ones who believe brutality is the key to gaining that status. I doubt any of them will survive past a century."

"Especially if you arrange for them to run afoul of hunters."

Jeorge shot him a sharp glance. "I had nothing to do with that."

"Of course you didn't. Valara's own actions led to her destruction. Oh, by the way, it would be wise to avoid letting the Westins capture you or any of your kiss you wish to keep in the future. To ease their minds, I examined their holding cell and pointed out its weak spots to prevent future escapes."

"Did you now?"

"Madame Westin is with child. She has enough to worry about without the threat of a vengeful vampire returning to her home. Of course, I don't think either she or her husband will be doing much vampire hunting in the immediate future. She would've fallen prey to Valara if not for His timing on the delivery of His edict to hunt me. Had that happened, I couldn't let it go unanswered." He let the menace color his voice.

Jeorge nodded. "I understand. I have to admit, it puzzled me to find your scent but not your power on them. It surprised me even more to find the former Miss Brumble free of any vampire's power. She has been cleansed."

"Aye, Jim and I sent them to a priest in Tortuga and freed them. Hurt like hell, too." Vik winced at the memory.

118

"*Oui*, it does. Captain, you continue to astound me. Yet, if you willingly freed them, why is their continued safety of concern to you? "

"They are family, of a sort. Mr. Westin and Jim are long lost brothers. Westin erroneously believed the Lady murdered his mother and brother. In actuality, She turned his father years after the man accidentally killed his wife and abandoned his younger son. Some vampire hunting priest in Europe offered the elder Westin the false story to serve his own purposes."

"That would explain the strong resemblance between the young *m'sieur* and Her pet." He turned and continued to the library. Just outside the door, he stopped and looked up at the taller vampire. "I give you my word none of my kiss shall be sent to harm the young couple or their child. I cannot, however, offer them protection from Him or His agents."

"My thanks, my friend. I have offered them my protection where He is concerned. I do not know if they will accept or opt to take their chances. I gave them my word I would not force it on them."

Jeorge shook his head. "I fear many will be lost before this war is ended. I give you my word I will not willingly side against you, *mon ami*; even if it means I perish. That is a far better fate than enduring His direct rule again."

Chapter 11

"Captain Brandewyne! What a pleasure to see you again!" the old man greeted him upon his entry. "I have been quite busy since my arrival."

"So I see, *M'sieur* Beaujolais." Vik made note not only of the order and cleanliness of the library since his last visit, but the set of fangs the former school master now sported.

"Please, Jean will suffice. I've not much need of a surname these nights. When you told me of Jeorge's library, I had no idea it was so extensive. I've barely gotten it organized, and much is still in need of preservation or to be copied before it becomes too fragile to handle at all. But I've eternity before me to do it now."

He found himself grinning at the old man. He had a certain infectious enthusiasm about him.

"He's been like this ever since I sired him," Jeorge said. "I still have to remind him to feed on occasion. He's like a child with a new toy."

"That must be rare indeed," Vik said in amazement. "I know how demanding the Hunger can be."

"Oh, it's unheard of," Jean responded. "I've poured over so very many annals, chronicles, and books of lore. As yet, I've found no reference to a similar case in any vampire as new as I am."

"Jean, what information have you gleaned about the Daughters thus far?" Jeorge prompted.

"Oh, there are lots of records of their deeds and formidability, but I'm sure you are already acquainted with that. However, I've slowly been piecing together an account of their unique characteristics and names. I've identified four so far, beyond the eldest, whom Jeorge tells me you've already had dealings with. I suspect there are several more."

"It's quite fascinating research," he went on as he rummaged about in the pile of books and papers on the table. "Now what did I do with that list? Oh, here it is. It seems He has a pronounced preference for unusually clever, strong-willed women. All those I've learned of thus far are named for ancient goddesses of the hunt. Although, given how far back some of the histories go, it is quite plausible these women were the source of the mythic beings whose names they bear."

"You mean like Diana or Artemis?" Viktor asked. While the latter wasn't, the former was a rather common female name. Finding the right one would be difficult.

"Oh no, not those." Jean waved his hand in dismissal. "No, these names are far older and obscure. I imagine that was on purpose, to make it harder to learn about them. Every historian learned about the Greeks and Romans. Their writings were prolific and better preserved. Other areas and cultures were largely the victims of those conquering races who sought to replace them with their own ways, lore, and beliefs." He handed the list to Viktor. "The attributes listed next to the names are those of the goddesses but not necessarily of the Daughters who bear the names, unfortunately."

"I will keep it in mind. By that reasoning, the countries of origin won't always be the best place to look for them, either."

"No," Jean admitted, "but they at least offer starting points."

"True," Jeorge added. "I very much doubt my library can offer where they might be now. I will assign Carmella to assist Jean in his research. He can teach her to read the myriad languages these books contain, and she can make sure he feeds."

"My thanks, Jeorge. That will save me time getting new information as well as prevent my presence from endangering your kiss."

"My thoughts exactly, *mon ami.*"

Viktor looked at the list again. "These all seem to hail from the eastern Mediterranean or Black Sea regions. Perhaps Circe might have some information on them, not that she's likely to be cooperative."

"Circe? Like the witch from Homer's Odyssey who turned men to beasts?" Jean asked, eager as a schoolboy.

"Not like," Vik corrected him. "She is the self-same witch. I had to use moly, just as in the story, to defeat her wiles. She didn't take my refusal of her bed very well, though."

"Was she not as beautiful as in the story?" Jean asked.

"Oh, she is extraordinary to behold. I was warned not to share power with her, however; besides, I watched her turn from woman to sow and back again"

Jeorge laughed. "*Oui,* I can imagine that would be off-putting!"

"Very." He rolled the list up and tucked it in his shirt. "I thank you again for your help, my friends. I plan to leave on the morning tide. I will not return to this port except out of absolute necessity until this business is finished."

Jeorge clapped his forearm. "*Bon chance, mon ami*, but I fear we may never meet again. It has been a pleasure and an honor."

"Likewise."

As they left the library, Viktor pulled Jeorge aside. "I thought you might like to have your clothes back that you left at the Westins'."

Jeorge took the offered garments, a look of genuine surprise on his face. "*Merci, mon ami*! I didn't think they would have saved them. I know these are far from the current fashion, but they are comfortable."

"Clever of you to turn to mist to escape. I didn't know you could."

After looking around, both with his eyes and his sense of the members of his kiss, he replied. "Very few know I have that skill. It took me centuries to develop."

"What about being able to take animal form?"

"Alas, other than your Childe, my sire, the Lady, and the Dragon are the only vampires I've known to exhibit that particular talent."

Viktor smirked. "Add me to the list, Jeorge."

The older vampire went very still. Obviously, this news unsettled him. Viktor decided to put his mind at ease.

"I'll share some information I recently learned. Dragon started as I am, a living vampire. His first Childe turned him, and he destroyed her for it. The ability to take animal form was a gift from Mother Celie, now the All-Mother, to allow Him to move freely in daylight and an apology for not warning him about letting another vampire feed on him. In truth, he was such a new creature, she didn't know to warn him."

"Mother Celie? Isn't that the witch you say raised you?"

"She is the very person. I will tell you the secret to taking animal form. You are what you eat." He grinned while he watched Jeorge digest that nugget.

"I cannot eat the flesh of animals, *mon ami*."

"You can drink their blood, however. If you can bring yourself to choke down a little of their hair, feathers, scales, or skin it should work. I found I can change into animals I've eaten the flesh of when I was a mere man."

"I shall have to try this." Without further notice, he transformed to a smoky mist, his clothing dropping to the floor unceremoniously.

Viktor watched as the mist almost took on the shape of a rabbit. Just as the texture of its fur started to become visible it collapsed back to an amorphous blob. A few seconds later Jeorge stood before him nude, a mix of disappointment and delight on his face.

"Perhaps with a few decades of practice, I might master the feat. Amazingly, I could almost taste the rabbit flesh. The experiment was worth it just for that," he said as he picked his clothes up and began to put them back on.

Viktor mulled over why the trick hadn't worked. Though disorienting the first time he did it, he'd had no difficulty accomplishing it. A stray memory of Celie transforming Jim into the cat, Lazarus, came to him. He remembered the powder she'd sprinkled over his body.

More specifically, he remembered the scent of it and recognized it.

"Moly!"

"*Pardon moi?*"

"Mother Celie sprinkled moly on Jim's body before she turned him into a cat. She fed the cat a raven, which allowed him those two forms. It wasn't until he drank some of my blood after I'd had too much moly at once and cut myself that he was able to reclaim human form and hold it at will. I didn't gain the ability to take animal form until after completing the box of moly she gave me. I'd be willing to bet that's how she gave the ability to Dragon. How Thia or your sire came to have it, I can't speak to."

Jeorge sighed. "I shall just have to practice."

"I'm sorry, my friend. I had hoped it would work. It would've given the daylight back to you and possibly the ability to eat food again."

"I appreciate the thought, Captain Brandewyne. I wish you success in your quest."

Chapter 12

Viktor knocked at the Westins' door about an hour before dawn. A very weary-looking Samantha opened the door. He knew immediately from his link with Jim and Thomas both she and her husband had stayed up the entire night.

"Madame Westin, you should get some rest," he said with some concern.

"I may never see my brothers again," she responded. "I will have what time I can with them, Captain Brandewyne."

"Of course; I understand. I regret I must end that time soon. Thomas and Jim need to return to the ship before sunrise. May I come in?"

She nodded and motioned him in. He bowed and stepped across the threshold just as Britt came to investigate her delay in returning. Vik caught a slight change in her scent and called out to his host, "Catch her."

Sam's legs gave out beneath her. Britt barely made it to her in time to keep her from collapsing to the floor. "What have you done to her?"

"She is merely exhausted, Mr. Westin. I have not touched her." He looked at the man and saw the dark smudges under his eyes, as well. "Have either of you slept tonight?"

Britt sighed. "No, she refused to. I couldn't very well be callous enough to go to bed without her."

"You prove yourself a good and faithful man, Mr. Westin."

"Thank you, sir. If you will excuse me, I need to get her settled."

"Of course; I merely came to collect my crewmen. Dawn approaches."

Samantha recovered at that moment. "I can stand, Britt. Why are you carrying me?"

"You collapsed, my love." He set her back on her feet, but Vik noticed he kept a steadying arm about her waist.

"Let me at least say my goodbyes to my brothers."

Britt sighed and nodded. Sam walked under her own power back to the other room.

"She's too stubborn for her own good."

Vik clapped him on the shoulder. "I've learned it's best to let them do as they will, Mr. Westin. You'd be surprised at how resilient some women can be."

"Were you able to secure our safety?"

"Jeorge has given me his word he will not send any of his kiss after you with intent to harm. He knows I'm more powerful than him. He will not break his word."

Britt looked at him then rubbed his face in an apparent effort to clear his mind. He gave a half smile and shook his head. "I believe I owe you an apology for my attitude, sir. Years of training and conditioning tell me not to trust you, because you are both a pirate and a vampire. Yet, I have seen enough of your actions and heard enough about your reputation to know you mean what you say."

"A wise observation, sir."

"I'm just grateful you didn't kill me outright. Of course, this isn't the first time my actions have brought me close to death. Would you believe I was jailed for killing a public official in Antwerp?"

Vik blinked at him. "Really? Did you?"

He nodded. "I did, in a manner. The man had just been killed by a vampire posing as a prostitute and would've risen the next night had I not beheaded him. I didn't know his status at the time of my actions."

"How is it you weren't executed on the spot?" Viktor found himself interested in the tale despite being pressed for time. The similarities between his longtime friend, Jim, and this man ran deeper than just appearances.

"They thought me a madman when I started gibbering about vampires, a ruse which has gotten me out of a few scrapes before."

"He's more pirate than he'd care to admit," Jim said from the doorway.

Britt rubbed the back of his neck and glanced over at his brother. "I would argue the point, but killing vampires doesn't exactly fit well with polite society. Unfortunately, the ruse only proved a delay to the inevitable. I was told they'd heard similar stories before."

"Oh, now this sounds interesting," Vik commented.

"It seems the dead man I beheaded was a member of some secret society which had been accused of vampirism in the past by outsiders."

"And what is this society called?"

"It is a hedonistic group called the Court of Bendis. I'd heard rumors about it, and deaths or disappearances associated with the group fit the profile of vampire activity. I never could get reliable information on where they operated out of. I strongly suspect he set up the encounter with one of his lesser vampires in order to get me out of the way."

Viktor perked up at the mention of the group. The name seemed very familiar. "He?"

"Yes, Bendis. The best I could learn, he's positively ancient. I did catch a glimpse of him once."

Vik pulled the scroll out of his shirt and scanned it. A chuckle escaped his lips. "It fits. Thank you, Mr. Westin. You've given me a very good starting point in my hunt for the Daughters."

"Beg pardon?"

"Bendis is one of the four names I have to go on so far. She's named for an ancient hunting goddess, in this case from Thrace in ancient Greece. Of course, there is the possibility she was the inspiration for the myth. I've met a few vampires with delusions of godhood before. One of the characteristics mentioned about her was her preference for masculine clothing. Another was that she was often surrounded by nymphs and satyrs, which led to her being mistaken for Dionysus from time to time."

"You are right. It does fit." He yawned. "My apologies. What are the other names on your list? If I've heard of them, perhaps I can give you an idea on where to hunt for them."

"The other three I have so far are Anat, Dali, and Diktynna. You are being extremely helpful of a sudden, sir." Vik said with raised eyebrow. Experience taught him to be suspicious of such sudden changes in the tide.

"You can understand my reasons for giving up Bendis. He, I mean she caused me quite a bit of trouble. I wish I could help you with the others. The more you eliminate, the fewer I have to worry about showing up to threaten my family. Unfortunately, I don't recall ever hearing those names being mentioned during my years of hunting vampires."

"I'll just have to try to get the information out of this one, then." Vik sighed. He needed to get his men back to the ship and be on his way. "You have not mentioned it; I assume you decided to decline my offer."

"We really haven't reached a decision, to be honest. We haven't had time to discuss it between ourselves."

Vik stroked his beard in thought. He'd hoped to have an answer by now; but he hadn't taken into account they would spend so much time visiting with their brothers. He'd also given Jeorge his word he would leave port on the tide and not return— except in a case of extreme need.

He quickly formulated a plan.

"It will take me at least a week to pass the Florida Strait and sail far enough up the east coast to catch the trades. I can send Melanie to receive your answer. You don't have to open the door for her. Just leave a note. If you decide to accept, I will return with all haste."

"Thank you, Captain Brandewyne. You will have your answer within that time."

He stopped by Celine's, careful not to alert Angelique to his presence. His business lay solely with Gloribeau's minion.

"Ah good, you're still up. May I enter?" He remembered not to shatter her wards.

"Of course." She reached into her pocket and gave a slight twist to the hidden talisman.

Viktor felt the magical barriers drop and entered the little juju shop beneath the brothel. "Thank you, Celine. I have Jeorge's guarantee he and his will not trouble you. However, he can offer no protection from our mutual foe or His get."

"I figured as much, Captain Brandewyne."

"I will not be returning to this port until this business is done. This is to at least delay any further presence from Dragon's forces. I do have a favor to ask. Do you have or can you get any moly? I need three small packages— for gifts."

"Gifts? You are aware moly is mildly poisonous?"

"I suspected as much, in too large a dose and to humans. To a vampire it is best delivered through the blood of another. It enhances certain abilities."

Celine crossed her arms and leaned against the counter. "What abilities, and which three vampires?"

He chuckled. "Glory chose wisely with you, pet. The ability to take animal form and move freely in daylight and eat solids *only* in that form. I wish to give my daughters this gift as well as Jeorge. He has sided with me against Dragon. Since that bastard has this ability, I thought it would help to remove the advantage."

"And it puts Jeorge in your debt. Very well, I will provide the packets you requested. I don't have any in stock, but I can get it."

Viktor concentrated briefly, directing his thoughts to his eldest Childe. "A courier will be sent to deliver them. When can you have them ready?"

"No later than next week."

He handed her a small pouch of gold coins, kissed her hand, and made his exit.

Later that morning, once the *Incubus* cleared the delta and reentered the Gulf of Mexico, Hezekiah noticed some of the men displayed sour attitudes. As first mate, he took his duties seriously; especially where the crew's discipline and morale were concerned. He was determined to get to the heart of the matter before it spread throughout the crew and came to the captain's attention.

"Mr. Jon, a word with ye."

"Aye, Mr. Grimm." Jon-Jon's face brightened until he saw the look on Hezekiah's. "What be the problem, sir?"

"I notice the men you took ashore seem particularly surly this morning, yourself included." He let the unspoken "why" hang in the air and awaited an answer.

Jon-Jon gulped nervously. To an outsider, the sight of giant of a man cowed by someone a full foot or more shorter might seem comic, but the quartermaster well knew the Reaper's reputation.

"Well, y'see Mr. Grimm, the lads are just tired and a little put out is all. They'll be right as rain come afternoon and a good meal."

Grimm raised one eyebrow and clasped his hands behind his back. "Put out, Mr. Jon? How so?"

Jon-Jon sighed and rubbed his stubbly scalp. "We all thought we'd have a little time for some drink and sport last night; but Mr. Trundle had us lade on enough victuals to feed an armada for a month. We were humping cargo into the wee hours. Then havin' t'set sail not long after dawn took what hope we had. That's all it be, sir. Like I said, once they've got some of Mr. Trundle's fine cooking in their bellies they'll settle down."

"Gather them on the fo'c's'le."

"D'ye think that's necessary?"

He gave Jon-Jon an impassive stare.

"Right away, Mr. Grimm."

In short order, the quartermaster had the small group of men assembled before the first mate.

"It is my understanding there is some, shall we say, disgruntlement about how your time ashore was spent yesterday," he stated.

Most of the pirates vigorously shook their heads. A chorus of, "No, Mr. Grimm," rang out.

One pirate, however, proved the exception. "Aye, sir. I'll admit it, even if none of these lily-livered swabs will own up and back a mate. We humped our arses off with not so much as a grog or a quick shag to show for it."

Had he left it at that, Hezekiah might've lauded his honesty; but he made the fatal mistake of adding the grumble, "Might as well be back in th' bloody Navy."

Silence quickly spread across the deck and even into the rigging.

"Mr. Walters, report to the Captain's cabin."

Walters grew white as the sails. Too late, he realized his predicament. "I misspoke, sir. It won't happen again, I swear."

Hezekiah Grimm, feared throughout the Caribbean and beyond as the Grimm Reaper, remained impassive. "I will not repeat myself. The rest of you, back to work."

Viktor sat at his desk, several charts to one side with one rolled open and held in place by a pistol on one side and a bottle of blood and brandy on the other. Belladonna lounged on the bed nearby.

"Good morrow, Mr. Walters. It has come to my attention that you feel cheated because you didn't have time for some sport during your duty ashore." He spoke with a deceptively reasonable, almost pleasant tone.

"Beggin' your pardon Cap'n, but how?"

"I know everything that happens on my ship— everything."

"I-I m-mis-sp-spoke, Cap'n." The man looked like he couldn't decide whether to cry or wet himself.

Viktor stood, walked around the desk, past Walters, and locked the cabin door. He then stepped up behind the trembling man and leaned in close to his ear. "Luckily for you, I'm not particularly Hungry at the moment."

He placed a hand on the man's shoulder. "Pet, are you hungry?"

The smell of urine filled the air as a wet spot grew on Walters' trousers.

Belladonna shook her head. "No, I had a good hunt while you were in port."

"So, what shall we do with you, Mr. Walters? I know the Reaper feels you've been ungrateful; after all, most of the crew didn't get to go ashore at all."

The man started blubbering.

"I have an idea." Viktor's voice brightened. "Since you didn't get any sport ashore, Belle here could give you some. What say you, pet?" He sent the siren a mental image of what he had in mind.

"I have no objections," she replied and began to disrobe.

Walters shook his head no, as she stalked towards him.

Viktor reached out through the temporary blood bond he shared with his crew to calm the man's fears. If he was too afraid, he wouldn't be able to perform. That would make Belle cut the game too short.

The siren stopped in front of Walters and gently pushed his hair behind his ears. She massaged his scalp, and his muscles began to relax. "That's better. I want you to enjoy this." She took one of his hands and guided it to the moist folds at the juncture of her thighs.

Viktor went back to his charts and ignored them.

"Oh yes, that's it," Belle purred as Walters let his fingers explore her. She smiled when he grew hard.

When he reached for the band of his trousers, she stopped him. "Allow me."

She undid the drawstring and slowly pushed the pants down past his hips, stopping at his knees and effectively hobbling him where he stood. She stroked his erection and gently cupped his balls as if weighing them.

"We must wash you first." She stepped away just long enough to wet a cloth in the warm water of the nearby wash basin and ewer. When she returned, she used the cloth to slowly clean the urine away. His cock jumped with every stroke.

He reached for her again, but she deftly avoided his grasp and dropped to her knees. She grasped him firmly and traced the underside of him from base to tip with her tongue. When she closed her lips around the end of him, he groaned in ecstasy.

She slowly slid his full length in, relaxing her throat muscles to do so. Just as slowly, she drew him back out, flicking the tip of her tongue from side to side in the process.

He buried his hands in her hair and began thrusting frantically.

She quickly took control back, so he wouldn't release too soon. Holding his hips steady with inhuman strength, she bobbed her head, taking him in and out at varying speeds.

Once she sensed he was near, she took him in deep again. This time, she held him there and opened her mouth wide to take in his balls as well, a feat no human could reproduce on a fully erect man.

Of course, this involved allowing her teeth and jaws to take on their true, siren form. He didn't notice.

As she toyed with his balls with her tongue, he gave in to his orgasm. The moment he started to release, she eased her jaws shut just enough to hold him in place with her multiple rows of backward curved needle-sharp teeth designed to force live food down her gullet.

He finished and finally became aware of the pain when he tried to pull out of her mouth. He screamed as she looked up at him with amber eyes and continued to slowly, inexorably close her jaws.

He screamed until he was hoarse. Blood flowed in rivulets from the corners of her mouth. Finally, she snapped her jaws shut and severed his sex from his body.

She chewed some, obviously savoring the snack, then swallowed it.

Walters collapsed to the deck grasping his bloody crotch and growing whiter by the minute.

Belle picked up the flask of seawater she always kept handy and poured it over the fresh wound. She hummed a single note. Angry red skin grew over the wound and put an end to the bleeding.

Viktor stood and unlocked the door. "I thought you said you weren't hungry, pet."

"All that work made me a bit peckish."

Two pirates entered at Viktor's unspoken summons and picked Walters up under his armpits. When one reached to pull the injured man's trousers back up, he said, "No. Take him up on deck just as he is."

He then addressed his victim. "That should take care of whether or not you have time for sport during important work details, Mr. Walters."

They took the man from the cabin. Viktor closed the door behind them.

Chapter 13

Melanie answered the summons to Jeorge's audience chamber. Her Sire had only been out of port two days, possibly never to return. She had her suspicions about what her master wanted.

The ancient vampire made her wait nearly two hours before he entered the room and took his seat.

"You may rise, child."

She stood from the kneeling position she'd held the entire time of her wait with fluidity as if it had been merely moments. "You called for me, my lord."

"*Oui*. I wish you to deliver a message to M'sieur and Madame Westin." He held out a sealed letter, which she approached and took. "Tell me, do you know if they accepted your Sire's offer of protection?"

"He has not seen fit to inform me, my lord."

"I hope they did. A storm approaches which will be beyond my ability to shield them from. I will be hard pressed to protect my own."

She knew he referred to the Dragon's obsession with her Sire. "Them."

He nodded in confirmation. "Wait for a reply when you deliver this."

"As you command."

On her way to the vampire hunters' house, she reached out to Viktor. He let her know the Westins hadn't reached a decision on his offer but promised him one before the week was out. He also informed her to leave the letter on the stoop. Chances were, they wouldn't answer the door. This frustrated Jeorge's instructions to await a reply. Viktor's wry amusement at her predicament did little to soothe her irritation.

Britt scribbled a brief missive to relay to Captain Brandewyne.

The decision he and Samantha finally reached had been hard to arrive at. She'd even joked that childbirth had to be easier.

His hand shook as he wiped the blotting sand from the paper and folded it over. For better or worse, the decision was made. There could be no going back now.

They'd argued and weighed their options for over a full day. They were free of the vampire pirate's influence thanks to the cleansing administered by that priest in Tortuga. All Britt's training told him it was foolishness to willingly allow their souls to be corrupted and imprisoned again.

If not for the very real danger they faced from the Daughters of the Dragon and Samantha's vulnerability due to her pregnancy, he wouldn't even consider it.

He'd had to remind his wife of how powerful Carpathia had been the one time he'd encountered her in person. Despite all their training and blessed crucifixes, he and his father had been powerless and defenseless before the eldest Daughter. Brandewyne offered them at least a partial immunity to that level of power.

Finally, Sam had relented to his arguments.

He took a deep breath and stood with the note. The darkness outside served to remind him of the price of procrastination. He had no idea what time of night the pirate's vampire daughter would check for messages.

He opened the door to a lovely young woman. She seemed as startled to see him as he to see her. The speed with which she vanished marked her as vampire. He wondered if she was the messenger for the Captain; then he spotted the sealed letter on the stoop. He picked it up and set his down before closing the door again.

Safely inside, he broke the seal and unfolded the letter.

"*Monsieur et Madame* Westin,

I wish to make an arrangement with you for the discreet— removal of certain vampires from my territory. While most are those of direct descent of the eldest of my kind, a few may be of my own line who've proven themselves intractable and troublesome.

I congratulate you on your disposal of Valara. I sent this message via Melanie, daughter of Captain Viktor Brandewyne; I believe you are acquainted with Him. She shall await your reply.

Jeorge"

"That ballsy bastard," Britt muttered. "I'll not wake my wife just to put this question to her. He can damn well wait for an answer."

Melanie relayed the message she'd retrieved to Viktor. She also let him know what she'd heard Britt say.

Viktor's mental chuckle made her roll her eyes. *"Just be tactful when you relay the reaction to Jeorge, pet. I'll talk with the Westins before sunrise."*

"Oh joy. I'm sure you don't want him to know about your return."

"I do not. It would only trouble him."

"As you command."

"Where are you going?" Jim asked when he entered the Captain's cabin.

Viktor stood at the window casement, obviously about to step out. "Your brother and his wife have seen reason, at last. Tell Mr. Grimm I will return before sunset." With that, he took to flight out the open window and soon vanished beyond the horizon.

"Damn, I didn't know he could fly that fast," Jim said to the empty cabin. "Good thing Belle isn't aboard right now. This would really put her in a mood."

Viktor took a few moments to neaten his clothes before he knocked at the Westins' door. Normally, he wouldn't care, but the speed of his flight nearly ripped the clothes from his body.

He found the thrill of speed intoxicating. Perhaps for the return trip he would strip and see just how fast he could fly.

Britt Westin answered the knock, bleary-eyed and clearly roused from slumber. He peered hard at his visitor in the low lamplight.

"Captain Brandewyne?"

"Aye; may I come in?"

"Oh, of course, by all means." The vampire hunter ushered the vampire into his home. He set the lamp on a table and turned up the wick. "Good heavens, man! What happened to you?"

Viktor chuckled. "Remember, I told you I would return with all haste should you choose to accept my offer. It seems my garments don't travel well at quite such a velocity. I nearly flew out of them, so to speak."

"That would have been awkward," Samantha said from the doorway of the bedroom.

The look on her face told Viktor she might not have complained had that been the case. His heightened senses suggested the burgeoning life in her womb accounted for some of the latent lust he read on her.

He bowed but gave her a wicked wink for good measure. Her blush and quickened pulse rewarded his effort.

Britt scowled at the exchange but held his peace. He closed the door behind them.

"Before we proceed, Captain Brandewyne, I must know; will this have an adverse effect on my unborn child?" Sam asked.

Viktor thought about it for a moment or two. Finally, he responded, "I do not believe so, Madame Westin. My son, Robert, seemed to suffer no ill effects from my feeding on his mother." He carefully omitted he'd fed on Alyssa before he impregnated her.

Sam cocked her head and crossed her arms. "I hear some doubt in your voice, sir."

He nodded. "True; my doubt stems from the fact Robert's mother was a mermaid, not human."

She looked as if she wanted to question him further. He knew he couldn't afford the time. "I hate to rush this, truly I do; but the less time I spend in this port, the better for all involved."

"Jeorge?" Britt asked.

"Partially; I did promise I wouldn't return to New Orleans until my business with the Daughters and the Dragon is finished, except in case of extreme need. I believe this situation applies. My presence poses a great risk to his kiss and the port, in general."

"I see." The man sighed. He pushed his collar open.

Sam spoke before he could. "I'll go first. Do it now, Captain, before I lose my nerve."

Viktor smelled her fear, and he saw her determination. He recognized her offer for the valorous act it was. She'd experienced his embrace before, under less than pleasant circumstances. During a loss of control of his Hunger, he'd attacked her.

Had Jim, his oldest friend, second oldest Childe, and Sam's brother-in-law, not risked himself and intervened, Viktor would have killed her.

He wanted to mitigate that offense and make this as gentle on her as possible.

He raised her hand to his lips and placed a tender kiss on her knuckles. She trembled at his touch. With his free hand, he cupped her cheek and directed her gaze to his. He did not try to take her will. He sensed how much of a challenge it would prove. He had no desire to brutalize her that way.

Instead, he turned her hand to bare her wrist. He sealed his mouth over it and softly ran the tip of his tongue over her pulse point. He felt her pulse quicken and watched her eyelids flutter. At that moment, he drove just the fine points of his fangs into her soft flesh only until he tasted blood.

Her soft moan reminded him of a virgin's after her lover's initial, penetrating thrust.

Her blood held a rich, sweet saltiness he rarely got to enjoy: pure, healthy, and full of nourishment for her child.

In a flash, he left her and stood as far away as the room allowed. He couldn't repress his own groan of pleasure.

"That was it?" Sam looked shaken, aroused, but somewhat disappointed.

"That was all that was necessary," he replied and added, "Your child remains free of my influence."

She looked at her wrist and showed it to her husband in the lamplight. "This isn't even going to leave a scar. How do I know it worked?"

Viktor sent her a very graphic, sensual, and visceral image of what he'd like to do to and with her.

"Oh! Oh—." Her eyes widened in surprise, and she drew out the second "oh" as comprehension set in.

"Your turn, Mr. Westin." He didn't give the man time to react to his wife's response. He stood behind him, placed a restraining arm around his chest and shoulders, and bit deep into the juncture of neck and shoulder.

He tasted the strength in Britt's blood and drank a little more than originally intended. Still, he withdrew before he could weaken the man. This exercise was for their protection and benefit, not to satisfy his Hunger.

"I believe your wife is in need of your services, Mr. Westin. Enjoy the rest of your night." He implanted the same image in Britt's mind as he had Sam's, but he made sure it was only the married couple engaged in the fantasy.

They barely noticed his exit.

On his flight back to the ship, he reached out along his link with Belladonna.

"I need you, Belle."

She sensed something wrong in his mental tone, an undercurrent of distress and urgency. *"What happened? Where are you?"*

"I will be in my cabin." He shut down communication. He knew the action ensured she'd return from her hunt as quickly as possible.

Less than half an hour later, he spotted the *Incubus*. He saw the siren beat him back by mere minutes and watched her transform her shark tail into legs.

He flew into his cabin through the open window just before she opened the door. He tossed his boots and the bundle of clothes to the side as she entered.

"I'm sorry for not knocking, but your summons held an unusual urgency," she said then stopped as she caught full sight of him. "Viktor?"

"Close the door."

The morning sunlight shone in behind him, and he used it to keep her from seeing his face clearly. He kept his mental guards tight. He did not want her to see his struggle for control of his passions and appetites. The siren didn't scare easily, but he knew that would terrify her.

"You're naked," she stated.

"As are you."

He saw her reach back for the door latch. He intercepted her and held her close. Rather than soothe him, the feel of her soft, cool flesh only heightened the fever heat in his own. His hardness throbbed, trapped between them.

Belladonna raised her face to his. He saw her welcoming smile and felt her skin grow warm in answer to his heat. She placed her hands on his shoulders and began to pull. He put his hands on the back of her thighs just above her knees. Together, they pulled her body up his until he could kiss her without stooping.

He sheathed himself deep inside her. A sense of peace and home swept over him.

Neither of them remembered much after that.

Viktor returned to his senses sometime later. Belle's body draped partially over his, once again slightly cool to the touch.

A jolt of concern shot through him for a moment. It quickly passed. He tasted no blood, nor saw any fang marks on her anywhere.

She woke with a small, satisfied moan and stretched. It took all his willpower not to take her again.

"Hello," she said with a smile.

"Hello, pet. You worried me for a moment."

Her hand brushed his stomach. He gently stopped her before she brought it lower. As much as he would enjoy another go 'round, he had questions and the state of his ship and crew to see to.

"What brought that on?" It seemed the siren had questions of her own. "You haven't been that intense since I helped you break free of Carpathia's hold."

"My arrogance and carelessness, I'm afraid."

She raised an eyebrow and sat up.

"Perhaps we should both dress before we continue this, Belle. I'm having a hard time concentrating."

Her responding laugh elicited an eager reaction from the most rebellious part of his body. "So I see. Very well, I'll return in a few minutes and give you time to compose yourself, Viktor."

He groaned appreciatively at the sight of her backside as she exited his cabin.

Chapter 14

Belladonna wore her usual shirt and breeches. She'd broken Viktor long ago of trying to get her to wear more feminine garb. She did own some but only used it for special occasions. Dresses weren't suitable for shipboard life, and he refused to let her go about in the nude on a regular basis.

Given that the crew of the pirate ship was off the menu, so to speak, she didn't complain overly much.

She gave a cursory knock before entering his cabin once again. Viktor sat at his desk fully clothed and slightly flushed. She knew he wasn't ill. His vampirism gave him immunity to disease. His scent told her he'd brought his own release shortly before her return.

That explained the flushness.

She took a chair opposite and crossed her arms. "Now what's this about your uncharacteristic admission of carelessness?" she began.

For a few moments she thought he would deny ever saying such. Silence filled the cabin like pure granite.

"That was unlike me, wasn't it," he said.

"You are avoiding the subject."

He grinned. "I'm enjoying it, too. You're adorable when you're peeved, pet."

She narrowed her eyes and gave him a sly smile. Her fingers extended into talons as she drummed them on the desktop. "Would you like to see just how 'adorable' I can be?"

He relented from aggravating her. "I kept my fresh bond with the Westins a little too open on my return flight—."

"You went back to New Orleans?" she interrupted.

"Yes, last night."

"You do realize how far away we are."

He nodded. "Which was why I was naked when you came in. I very nearly flew out of my clothes on the way there. I stripped for the return flight so I could see just how fast I could go."

She just stared at him, stunned and a little frightened.

"Belle?"

Her voice came out as a low whisper. "I cannot travel that far in the amount of time you were gone, even if I were to only turn around immediately upon my arrival."

Concern painted his features. "You are frightened. I never intended that, pet."

She knew from his scent and body language he truly meant it. This fact helped her regain self-control. "What did Jeorge have to say about this?"

"I did not let him know. He is wary of me enough, as it is. Melanie knows, but she is skilled at careful omissions. I've instructed her to let him know the Westins are mine, but to omit the fact I made them so well after I left port."

She pulled up her knees and rested her chin on them as she pondered the situation. "Hmm. They have been useful sources of information, and I'm sure their brothers will appreciate you giving your protection."

"They will definitely need it," he stated. "Jeorge sent Melanie to them to make an arrangement. He'd like to use them to weed out the Dragon's get from his territory. He plans to send those of his own kiss who've gotten out of line their way to deflect any suspicion of collusion."

"I see what you mean. For only direct descendants of the Dragon to fall prey would draw His attention and give the impression Jeorge has sided against Him." She then steered the conversation back on course. "So, tell me, how exactly did keeping your new bonds too open play into what we did?"

"Do you have any idea how potent a healthy, pregnant woman's blood is; especially one I find attractive?"

Understanding dawned on her. "I sometimes forget you are incubus to my succubus. You feed on blood or sex just as I feed on flesh or sex."

He nodded. "Samantha doubted I had truly claimed her. My bite had been too gentle, and I only permitted myself a small taste to prevent losing control. So, I sent her a little fantasy to prove the connection. To keep peace with her husband, I sent him the same fantasy but put him in my place with his wife."

"Then you eavesdropped."

"Aye."

She noticed he showed no true remorse for his actions. The only thing which puzzled her was why Viktor would care what Britt Westin thought of his lusting for Samantha, now that the man was his thrall. She decided not to broach that topic, however. It really wasn't that important, and she recognized Viktor had grown beyond the predator she'd bound herself to so many years ago.

She stood and stretched, fully aware of his eyes on her.

"Well then, since you gifted me such a satisfying morning, and your business in these waters is concluded for the time being, I believe I shall sing up a wind to speed us across the sea."

She turned and strode out of the cabin heading topside.

She heard his mental warning to his mates and the riggers.

Samantha Westin woke up nestling against her husband's body. The light streaming through the closed shutter slats told her the day was well advanced. The room felt stuffy, and a fine sheen of sweat covered their bodies.

Britt didn't stir when she climbed out of bed.

She made her way quietly to the wash basin. The water in the ewer felt tepid. She washed anyway.

While the bath provided some relief, the room grew hotter. She went to the window and opened the slats to let a breeze in. She thought about opening the shutters altogether but decided against it. Even though their bedroom faced the rear of the house and was a good bit above the level of the alleyway, she heard children playing somewhere nearby. It was best not to risk being seen until she had some clothes on.

"You are magnificent."

She jumped at the words and turned to see her husband watching her.

"I am fat and unwieldy."

"Nonsense," he countered and got out of the bed. He strolled over and kissed her cheek before turning to make use of the wash basin as well. "You are glorious, radiant, and filled with love, light, and my child."

She noticed he remained flaccid; unusual for him on waking. "It looks like part of you does not agree with your statement."

He looked down and laughed ruefully. "He's just exhausted. I'm surprised either of us can stand, let alone walk, this morning."

"Afternoon."

"What?"

"It is afternoon, my love. We slept half the day away."

"It doesn't surprise me after how we spent the latter part of the night."

"That wasn't us." An angry chill spread through her at the certainty of that thought.

"I beg to differ, my love. It most certainly felt like us."

She shook her head. "No, that was Captain Brandewyne's doing. He— showed me things to disprove my doubts. You," she stabbed a finger in his direction, "performed every act verbatim. He used your body to have his way with me. I felt his presence throughout our lovemaking, and some of the things we did I never would have thought possible; especially in my condition."

He gazed at her, and she saw the realization grow in his eyes. "Now you mention it, I felt it, too."

She walked over to him and tentatively touched his chest. He did not recoil. He embraced her and held her close.

She mumbled into his chest, "Britt, I think he used me to have his way with you, as well."

"I know. Oddly, I'm not as bothered by that as I would've imagined I would be. I mean, if someone had postulated the possibility beforehand. I got the sensation he was more curious about how a woman's body reacted than satisfying some hidden desire to have a male lover. I definitely sensed his intrusion to both of us was neither malicious nor to show dominance."

She bit her lower lip. "So, you don't feel violated?"

He stroked her hair. "I know I should; but no, I do not. I hope you don't think ill of me for that. Do you feel violated, love?"

She shook her head. "I felt afraid I would lose you over this. I don't and didn't feel violated. I do feel conflicted, however."

"How so?" He pulled back from her without breaking contact and studied her face.

"You know how much I truly love you, Britt, but I wouldn't hesitate to go to his bed if he invited me." She rushed to finish before he could say anything. "I don't love him, but he excites me. Please don't think me a wanton."

He smiled, leaned down, and kissed his wife soundly. When he pulled back, he said, "Before last night, I would have been hurt. Given what we experienced and to what depth, I don't blame you. I'd fuck him, too, if I were a woman. I honestly didn't know about some of the things we did last night, or that they could be done."

She laughed in relief. "I agree, but let's not do them again for a while. I don't think I'd have the stamina right now."

"Nor do I, my love, nor do I."

About mid-Atlantic, Viktor finally brought up something to Belladonna which had puzzled him since leaving New Orleans. He couldn't figure it out and realized he needed a female's perspective, even if the female wasn't human.

"Pet, I experienced something odd, or at least odd to me, when I was in contact with Samantha Westin's mind."

She gave him a look which said, "this better be good." Knowing her territorial nature regarding him, he'd expected the look and chose to ignore it.

"Is it common for women to be aroused by the sight of two men together?" he plowed ahead.

Her reaction of stunned silence, mouth slightly agape, told him she definitely hadn't expected that particular question. While he found this amusing, he really did want an answer to the question.

"Well?"

"I suppose it depends on the woman. Why? What happened?"

"When I bit her, I was extremely gentle. When I bit her husband in front of her, I wasn't. She almost came just at the sight of our embrace. Granted, I probably started the process with the fantasy I implanted in her mind, but her physical reaction was definitely tied to the sight of my arm around her husband and my mouth on his neck."

"Did you find it arousing?" Belle asked with an impish smirk.

"I," he began, about to vehemently deny it, but stopped short.

"You did." She cocked her head to the side. "Interesting; I should have seen this coming."

He scowled at her. "Fine, I did find it arousing. The stimulus of feeding on fresh, healthy blood is very similar to sexual arousal. That still doesn't explain why she found it arousing."

The siren tapped her lip in thought. After some time, she spoke again. "I think I may have a theory about that; well, about this instance specifically."

"And that would be?"

"She loves her husband. She fantasizes about being with you. Something I've noticed about human males is their reluctance to show any tenderness publicly. Your sexual aura probably provoked a physical reaction in Mr. Westin at the time. Plus, her pregnancy has advanced. The combination of these things was enough to bring her to climax."

"I have a slightly different theory."

They looked over to see Jim Rigger, naked, leaning against the shelf he'd been napping on as Lazarus in his feline form.

"She loves him. She wants you. She got excited by the sight of you together and the thought of fucking both of you at the same time," he said with a grin. "I speak from years of experience having multiple lovers at the same time."

Vik narrowed his eyes at his friend. "Do you say that because you figure a woman would think like you, or are you hoping Belle and I would let you play with us?"

Jim chuckled and blew a kiss at his captain. "Both, of course. You know how pretty I think you are, Vik."

The vampire and siren both laughed at his foolishness.

Not to be deterred, Jim looked at Belle and asked, "What say you, Belle?" He put his arms around his captain and leaned his head against Vik's cheek. "Does this make you want to have us both at the same time?"

She rolled her eyes.

Vik's hand found its way around his friend's throat. He gave his most lethal smile. "You will never mention this conversation or subject to anyone else."

"Of course not, Vik." Jim's face showed no sign of repentance, but Viktor knew he would obey.

Chapter 15

For three days Carmella awaited news from the street urchin she'd bespelled. Finally, he arrived at the rooms she'd rented for when she wished to make daytime excursions without alerting Jeorge's household.

"Mistress! *Madame* Thibideaux says she'll have your package ready by noon!"

"*Bon*, Phillippe," the vampire replied. She handed the lad a small pouch that jingled a bit. "Take this to her when you go back to pick it up. Tell her Captain Brandewyne sends his thanks."

The boy's eyes grew large. "Bloody Vik Brandee, the pirate? You know him?!"

She laughed at his enthusiasm, careful not to reveal her fangs. "*Oui*, I have known him for many years. Long enough almost to consider him my father."

"*Mon Dieu*! Do not worry, mistress. I will not fail you or Captain Brandee."

"*Merci*, Phillippe."

Phillippe returned that early afternoon with the promised package. Carmella had him wait while she inspected the contents. She separated two of the three smaller packets and set them aside.

Taking up a scrap of vellum, quill, and ink, she composed a brief note.

Jeorge ,

I arranged to acquire some moly. I trust it will aide your efforts.

Viktor Brandewyne, Captain.

She placed the note with the remaining packet and handed it back to Phillippe. The other packets quickly vanished into her pocket.

"Do you remember where to deliver this?"

The boy nodded.

Her eyes took on a warm brown glow. She made sure to capture his gaze. "After you finish the transaction, you will have no memory of ever meeting me or why you are there."

"*Oui,* mistress."

Once she made sure her wrappings were secure and no one was present to see her, Carmella flew back to the roof of Jeorge's mansion near the necropolis.

She crept back in through the garret window she'd left open and quietly made her way back to her room.

Melanie never stirred, still dead for the day.

Jeorge looked up from the book he was reading after his initial feeding of the night. A mortal servant stood at the doorway of the library awaiting his notice.

"*Oui,* Maurice? What is It?"

"Your pardon, master. A boy just delivered this for you. He immediately seemed confused as to his whereabouts immediately after handing it over."

"Interesting." He held his hand out for the package. Maurice surrendered it. "Thank you, that will be all."

The servant bowed and exited the room.

Jeorge found the note and read it. He smiled but raised an eyebrow. He recognized the handwriting and knew the pirate was not the author, although he may have indicated what to write.

He returned to his book and waited patiently.

Carmella and Jean entered the library together. The librarian headed to his workstation. Jeorge motioned for the former prostitute to join him.

"*Oui?*"

"A package arrived from your sire. However, I know he did not have it delivered personally. He has been away from this port too long for any bespellment on the courier to last."

She frowned. "Are you sure the courier was bespelled?"

He smiled patiently. "Most definitely. Captain Brandewyne is considerate enough to not compromise our location with the uninitiated. That is why he had you arrange for the delivery, *mon amor*. Did you think I wouldn't recognize your handwriting, Carmella?"

She stood there, a look of dread, or more accurately, terror in her eyes. This puzzled him.

"You need not be frightened. I am not angry. I merely wonder why you didn't have it brought to me yesterday."

"Forgive me, master. It did not arrive until midday today."

"Today." Now he had reason to justify her fear. "Jean, please leave us for a time. Have Melanie sent to us. I have need for a private discussion with Captain Brandewyne's daughters."

The librarian left but gave his student a worried look as he passed.

"Is there a problem, my lord? Jean seemed quite distressed when he found me," Melanie said when she arrived in the library.

"That is what I wish to learn. Secrets have been kept. Secrets I was previously unable to detect despite both your blood oaths to me. I find this troubling."

"What we failed to reveal, we did so at our sire's behest. He did not wish us to frighten you and thereby place ourselves in danger. It was not done with malice on his part or ours," she replied.

Carmella added to her sister's revelation. "Neither he nor we have any desire to overthrow you, master. We are honor bound to serve and protect you. He has very few friends, and he numbers you among them."

He gazed at them, expressionless. They stood patiently, awaiting his decision.

"Is your sire aware of the predicament he has placed you in?"

"I have informed him, my lord," Melanie answered. "He is observing but will not interfere. He wishes to maintain your trust and friendship."

"Very well. First, I ask if there are any further secrets either of you have kept from me."

"I am the only one of us able to remain alive during daylight," Carmella replied.

Melanie proved unable to hide her surprise at the revelation. "How long have you been able to do that?"

"Since before I came here. I don't know if it's because I'm the Captain's eldest Childe or because of being forced to remain alive during the day by the cursed necromancer who enslaved me."

She continued, "We both can fly."

"Intriguing but not surprising, given your sire. He taught you to fly before he brought you to me. I knew it was just a matter of time before Melanie gained the ability, as well."

"There is one last bit of information about us I have not shared yet, master. The Captain purchased three doses of moly; one for you and one each for us. He wanted to make sure we both had a means of escape, should the city fall to our mutual enemy's forces."

Jeorge regarded the two vampires in silence but no longer stone faced. Other than keeping secrets from him, neither had ever tried to undermine his authority. In fact, they were less questioning than some of his own line.

On more than one occasion, Melanie's political acumen had served him well. Carmella was proving an able assistant and caretaker to his librarian, Jean.

He decided to forgo any punishment for either.

"I do ask that you not keep anything from me in the future. I understand your misgivings about divulging your advanced and unusual abilities. However, I have had both of you in my service long enough to know you meant me no malice. Do you have the other packets of moly with you, Carmella?"

"*Oui.*"

"Then I shall arrange for the experiment to commence."

Jeorge signaled for Jean to return to his duties and reassured the librarian that his student and caretaker was in no distress. He then sent for three fresh victims to be brought to his throne room along with meals for the humans.

The three vampires retired from the library to the throne room to await their meals.

When the humans and the food arrived, they handed them each a packet of moly.

"Welcome, honored guests," Jeorge greeted the unwitting victims. "Please accept this bounteous meal. This is a very rare spice designed to enhance the flavors. Only the very wealthy can afford it. I have selected you to experience this gift normally beyond your means."

The human, obviously chosen from among New Orleans' poorest, wasted no time pouring the fine powder all over their food. They tasted it and began to eat ravenously. It never occurred to them to question why their hosts weren't eating.

The vampires found they had to compel their victims to remain awake long enough to complete the food. As soon as they finished, they dropped into a stupor.

"Viktor did experience something similar when he finished his dose. I remember being alarmed by what I felt from him at that time," Carmella commented. "There is a possibility we may momentarily weaken after we feed on these."

"Melanie, go lock the doors," Jeorge ordered. She immediately complied. None of them wanted to be incapacitated while others could access them.

"Which of you would like to go first?" he asked once they secured the room.

"I will, my lord," Melanie volunteered. "I am the youngest and least advanced. Therefore, I should be the most accurate bellwether."

He nodded, and she chose her victim. He observed her intently as she fed, watching for any signs of weakness or faltering.

When her victim lay dead in her arms, she looked up with eyes dilated to the point of appearing black. She licked her lips. "What an interesting flavor."

"Do you feel faint?"

"No. I feel invigorated. Shall I attempt to change form now?"

"If you feel ready."

She closed her eyes and concentrated. Moments later, a peahen stood on the now empty dress. She craned her head around and began to preen her feathers.

"I have never seen a bird such as this," Carmella commented with wonder.

Jeorge laughed with delight. "It is a peacock, or more accurately, a peahen."

The bird pecked at the crumbs on one of the plates. Shortly after, she turned back into Melanie.

"You have an excellent chef, my lord. That tiny morsel of beef tasted amazing!"

Carmella went next. Soon, a sleek, black dog struggled to walk out of her dress and get to the plates. She finally got free of the garment and lapped at some residual gravy.

Once again, the change back to human form came quickly.

"That was even better than Edmina's cooking."

"I try to acquire the most skilled for my mortal household staff. Well-fed food enhances the flavor of the blood. Why did the transformation reverse so quickly?"

Carmella answered for both of them. "I believe it was because we ate so soon after the initial change. There was still some moly on the food, and the taste of solid food after so many years of going without shocked me and broke my concentration."

Melanie nodded her agreement.

"Very well, I shall abstain from the crumbs." With that, he transformed into a rabbit. He hopped around the room, experimenting with the different perspective and variations in his senses.

Once satisfied, he shifted form again, this time to a stag. Finally, he returned to human form.

"So, I truly can take the form of any beast I've had the flesh of." He turned to the female vampires. "The peahen I understand. Gilded roast peacock is a popular dish among the higher classes. What about the dog?"

Carmella's face grew livid. "Dog?! That *batarde* Henri! If he wasn't dead already, I would go back to Terra Beau and kill him myself!"

The other vampires looked at her in confusion as reddish tears streamed down her face.

"My poor, sweet Jasmine!"

Jeorge reached out and gently wiped away a tear. "Please, my dear, who are Henri and Jasmine, and why does this upset you so?"

Carmella sniffled and snarled. "Henri was my pimp when I was still mortal. Jasmine was a sweet, little, black puppy a customer gave me as a gift in addition to my payment."

"Henri said we could not keep or afford pets. He took her away and told me he would give her to a farmer he knew far inland."

"A few days later, he said he'd gotten some beef from this farmer and had Edmina make it into a stew for us. I'd never had beef before. Fish, chickens, and the occasional goat were the most available meats in the village."

"I remember how flavorful that stew was and wanted to take the form of the animal whose flesh I'd tasted. Now I know why this gravy tasted so much better. He made her cook my dog!"

Melanie rubbed on her back in an effort to calm and comfort her. Her expression showed her incense for such a vile, cruel trick.

Carmella laughed bitterly. "We thought we were the best fed whores in all of Hispañola that day."

"Why didn't this Edmina tell you?" Jeorge asked.

"I do not hold her at fault. Henri could be a cruel bastard. She tried to run away with a British sailor once. His captain had the man beaten when he found her aboard. Then he let his entire crew have her. They left her ashore broken and bleeding, not caring if she survived."

"Henri took her back in because she was a good cook and as an object lesson to the rest of us. She was terrified of being with a man after that. Henri always threatened that if she ever 'got out of line' again, he would lock her in the stocks in the village naked and let every man who wanted have a go at her for free."

Jeorge cupped her cheek and kissed her gently. "*Ma cherie*, we all have bad things in our past, some worse than others. Remember that they are past. The man who tormented you is truly dead, is he not?"

She nodded. "*Oui,* our brother, Jim told me he killed Henri before *mon Capitan* turned him. They wanted no word of their presence in Terra Beau to reach the pirate hunters."

"*Bon.* A wise decision."

He unlocked the door.

At a silent command from Jeorge, servants entered the throne room to remove the dishes and the bodies. One remained behind to gather the clothing from the floor, neatly fold it, and set it aside. They then drew back the drapery which concealed the large bed. The same bed Melanie shared with Viktor the night he sired her as a vampire.

She smiled at the memory.

Carmella wiped the tear stains from her face and stared at the bed. She then looked at her sister and Jeorge with hopeful curiosity.

Jeorge smiled and took both their hands in his. He kissed each woman's hand in turn.

"*Mes amours*, have either of you been with another woman before?"

"*Non,*" Melanie replied. "Captain Brandewyne was my first lover. You have known of all since then."

Carmella shook her head with a wry smile. "*Non,* but almost once. Henri stopped us. He didn't want us wasting our energy on anyone not a customer. No one in our village could afford an additional whore if they paid for my services. Is that what you have in mind, my master?"

"*Exactament.* A *menage a troi* if you both are willing."

The women exchanged a glance, Melanie shy but curious, Carmella curious and excited. They turned back to him and nodded in unison.

"*Bon!* This will help banish sad memories and melancholy." He led them to the bed.

Tamara A. Lowery

Chapter 16

Against Grimm's arguments, Viktor and Belle entered Antwerp alone, save for Lazarus' companionship. The latter agreed to stick to his feline and corvine forms only. Viktor knew well how tempted and distracted his friend could grow among the Court of Bendis should he take his human form as Jim Rigger. Jim was a hedonist at heart.

Grimm remained with the ship. With only the narrow North Sea between them and England, Vik wanted the most skilled and cunning of his mates in charge of the ship should Britain's Royal Navy choose to investigate. Besides, Grimm was one of the few men Vik ever knew to honor their wedding vows faithfully. He found that aspect of his first mate both appealing and precious. He refused to be the cause of those vows to be broken.

To keep from drawing attention to the *Incubus*, captain and first mate agreed she should keep to sea. Antwerp's harbor had closed long ago for political reasons.

"This is certainly a dreary place," Belle commented as they made their way into the city. "It almost feels abandoned."

"I imagine parts of it are. The port closed nearly a century and a half ago because of a treaty agreement. That effectively killed all the trade," Viktor said. "I wish I could've seen it in its glory days. The warehouse district would've been a pirates' paradise."

She glanced at him. "And you would know all this how?"

"I'm a voracious reader. Believe it or not, I almost always returned any books I took during my youthful forays into burglary— after I read them, of course."

She smirked and raised an eyebrow. "Why would you do that? It seems out of character."

"On the contrary; trinkets, trade goods and valuables are easy enough to dispose of. Books are not. They draw attention, especially if in large quantities. Besides, Celie would've hided me had I cluttered up the place with books. I knew where to find them again if I wanted to re-read one."

"So, I take it the history of this particular port resides somewhere in Savannah."

He laughed. "No, I learned about Antwerp's former fame in a book on the history of world trade I came across in Charleston some years back. A local trader had bought it to help teach his son. The lad had neither the aptitude nor the desire for the family trade."

She cocked her head in thought. "Did you return it?"

"The boy didn't want it and had no brothers. I kept it."

"I see how you would find such a book valuable."

"Indeed. It allowed me to expand my hunting, for one thing. Current trade routes were listed along with the historical ones, after all. That let me know the best places to get top price for whatever cargo I took."

"Clever."

He smiled and nodded at the praise. Finally, he spotted what he was looking for. "This looks like a promising spot. Let's see if they have a room available." He leaned down and whispered, "Thank you for agreeing to wear a dress, pet. I know how much you loathe the cumbersome things."

"They have their uses. I already know my usual attire would draw too much of the wrong kind of attention," she murmured back. With that, she schooled her features to appear as an innocent maiden.

Viktor envied her that ability. Though centuries, if not millennia older than him, the siren appeared to be but a young woman in her human guise. The sea had weathered his features and stripped him of the illusion of youth. Still, his vampirism kept him looking younger than his nearly forty years. He'd been cursed with it when he was thirty-two. He consoled himself with the fact he would never grow gray-haired.

They entered the inn he'd spotted and soon procured rooms. The innkeeper kept his prices low since they brought no animals requiring fodder.

Once settled in, Viktor went down to the common room and discreetly inquired about the local brothels. The innkeeper seemed dubious until Vik slid a few gold coins his way.

The innkeeper bit the coins and quickly pocketed them. "There are a few in this part of town. If you'll tell me what your tastes run to, I can better direct you, sir. I admit, I'm surprised by your request, considering the beauty you brought with you."

Vik gave the man his best worldly smile. "She is part of the reason I ask. I am a procurer. The client I brought her for had an— unfortunate accident. Antwerp was close, and I thought I might find a new buyer here."

"Accident?"

"Aye. He accused me of despoiling her and tried to pay only a quarter of the agreed price."

The innkeeper gulped. Clearly, he understood the implication. "I will bring you a list according to each house's reputation and business practices."

"I appreciate it."

☠

At the fifth brothel he visited, Viktor finally got information about the Court of Bendis, in a roundabout way.

"How may I help you, *minnaar*?" the madam greeted him in Flemish.

"*Spreekt u Frans*?" he asked in clumsy Dutch.

"*Oui*, or English, if you prefer."

"Good; that will make this much easier. I have something you may be interested in."

She gave a sharp bark of laughter. "You are definitely not the modest type, *minnaar*. Show me your coin, and I'll let you know how interested I or my *meisjes* may be."

He gazed at her with one of his more seductive looks. "You misunderstand. I am selling. Would you have need of a red-haired virgin?"

"Red-haired, you say; have you brought her with you?"

He reached out through his mental link with Belladonna. True to plan, she waited nearby but out of sight. "I have her close by."

"And you say she is virgin? Is she that ugly? You, I think, would be hard to resist." She eyed him appreciatively.

"Belle, come in, pet."

The siren stuck to her role and eased into the room. She sidled over to him and looked around fearfully.

The madam approached with a speculative gleam in her eyes. She appraised the siren then stepped back, definitely interested. "If she's half as skilled as she is beautiful, she's worth whatever you're asking, virgin or not." She smirked at him. "And I do not believe she is virgin, though she plays the part well. Those who want to believe it would fall for the act."

Despite his earlier words to the innkeeper, Viktor took no offense at the madam calling him on the lie. She hadn't insulted him in the process. He smiled and nodded in acknowledgement. "No, in that I did lie. Belle is no virgin, and she is far more skilled than one would imagine."

He buried his fist in Belle's hair and forced her head back. "Would you like a demonstration? She is equally at ease with a man or a woman for a lover."

"That won't be necessary. I see she doesn't mind rough handling. I have some clients who would value that greatly. Paired with her virgin act, they would pay handsomely for the fantasy of breaking her."

He smiled. "One of the reasons I brought her here were rumors of a group who revel in all manner of depravities."

To his surprise, the woman blanched a little. "I know this group you speak of. I have only ever sent two of my *meisjes* to them. One came back unable to perform for months. The other never returned. I was paid an obscene amount to forget about her."

"What does this group call themselves?"

She looked away and shook her head, frightened. "I will not say. They are too powerful."

Lightning fast, he reached out and grasped her chin, forcing her to meet his gaze. "The name."

"The Court of Bendis," she said in a hoarse, terrified whisper.

"Where?"

"They move from time to time, but they're always somewhere in the old guild district. Most of the buildings stay empty. If they do not want to be found, you will not find them."

"We shall see."

He released her from his gaze and his grasp. By the time she came to her senses, he and Belle were long gone.

It didn't take that long to reach the portion of the city where the old guild houses were located. Picking out the abandoned ones proved more difficult than expected. Apparently, those who held power in the city felt some over developed civic duty to prevent blight. Nearly every building looked stable and well maintained.

Viktor wondered if the inhabitants still held some hope Antwerp would once again rise in importance to trade and wanted to be ready for it.

He sent Lazarus to methodically scout each guild house while he and Belle took up a vantage point from which to observe the people. They paid attention to which buildings had the lightest traffic in and out and which ones had none or only a little.

"This place reeks of vampires," Belle commented mentally. They'd already agreed to keep all but the most mundane conversation to this silent mode. It gave them

the freedom to coordinate the hunt without revealing the true nature of their presence.

"Indeed. Perhaps they've spread their daytime nests throughout the district. It would definitely confound any hunters looking to eliminate the local kiss."

"I never considered that, but it makes sense strategically. I'm surprised Jeorge never employed the tactic."

"I'm hungry. Stay here, pet. I'll get us something from one of the street vendors," he said aloud. Silently, he replied, *"Actually, he does. While a large portion of his kiss resides with him, he has several outposts throughout New Orleans and the surrounding countryside. It keeps the feeding pattern dispersed so as not to draw attention to any one particular area."*

After a few minutes, he returned carrying two clay bowls brimming with some sort of fried meat and chunks of fried potato. "The vendor said this is called *Mosselen-Friet*. My Flemish isn't that good, so I'm not sure what the meat is, but it smelled good."

"It does smell good," she admitted, which surprised him. Usually, the siren didn't care for human fare, particularly cooked meats. Her tastes ran more to still screaming and quivering flesh.

He handed her one of the bowls and tested the contents of his own.

"These are river mussels," he said after a bite.

Belle peered at hers and tilted her head. "Really? I wonder why they discarded the organs; the shells, I can understand."

"Those tend to make people sick, pet. Why do you say you understand not eating the shells?"

She looked at him as if he was daft. "Human teeth generally aren't strong enough to bite through something like that."

"How do you like your mussels?"

"Interesting flavor for something dead. I suppose I could get used to them. I usually don't bother with any kind of shellfish. Too small; it would take far too many to satisfy my appetite.

"I see your point. I've seen the volume of meat you can eat." Silently, he added, *"I also remember your claim of eating the entire crew who took my ship on her maiden voyage."* He'd had to increase the size of his crew when they'd transferred to the *Incubus* from the much-damaged *Barracuda*.

"That was a good feed. There are a couple of rather underfed women watching us from the narrow alley between the red building and the yellow one."

He looked where she directed. Two gaunt women dressed reasonably well, save for how their clothes hung loose on their frames, lurked back in the shadows clearly looking at him and the siren. When they realized he stared back at them, one shrank back deeper into the alley. The other pulled her breasts out of the top of her bodice and leered at him.

"Whores."

"They smell diseased," Belle replied.

"Aye, and the bold one has fang marks on her breasts. We may have found our way in."

Belle made a slight gagging sound. He turned to her with some concern. "Pet? Is the food not agreeing with you?"

"Oh, this is fine. Those two examples of walking carrion are what I find unappetizing," she whispered.

"Trust me, I have no desire to bed either of them, and certainly not to feed on them, either. I am, however, willing to use them to my advantage. Shall we continue that way once we finish this?"

She nodded.

He noted with wry amusement that she slowed her eating considerably. He paced himself with her so as not to appear impatient.

Shortly after this exchange, Lazarus confirmed both the prostitutes and the alley were a way into the Court of Bendis.

Tamara A. Lowery

Chapter 17

Viktor and Belladonna entered the alley where they'd spotted the two prostitutes. The women had returned to the shadows by the time they'd finished their meal. Still, they knew the women hadn't gone far. They could still smell them.

The sounds of quiet moans, grunts, and flesh slapping against flesh traveled from further down the alley.

"Sounds like they found some business to tide them over," Viktor muttered.

They came to a niche in the alley and the aromas of sex hit them full force. The shyer of the two prostitutes stood bent at the hips with hands braced against the wall. Her skirts hung bunched at her waist, baring her lower regions. A fat, middle-aged man stood behind her with his hands on her hips and plugging away at her rump. The bolder prostitute, still with her breasts bared, held a leather flogger and periodically struck the man's bare buttocks while commanding him, "Harder! Faster!"

Vampire and siren watched the display in silence. Finally, the man cried out in release and withdrew. He pulled up his trousers and mopped the sweat from his face. He then handed some coins to the flogger-wielding whore and went back toward the square.

After lowering her skirts, the formerly shy whore sauntered up to Viktor. "Would you like to play? We noticed you both visited several *bordelen* but didn't stay long enough at any to do anything. We know where you can find those willing to sell you what you want."

The dominant of the pair approached Belle and grasped the siren's breast. "I heard you like it rough."

The siren gripped the woman's wrist hard enough to elicit a surprised gasp. Behind her back, she extended a single talon. Viktor noticed she worked some kind of glamour to make it appear as if she wore an elongated metal finger sheath.

"You heard right." She purred and stroked the woman's cheek with the back of her taloned hand. She drew the tip of her talon down between the woman's bare breasts and raised a line of blood.

A moan of pleasure escaped the whore's lips, and her eyes fluttered closed.

"She likes blood play; giving or receiving," the one by Viktor explained.

He raised an eyebrow in a sardonic smirk. "So I see. That's enough, pet," he called the siren off. To the prostitutes, he continued, "We would like to visit this place you mentioned. I am curious to see what delights there are to enjoy."

"Follow us."

The prostitutes led them to a crossing alley, on to another hidden alcove, down a flight of stairs to a doorway, and through a maze of short corridors. The images Lazarus sent during his earlier exploration let Viktor know they'd passed under the alley to the building opposite the stairwell.

They came to a long corridor. Multiple doorways, with beaded curtains in place of doors, lined the hall. The smells of sex, blood, animals, and excrement hung thick in the air. Underlying it all, but only recognizable to those who knew what they smelled, was the copper-cinnamon scent of vampires.

While Belle ignored the doorways, Viktor made cursory glances into some of the unoccupied rooms. Even though he'd spent a good portion of his youth working for old Billy Black at the Black Flag in Savannah, he found some of the— furnishings, for want of a better word, puzzling. A few looked more like torture devices than anything else.

He didn't have to look to know what one room held, however. The unmistakable scent of various types of livestock accompanied their muffled lows, bleats, or whimpers. He knew of bestiality, having encountered it among a few former crew members. It was one of the few things he did not tolerate on his ship, hence the "former" qualifier.

At the end of the hallway, they mounted another stair. They climbed to the third floor, a fact he found unexpected. Up was not, generally, the direction vampires took to hide from daylight; yet their scent grew stronger, the higher they climbed.

Finally, their guides stopped before a wooden, double door. Each took a handle and opened the doors in unison.

"Welcome to the Court of Bendis, where all of your desires can be fulfilled," they said in perfect chorus.

Belladonna shivered. Viktor felt the same surge of energy she did. They'd just entered the lair of an ancient power, and it just woke for the evening.

"*She's awake. Damn, but she's old,*" Belle warned him silently.

"*I felt it, too. Sunset is still over an hour away,*" he replied in kind. "*She is not as old or powerful as Thia, however. We should try to get her away from her followers. I want to try to learn where Dragon is from her, if possible.*"

"*I'm going to tone down my power as much as possible, to hide my true nature. We already know she'll recognize you eventually, thanks to the information the Westins gave you.*"

"*Thank you for reminding me of that. It may explain why we got in so easily.*"

"*You think this is a trap?*"

"*I think everything is a trap. It is a survival tactic.*"

They entered the room before them with the full knowledge they might have to fight their way out.

The former warehouse space appeared to occupy most of the building's third story. Floor-to-ceiling stained glass windows lined three of the walls. Viktor recognized them to be false, possibly concealing a passageway between them and the true windows visible from the exterior. The flickering light of numerous candles behind the colored glass confirmed at least part of his suspicions. He surmised the outer windows had been painted over or boarded up to keep out the sunlight.

He noted with wry amusement the false windows depicted various scenes of revelry and debauchery. It reminded him of the room Circe had put him in when she tried to seduce him.

A curving, gold-trimmed staircase descended from an upper floor to a dais, complete with an ornate throne, at the far end of the room.

Several men and women in various stages of undress lounged or stood about the room, watching the golden stair in anticipation. A few wore only a few leather straps, formed into odd harnesses with metal rings at various points. He wondered what purpose they served, seeing as how they did nothing to cover their wearers' nudity.

"Do not feed here. I feel her power riding all of them," Belle warned.

He felt grateful. He'd already grown aroused by the sheer decadence of the scene before him. Well he knew how quickly his sexual appetite could give way to the Hunger, especially since he could feed on blood or sex.

He determined to maintain restraint. He would not share power or feed during any sexual encounters in this place.

All eyes were drawn to the stairwell. Someone sounded an unseen gong. What appeared to be a well-dressed young man descended the stairs and draped themselves indolently on the throne.

"My faithful, whom shall provide me with sustenance this evening?" the vampire spoke with a rich contralto, belying her gender. Her accent reminded him of Belladonna's.

"She is from the Aegean region," the siren confirmed.

No shortage of volunteers stepped forward. Some carried the scars of multiple fanged bites. A small handful bore no scars at all. She picked a girl from the latter group.

Bendis led the girl to a framework and attached leather manacles to her wrists and ankles. She turned a crank on the side of the frame until the chains connecting the manacles to it drew the girl into a suspended spread-eagle; then, using a small knife, she cut away what little clothing her victim wore.

She grasped the young woman's hair and forced her head to one side. She then bit into the juncture of neck and muscle savagely enough for blood to flow down from the wound when she pulled away.

Viktor's Hunger flared at the scent of fresh blood, and Bendis stared directly at him for a moment. Her non-expression never changed, as if she were looking through him rather than at him.

He used it to focus his attention and force his Hunger to the back of his mind. Only then did Bendis lift one eyebrow as if impressed or perhaps surprised.

She withdrew from her dying victim and turned her attention back to her followers. "I am finished. Any and all may do with this one as they please. Let the evening's revel begin."

She retired to her throne and watched the ensuing debauchery with detached indolence.

"Interesting; she had no arousal at all during that little display until you reined your urges in," Belle commented silently.

"I noticed as well, pet. I think my control surprised her. What say we test hers?"

"I've no objection, since this playground isn't exactly safe."

"Very well, I'll go first, since I've already gained her interest. Just remember you're passing as human."

Her mental chuckle felt slightly unsettling.

Viktor felt the experiences of his youth might serve him well in his current efforts. He practically grew up at the Black Flag back in Savannah. He'd secured a job with old Billy Black in order to learn piracy. The fact the place was more brothel than tavern had proven delightfully educational. Billy ran him off to sea just to keep him from wearing the girls out.

If he could use the skills he'd learned back then to seduce Bendis, he could enlist her aid in getting to Dragon.

He approached the dais and gave the enthroned vampire an elegant bow. "Greetings, milady. I have come to pay my respects."

"You surprise me with your boldness, Viktor Brandewyne. Still, if you were able to ensnare Lady Carpathia, I should've expected you would seek out the pleasures of my Court."

"Actually, I'm more interested in the pleasures of you, Lady Bendis."

She raised an eyebrow at him but otherwise kept a neutral expression. He smiled in turn, took her hand, and raised it to his lips. "You will find I am quite skilled."

"If you say so," she said with a bored tone.

His brief moment of irritation never showed. He determined he would rise to the challenge. He would arouse her despite her icy manner. A woman who surrounded herself with this much decadence had to take some pleasure in it.

He reached out to caress her face. She grasped his wrist with an iron grip, reminding him she was vampire not human. He didn't try to pull away, nor did he try to force things. He wanted to seduce her, not rape her.

"What is your pleasure, milady?"

"Do not think you can seduce me. I am beyond that. Nor do I intend to fall into the same trap Carpathia did. That is why you are here, is it not?"

"You have not wounded or betrayed me as she did, milady. I have no desire or reason to subject you to her fate."

She released his wrist. He cupped her cheek gently, but she did not respond to his touch. Her expression remained bland and bored.

He'd had reactions from women in the past which ranged from ardor, to excitement, to fear, and to anger. Never in his life had he encountered such a— non-response. It puzzled him.

Still, given her preference for masculine clothing, perhaps she preferred female companionship.

Within moments, Belladonna approached the dais. A few men and women, their guides among them, trailed behind her. They all stopped several feet away as she continued on. Raw sex and violence seemed to radiate off the siren in equal parts. Viktor had a moment's surprise at the effect it had on his body. He maintained his self-control, but only just. It made him wonder just how formidable Belle was.

"Lady Bendis, it is an honor to make your acquaintance." Belladonna's voice came out at its most sultry. "How may I please you?"

Bendis barely acknowledged her. Instead, she turned to Viktor. "Send your whore back to her playmates. I have no interest. You impress me with your ability to channel your powers through her, however. I can see why my Sire desires your destruction."

He gave her a wry half smile. "At least I've gotten some sort of reaction from you, milady." He turned to Belle. "You did your best, pet. It seems the lady is not interested in either of us."

Belle pouted and returned to the group she'd so recently left.

Viktor returned his attention to his hostess. "It seems you truly are beyond seduction, Lady Bendis. Tell me, since you know who I am, why have you not acted according to the Dragon's decree to destroy me?"

She smiled, a cold thing, and replied, "The night is still young."

"You didn't answer my question." He kept his voice calm and reasonable as he returned her smile with an equally cold one. Any who knew him would recognize him at his deadliest.

"I like to assess my prey. Why did you seek me out, if not to destroy me? You obviously are aware of my Sire's command."

"I did not come here planning to destroy you. Rather, I hope to enlist your aid in locating Dragon. Why should you or your sisters fight his battles for him? Is he such a coward as to hide behind women?" He dearly hoped the bastard was listening in through his Daughter. The words were intended to goad him.

Bendis laughed. "He isn't listening. I have not alerted Him to your presence— yet. Return to me tomorrow night, Viktor Brandewyne. I will speak more with you then."

He bowed. "I look forward to it."

Looking around the room, he spotted Belladonna among the revelers. The group around her had grown considerably.

"Bring your whore. My children seem to enjoy her. Perhaps I may buy her from you."

"I will keep that in mind." He moved among the hedonists and extracted the siren from among those clamoring for her attention. "Time to go, pet. We'll return tomorrow."

She made a point of pouting but came along with him.

Chapter 18

"Jacques." Bendis summoned one of her older Children.

The vampire arrived almost immediately. "My Lady?"

"Have Viktor Brandewyne and his guest followed discreetly. I want to know where they are lodging and what they discuss."

"It will be done."

He bowed and left her presence.

"Ah, there they are." Viktor spoke through his mental link with the siren.

"Shadows?"

"Aye. Male vampire, judging by his scent. He's good, but I think he's not used to hunting another vampire. I smelled him before I spotted him. A human would've never known he was there."

"Should we lodge elsewhere today?" Belle asked.

"No; I don't want him to know he's been spotted. I fully expected Bendis to assign a spy to us." In truth, he would've been surprised if she hadn't.

They continue to the inn. Viktor gave the innkeeper extra coins to ensure they would not be disturbed during the day.

☠

Belle rubbed her arms once they were safely back in their room. Clearly something had her upset or agitated, but her mental shields let Viktor know she didn't want him in her head at that moment.

Still, she was part of his crew, as well as his lover. As captain, he needed to know what the problem was.

"Something vexes you, pet. Out with it."

She glared at him. "We aren't in the Court of Bendis, Viktor. Stay out of my head."

He reached to caress her face, and she flinched. He saw fear in her eyes. In his most gentle tone, he said, "I did not have to touch your mind to see you are troubled over something, Belladonna. As your captain, I need to know what it is, so we can prepare for it."

She flopped in a chair and stared at her hands for a moment. Finally, she said, "Her Court awakened dangerous appetites in me. I enjoy blood play; giving, anyway. I had to fight not to feed off the tantric energy in that place."

"Tantric?"

"Sexual: lust: same thing."

"Oh." He'd never heard the word before and wondered what language it originated from. He chose not to indulge his curiosity, recognizing it as a diversionary tactic on her part. "I know it presents a risk for me. You do not have a bond with Bendis, however. I would think you'd be immune to her taint on her people."

"I am, but it would draw her attention and reveal my true nature to her."

"Damn, I should have thought of that, pet." He shook his head. "This is no time for me to be off my mark like that. I wish I'd had foresight to bring a few bottles of my blood-brandy mix, too."

She sighed. "Hopefully we won't have to stay here too long. Otherwise, you'll have to go well outside the city to hunt."

"I know. Now that I have her scent, I've caught it on most of the humans here. Our host seems clear of her power for now, at least."

"Mrrow!" Lazarus announced his presence. The cat grew amorphous and reformed as a rat. Viktor had never seen him take that form before, but he understood what the creature meant by that action.

"That is an alternative I will keep in mind, my friend. I'm not quite Hungry enough to feed on animal blood right now."

"Ugh, I hope we're not here that long," Belle said with a groan.

Viktor suspected he knew what would calm her frustration, at least temporarily. "Lazarus, return to the ship for now. Let Mr. Grimm know it may be a few days."

The rat turned to smoke and then to his familiar raven form. With a brief *"caw"*, he flew westward from the open window.

Now with a modicum of privacy, Vik turned his full attention to the siren. The scrutiny did not go unnoticed, although she kept her shields tight against his mental presence.

"I believe we can both satisfy one of our hungers, Belladonna." He deliberately used her name to let her know the choice lay with her.

She relaxed visibly and gazed at him hungrily.

"Today, I am yours to command."

She rose and stalked to him. "Do you trust me?"

He heard a tone in her voice she'd never used with him before. It gave him pause. She knew he rarely trusted anyone and preferred to be in command of any given situation. He realized she was asking him to surrender completely to her will; that if he offered it, he best mean it.

"Implicitly," he said with conviction. He kept his mental shields down so she could see the truth of his words.

"Good," she growled. She reached behind his head and undid the leather tie holding his hair back. She ran her fingers up into it, caressing his scalp and raising gooseflesh and other things on his body.

Without warning, she made a fist in his hair and pulled his head back, forcing him to arch his back in the process. He grunted in surprise.

She ran the tip of her tongue from the dip between his collar bones slowly up to where jaw met neck. He groaned when she blew lightly on the moist trail she'd made on his skin.

She released him, and only his quick reflexes kept him from falling over. He occasionally forgot her strength nearly equaled his.

"Strip," she ordered, "slowly."

He smirked and obeyed. Soon, he stood before her completely exposed. Only a slight furrow of his brow gave indication of his disappointment she remained clothed.

She stalked around him. When she stopped in front of him again, he saw her pull a small flogging whip from the pocket of her skirts. Several leather straps no longer than his forearm were braided into a solid handle halfway up their length.

"Where did you get that?"

"I borrowed it." She trailed the straps down his chest and stomach to his groin. She then moved her arm around behind him. With a quick flick, she struck him with the flogger.

He felt the light sting as the soft leather strips molded to his left buttock then fell away. To his surprise and her delight, his erection gave a happy little jump at the sensation.

"Oh, you liked that, did you?" Belle's words came out as a wicked little chuckle.

She struck him again, the right cheek and a little harder this time. This elicited a growl from him. She cupped his balls and traced the very tips of the flogger along the length of his erection, staring him down while she did so.

"These are mine to do with as I please today. I intend to test your self-control to the limits."

"Oh?" He felt the corner of his mouth quirk up.

She let his balls slip down out of her grasp and traced one fingertip from base to tip along the underside of his shaft, never breaking eye contact. "You are not to cum until I give you permission."

"Oho! A challenge! I'm sure you are not going to make this easy, either."

She laughed. He felt the magic in the musical sound and knew he was in for a day of delicious torture.

"I intend to make you beg for release, my love."

He kept silent, biting off the temptation to tell her he would never beg. Well he knew how formidable a lover Belladonna was. A very real possibility she could do what she said existed.

"Then let the game begin, pet."

The innkeeper watched through a hidden peephole until his muscles cramped. Finally, he had to go relieve himself about midday.

Having no wife, he found his favorite chamber maid and took her to his rooms to work off the lust his voyeurism brought on.

He never knew the objects of his observation knew he'd done so.

Shortly after dusk, Jacques paid a visit to his new slave. He'd taken the man's mind and given his blood to ensure the innkeeper remained in his thrall long enough to fulfill his purpose.

He did not, however, feed on the human.

Jacques knew he was weak by vampiric standards. He knew making Children would increase his power, but he knew weak Children did little for a vampire's power base except in sheer volume. He preferred to be selective about who he brought over; the innkeeper did not meet his standards.

The man met him in the alleyway behind the inn. What he had to say, while over detailed, proved quite informative.

Jacques confirmed his targets had left to pay Bendis a second visit before he flew ahead of them to pass the information on to his Mistress

"You have served well. Go start the evening's revels. I shall join later. You've given me much to think on," Bendis instructed her Childe.

"As you wish, Mistress." Jacques bowed and left her presence.

Brandewyne puzzled her. His power felt very like her Sire's yet very different. Perhaps there was some truth to the rumor he was a living vampire.

The fact he obviously trusted the red head with him marked him as very different from Dragon. She'd never known Him to trust anyone or let them have true control. By His own admission, He'd killed the vampire who made Him to avoid being under their control.

Bendis doubted even more that Brandewyne brought his companion with the aim of selling her. More likely, she was a ruse to gain entry to the Court. It hadn't been necessary, but it would make it easier for her to fulfill Dragon's directive regarding Brandewyne— should she choose to obey it.

One of the lesser vampires greeted Viktor and Belle when they arrived at the Court. To their surprise, Bendis remained markedly absent while the orgy progressed without her.

The greeter soon explained his mistress' absence. "My Lady desires your attendance in her chambers. Your pet human is welcome to join in the revels here. There are several who hoped for her return tonight."

"Very well; just see to it they do not damage the merchandise. If Lady Bendis has no interest in her, I would like to be able to get a good price for her in another market," Viktor agreed, keeping up the ruse.

"Don't worry about me," Belle said with a chuckle. "Worry about them."

As they worked their way deeper into the room, the sound of a goat bleat drew their attention. A naked man stroked himself, apparently in preparation for violating the poor animal.

"Barnett?" Belle questioned mentally. *"But Venoma killed him a few years ago, so it can't be."*

Viktor's mental tone held a note of disgust. *"I do seem to recall him mentioning an uncle whom he favored that had been disowned by his family. He never said why. It's quite possible this— man may be that relation. The resemblance is far too strong for him not to be, really."*

"I never really understood this particular deviation when willing partners are available."

"Nor I, pet. Watch yourself with this lot."

"Oh, I will, Viktor. I will."

She split off from him as he continued to the dais and grand staircase. When they reached it, his guide bowed and motioned upward. "The Lady awaits above."

Viktor didn't know quite what to expect, but the austerity of the windowless room surprised him. It made a stark contrast to the opulent den of decadence below.

"Greetings, Lady Bendis." He gave a formal bow.

"Captain Brandewyne. You seem disappointed by my chambers." She inclined her head with a sardonic smile.

"On the contrary, milady; it is a refreshing surprise. Even without windows it has a pleasant feel of openness and freedom about it."

"So, you approve?" She arched an eyebrow. "I would think a pirate would like to be surrounded with all his plunder."

He smiled and shook his head. "Some pirates perhaps, but that sort doesn't survive long. I do what I do because I enjoy doing it; and I'm very good at what I do. Any prizes go for the maintenance of my ship and crew or to be spent on our pleasure."

"You intrigue me. Your words are boastful, yet your demeanor is not." She stalked around him, more in examination than to intimidate. She even sniffed at him, something which might've made a human uncomfortable. He knew she merely tested his power.

Finally, she stopped in front of him with a look of curious puzzlement on her face. "You present me with quite an enigma. Your power tastes so very like His, yet you seem to lack His cruelty or need for dominance over all those around Him. You've been alone with me in my private chambers for several minutes now; yet even after being rebuffed by me last night, you've neither tried again to seduce me nor forced yourself on me."

"When I first came into my power, I may very well have done so. Mother says I've grown. I know now it would only gain your enmity further, something I have no desire to do."

He watched her reaction. Both it and her words gave him a small revelation.

"Dragon raped you." He made the words a statement rather than a question. "I imagine he turned you against your will, as well."

Bendis showed shock for just a split second then hid it so well one would doubt they'd seen it to begin with. Viktor didn't miss it, but he gave her no indication he'd seen.

"Why are you here? My watchers have seen how much the woman means to you. I do not believe you're just trying to sell her."

He inclined his head slightly. "I admit that was a ruse. I am hunting your maker. He presents a threat to the All-Mother. I seek to neutralize that threat."

She gave a cold laugh. "I have never heard of this All-Mother. If she was someone he would want dealt with, she would already be dead. I do not believe you."

"Did he ever tell you about how he became vampire"

She blinked at the abrupt change of subject but recovered quickly. "As a matter of fact, He said He destroyed the vampire who turned Him, so as not to be under their power."

Viktor smiled tightly. "That is how he became undead. Once, Dragon was as I am: a living vampire with all the power and none of the weaknesses. He made the vampire who turned him."

Bendis went very still, so still she seemed turned to marble.

He knew from her pallor she hadn't fed yet this evening. He also knew she was trying to both sense the truth or fallacy of his words and to unnerve him.

"You speak truth or at least believe it's true." Her voice held quiet awe when she finally spoke. "How did you come by this knowledge?"

"Before she became All-Mother, Mother Celie chose Dragon to be her champion and aid her in becoming what she is now. After his first Childe turned him, he vowed to thwart Celie in any way he could. For thousands of years, he succeeded in preventing her Becoming."

Something in his words apparently struck a chord of memory. She began to pace in a stalking manner, watching him the entire time. Again, he returned her scrutiny with calm patience.

She narrowed her eyes. "You are not the first He has charged us to hunt. I can remember at least two others. If I recall correctly, they bore the same name, Viktor Brandewyne."

He nodded in confirmation. "Celie made me aware of my predecessors, all of whom failed at some point or other. I am the last Viktor Brandewyne. Dragon was the first. He rejected the name when he began his feud with her."

Bendis stepped back and cocked her head to the side thoughtfully. "Your words ring true, but they puzzle me. Why would He be angry at this Celie if His Childe made Him? Was it because she failed to protect her champion?"

"She says he does blame her for not warning him of the consequences of the powers she gifted him. He killed his first Childe on impulse for turning him. She believes she holds her responsible for his Childe's death more than anything."

Bendis snorted. "You make it sound as if He cared for or maybe even loved the one who turned Him. That is not the Dragon I know. He knows only domination."

"I shall bear that in mind. I admit, it does have its appeal and usefulness; it is dangerous to just take it as a given, however. It is better if those who claim loyalty do so out of desire to, rather than just out of fear. There comes a point where fear no longer presents a deterrent to betrayal. You would be surprised at the chances some people will take in the face of certain death."

"You sound as if you speak from experience."

"I do. Sometimes I've even spared lives for the reckless bravado they've displayed; sometimes."

"If you think to entice me to betray Dragon to you, it won't work. He has already killed me, and He is not merciful enough to end my existence. There are far worse things He can do."

"What did he do to you, Bendis?" His question came out as a whisper colored with genuine concern.

He must've touched a nerve with her. She gave him a pained, haunted look, like a child who has witnessed unspeakable horror.

Then, she closed off all emotions and returned to a *blasé* demeanor of indifference. "You have not fed since you entered my territory. Perhaps you fear falling under my thrall or perhaps not."

"I am in your territory. It would be rude to hunt here without your leave."

She raised an eyebrow at the comment. "You truly are a study in contradictions, Viktor Brandewyne. You are a pirate, taking what you want, yet you show yourself to be a skilled diplomat."

He gave her a half-smile and a slight bow. "I have learned that diplomacy often can gain me what I seek far faster and in greater quantities than use of force. It all depends on the situation."

"Spoken with wisdom."

She grew thoughtfully silent for a time. Viktor gently opened his senses and found he could "taste" the subtle flavor of her power reaching out. Somehow, he knew she didn't direct it at him, but out among her followers.

He remained deliberately relaxed and hoped she wouldn't sense his intrusion.

"I remain undecided about what to do with you. As of yet, I have not alerted Him to your presence here. For now, I shall play gracious host. Allow me to offer you a young morsel I recently acquired. She is untouched by my power or by any of my followers. Your candor with me earned you this meal."

She snapped her fingers, and doors at the far end of the room opened.

Viktor caught their scent before they entered. A male vampire gripped the arm of a nude girl and led her into the room. She wore a blindfold and struggled in vain to cover herself with hands bound at the wrist.

His senses confirmed her virginity immediately. She looked to be barely old enough to know anything of sexual desire. Her budding breasts were barely formed, and her mound bore no hair.

He thought he'd kept his face impassive, but some of his disgust must've shown.

"You don't care for her?" Bendis seemed almost amused, the hint of a smirk curling her lips.

"As sport, no; she's just a child. I prefer something a little older and more experienced."

"Interesting. I would've thought you liked taking virgins."

"It depends entirely on the virgin. This child's body is hardly ready to experience any pleasure like that. She would get more pain and fear from it than anything else. I do not inflict such on one who has not earned my complete disdain and indifference."

He took the girl's hands and gave the victim's escort a cold stare. The male released her and backed down from the raw power of that simple gaze.

"Still, I accept your gift. I do Hunger."

He untied the girl's hands and removed her blindfold. She crossed one arm across her chest and lowered her other hand to cover herself. He caressed her face and brought her gaze up to his. The emerald glow from his eyes reflected on her skin in the dimly lit room. Once he felt her will fall to his and saw her face grow slack, he lifted her in his arms and bit deep into the juncture of neck and shoulder.

His victim didn't even emit a whimper of pain.

When her breathing grew labored, and her limbs twitched in quick spasms he adjusted his grip to nearly crush her against his chest. Finally, she grew still and pale.

He held her lifeless form by the neck in one hand and plunged the other up under her ribs and grasped her heart. With a twist and a hard yank, he pulled the now bloodless organ from her body.

"Why did you do that?" Bendis' voice held only curiosity, not scorn or anger.

"She was too young to adapt well to existence as a vampire, and I do not wish to leave a Childe in a place where I cannot guarantee their safety."

"That is reasonable and responsible. I imagine you don't wish to leave behind a means to spy on you, either."

"I learned that lesson long ago."

She nodded and drifted into deep contemplation. He felt her power close in on itself, as if she sought to wall herself off from something— or someone. It felt vaguely like when Belladonna shielded herself from him. It made him wonder if his host was blocking out her Sire.

After a few moments, she spoke again. "I hold no love and only the loyalty fear demands for my Sire. I did not ask for any of this."

He knew she meant the nature of her continued existence. "Will you help me against him?"

Her smile held true sorrow. "I don't know how. I have tried to stay at the periphery of His perception for millennia. I have no way of knowing where to find Him without drawing His attention."

"I think I understand what you're saying. You've avoided him for so long, he would know any supposed casual contact from you was anything but, and it would make him focus on you sharply. Am I correct?"

"Yes."

"Then, I will not ask you to take that risk. He would change his location long before I would have a chance to reach Him. You can still help me in my quest, however, without alerting him."

"How?"

"Tell me what you know about him; his habits and preferences, that sort of thing."

She tilted her head to the side. "How will that help you?"

He crossed his arms and leaned back against the wall. "You already know the answer to that, Bendis. You've been studying me, trying to understand me better."

She continued to play coy. "What has that to do with why you want me to tell you about Him?"

"A very wise woman once told me one should try to understand their prey. I know he ordered the Daughters to hunt me down. That makes me your prey by definition, just as he is my prey."

To his surprise, she grinned at him. "You know, I think you might actually stand a chance against Him. He has always been arrogantly condescending toward females, as if we were lesser beings and less intelligent. You do not seem to fall into that trap. Have a seat, and we will talk. This will take some time."

Chapter 19

Jacques watched Brandewyne's whore work the room. Something about her didn't smell right to him. Her scent spoke of salt water and her master, but it held some subtle quality he'd never encountered before. It almost made him wonder if she might not be human.

After a while, satisfied the revels would carry on without him, he selected a meal from the human cattle. He finished his victim quickly. Unaware the action was mirrored in the chamber above, he ripped the victim's heart out with a practiced twist. The man had been diseased and weak-minded, a creature unfit to make his Childe.

He knew some of the revelers enjoyed necrophilia; however, he preferred to dispose of his leavings as quickly as possible. Even in a city as controlled by vampires as Antwerp, dead bodies tended to draw the wrong kind of attention; especially if they had gaping holes where their heart should be.

He stuffed the organ back in the cavity for easier carrying and slung the bloodless body over his shoulder. He decided this one could go in the North Sea. If it washed ashore, it would be far, far away.

A niggling sensation ate at the back of Dragon's mind. He'd kept his links with his Daughters partially open since delivering his edict concerning Brandewyne.

As he'd expected, the bond with Bendis remained muted. She'd never been shy about her loathing for him. She tried to keep him out of her mind as much as possible. Still, she felt particularly quiet this evening, almost as quiet as Carpathia.

He wondered if it was deliberate, or if she, too, had fallen prey to his rival.

Since he knew she would actively block him if he tried to probe her, he reached out to some of her Children, instead. The first, and most powerful one he found was Jacques.

Sails on the horizon accompanied by the inexplicable scent of vampires on the sea breeze drew Jacques' attention just after he dropped his victim's body into the brine below.

As he flew to investigate, he felt a powerful presence surrounding him. He knew right away it wasn't Bendis. The presence felt much stronger than his Dam.

"Perceptive. I like that," a distinctly male voice spoke in his head.

"My Lord Dragon? You honor me," he replied to the unseen presence.

"I wish to know how my Daughter progresses in the hunt I have set her and her sisters. As ever, she avoids my will and refuses to answer."

Jacques felt the very human urge to vomit his recent meal. Dragon's presence felt closer.

"This troubles you, young one. Why?"

"I fear my Dam will view this as a betrayal. Brandewyne is in Antwerp and has been in contact with Her. I do not know Her intentions toward him."

An ephemeral image of a dragon's head appeared before him. *"You need not fear Bendis' wrath. I sense you wish to be free of her, just as she wishes to be free of me. If you have a safe place to spend the day away from the city, I advise you to go there at dawn."*

The apparition looked about then asked, *"What reason brings you so far from land?"*

"Disposal of the remains of my last meal, my Lord. By chance, that ship carries the scent of vampires. I was about to investigate."

He sensed his ultimate master's power stretch towards the vessel in question and felt baffled frustration enter Dragon's aura.

"They must be of Brandewyne's making. I cannot touch their minds. Investigate that ship. You shall be my eyes and ears in this."

"As you command, my Lord."

Jacques flew high to avoid being seen by the ship's watch. He descended towards the most shadowy area, intent on alighting on deck. An unseen barrier prevented him from even landing on a spar. He had to satisfy himself with drifting among the rigging.

A squat, malodorous form caught his attention as it descended rapidly toward the helm. Despite the man's truncated legs, he moved with the speed and agility of a monkey among the ropes and sheets.

"Vampire in the rigging!" the smelly creature cried in alarm.

The man at the helm answered with a tone of amusement. "Of course there are vampires in the rigging, Sniff. You don't expect them to stay in the hold all the time, do you? You're too rancid to drink anyway."

"No sir, a strange vampire. He's hoverin' 'round up there."

"Mr. Rigger! Sniff says we've an uninvited guest," the helmsman called out. Before Jacques knew where to look next, a raven appeared, as if from thin air, and flew in his face. He batted at it, but it dissolved into smoke and coalesced back to solid, avoiding the blow. He tried again, with the same result.

"Leave here. I have seen enough," Dragon instructed him. *"Go to your safe place. I will speak with you later."*

Sometime later, in the cellar of an abandoned chalet, Jacques fervently hoped Bendis wouldn't summon him for the rest of the night.

Viktor gave his hostess a formal bow. "I thank you for your information, milady, and for the meal. You've given me much to think about. If you don't mind, I'll collect what's mine and retire for the evening."

"Of course. Will you be returning to my Court tomorrow? There is still much more to the story."

"As you wish, milady."

"Come, pet. It is time for us to depart." He beckoned Belle.

She came to him reeking of sexual energy. After his prolonged time in the asexual presence of Bendis, Viktor found his control sorely tried. He felt himself grow instantly hard and fought the urge to take the siren on the spot. Knowing no one present would be shocked or offended by such an action did not make the task of avoiding it any easier.

Belle seemed oblivious to the predicament she posed for him. "Do we have to leave so early? Dawn is still a few hours away."

"Yes, we do. Don't worry, pet. We'll return tomorrow night."

"Oh good! I spotted a toy I'd really like to try out!" Her enthusiasm reminded him of her behavior the one, and only, time he'd given her rum. His navigator, Zachary Brumble, had been offered up to slake her lust then. The poor man had been too sore to walk or even stand for several days afterward.

"I've a feeling I should be worried."

Without further preamble, he grasped her arm gently, but firmly, and led her out the door.

Viktor kept his silence and his mental shields firmly in place until they reached their rented rooms.

"What is troubling you?" Belle demanded as she jerked free of his grip and rubbed her arm.

"Did you have anything to drink?"

Realization showed on her face. He felt her aura mute immediately. "I did accept the offer of some absinthe. It tasted even more vile than gin, so I only had a sip. I didn't realize such a small amount had affected my self-control."

He felt tension release from his back and shoulders. "Thank you, Belle. I had all I could do to control my urges back there. You are a formidable force."

She grinned impishly. "Wait until you see the toy."

"It won't be right away, pet. Bendis and I haven't finished our conversation. I broke it off with the excuse of mulling over what I've learned thus far."

She narrowed her eyes at him. "What was the real reason?"

"This needs to be kept private. Are you enough in control of your abilities to manage it without us falling prey to our lust?"

She appeared to consider the question seriously, her expression growing more sober. Finally, she nodded.

He felt her shields lower and wasn't overwhelmed with a flood of her desire. He steeled himself and lowered his, as well, allowing their minds to touch.

"In truth, I was more worried about my ability to maintain control of my hungers," he admitted.

She smiled. *"While alcohol does seem to impair it, I've had much more practice controlling mine."*

"I knew you would understand, pet. Lazarus informed me of an uninvited vampire among the shrouds back aboard the ship. I recognized the visitor as Jacques."

"So, Bendis is spying on you."

"Possibly, but I don't think that's the case. Lazarus sensed a second presence that didn't smell like her. I think it might've been our prey riding her Childe."

Belle's eyes grew wide, and he thought he saw a touch of fear there. He reached out and cupped her cheek. *"I've called for Jim to join us outside the city, away from prying eyes and ears."*

She relaxed under his touch. *"The game just got more complicated, it seems."*

"True; but we can't let them know how much we're aware of. Now, let's go meet Jim."

"Why didn't we just come here straight from the Court?" Belle complained just before Viktor landed and set her on her feet.

"I know you hate to fly, pet; but surely you can understand my reasoning. First, I wanted to make sure we weren't being followed. Second, I had to be sure you were back in control of your urges. If you hadn't been, I would've left you at the inn."

"What did I miss?" Jim asked once he shifted from Lazarus' raven form and pulled a pair of breeches out of the bag he'd carried in his erstwhile talons.

"Someone at the orgy gave Belle some absinthe."

Jim grinned wide enough to let his fangs gleam in the semi-darkness of pre-dawn. "Sounds like someone got more than they bargained for. Wish I'd been there."

"Lecher." Vik laughed despite the siren's scowl.

"Yes; yes, I am."

Viktor sobered instantly. "Dawn is less than an hour away. You send vivid images and other sensations as Lazarus, but sometimes I need a verbal report. What did you observe about Bendis' lackey who invaded the rigging?"

"His movements were not smooth. It reminded me of how Melanie or Thomas move when you're riding them, like a puppet. I could smell he belonged to Bendis, but I caught an overlaying scent like sulfur and snakes. I noticed he never landed on any of the spars or lines, although he seemed to try to."

"Anything else?"

"Bugger tried to swat me away a couple of times. I went smoke on him and held my position. When his hand passed through me, I felt a presence try to make contact like we do. I didn't even have to block it. There already seemed to be some unseen barrier."

Viktor mulled this over for a while. Finally, he said, "We'll try to work this to our advantage, somehow. If I guess right, the presence you sensed was Dragon. I'm sure it puzzled him to not be able to reach you, let alone control you. I'm also sure it irritated him to no end to not be able to set foot on my ship. He knows I'm a vampire, and I recall Thia telling me she could go on any ship owned by a vampire, but not one owned by a human without an invitation."

"He did seem consternated when he left," Jim said.

"You've done well, my friend. Help yourself to a bottle from my private stock when you get back to the ship."

"Aye-aye, Cap'n!" he said with enthusiasm. He immediately transformed back into a raven.

Viktor picked up the discarded breeches and stuffed them back into the bag. He held the bag so the bird could get a good grip.

Once Lazarus flew off, Belle posed a question. "Why do you think Bendis wasn't part of that, as well? She is Dragon's Childe."

"During my audience with her, she went still for a time. I could sense she'd closed all her mental shields as if to hide from someone or at least shut them out. The power tasted much like when you or I do so to each other on occasion. She's made it quite plain how much she loathes her Sire and what he's done to her. He very likely latched onto Jacques when Bendis wouldn't let him in."

"Now that he knows where you are, do you think he'll make an attack?"

"I believe he will by proxy, possibly as soon as this evening. He considered me enough of a threat to first send Thia after me, then the rest of his Daughters. I don't know that he considers me enough of a threat to come after me in person, though."

"Yet," Belle pointed out. "It could also be he sees you as too dangerous to stage a direct attack on."

"Possibly, but I doubt it at this point. Remember to be careful tonight. They still think you are human."

"I'll remember to play the part. I won't get myself into a situation I can't readily get myself out of," she replied.

"Good, since I don't know how quickly I could come to your aid."

Chapter 20

The following night, Dragon visited Jacques briefly.

"Do not return to your Dam tonight. Hunt the countryside for clean prey rather than the diseased fare you've subsisted on. Afterwards, return here. My Daughter will not summon you this evening. I will not permit it."

"As you command, my Lord."

Later, as he drained a healthy young stable boy, he pondered the previous evening's encounter at sea.

He knew the ship must belong to Brandewyne, else there wouldn't be vampires aboard. Given that, he didn't understand why he couldn't land on it. Vampires only required an invitation to enter a structure owned by mortal humans.

Another odd thing was how Dragon could not sense the sea-going vampires. He was the First; all vampires descended from Him. Yet these had been outside His influence; alien to Him.

Finally, what had that bird really been? It smelled like a vampire, but it looked like a raven. The way it dissolved and reformed when he'd swatted at it truly unnerved him.

He'd gotten the sense Dragon recognized what the creature was, but He'd not shared the information with him.

The one thing he knew for certain; he would not want to be in Bendis' position tonight. He got the distinct impression Her Sire was less than pleased with the status of her hunt.

Viktor and Belle arrived at the Court of Bendis about an hour past sunset. He'd wanted to give his hostess time to feed before continuing their conversation from the previous evening. Both remained on surreptitious alert for any attack.

"Go try the toy you were interested in, pet. I've a feeling this may take a while yet." He watched her smile and sashay off through the revelers, some of whom greeted her enthusiastically.

Satisfied she would prove more than a match for any of them, human or vampire, should they try to turn on her, he ascended the stairs to Bendis' chambers. Though unbidden and unannounced, no one tried to bar his way.

"Captain Brandewyne, I thought perhaps you'd changed your mind about tonight's visit."

Bendis rose from beside the supine form of a young man on the floor. Viktor noted the lad still lived; more, he smelled disease free.

"Forgive me, milady. I did not intend to interrupt your meal." He flourished a bow in apology. "In fact, that is the reason for my tardiness."

She smiled in surprise. "You seem unusually considerate for a pirate."

"I will take that as a compliment," he replied with a wry smirk. "I find it useful to keep others a bit confused as to my nature and motives until it is too late for them to take precautions. The practice has become habit over the years, regardless of who I'm dealing with; friend, foe, or prey."

"I see." She clapped her hands, and a pair of servants entered. "Take Pierre back to his room and see to it he is cleaned and fed." She indicated the figure on the floor.

In minutes, only she and Viktor remained in the room.

"Have you fed this evening?"

"I've had no blood, but I found a tavern which serves ample meals. I am sated for the time being."

"Ah yes; I remember some of my servants informing me they saw you eating mortal fare shortly after entering my city."

"Do you miss solid food?"

She smiled and shook her head. "I do not even remember what it feels like in the mouth, let alone how it tastes. Please, have a seat."

He took one of the chairs she motioned to. "Shall we continue our conversation from last night, or do you tire of the subject?"

She sighed and gave him a sad smile. "I had no intention of betraying my Sire to you, when first you entered my Court. I merely wished to study you before I destroyed you."

"Do you still intend to destroy me?" He maintained his outward demeanor but felt himself go very still inside. He watched his hostess closely, ready for anything.

"No; I now see you as my last hope of freeing myself from His yoke. I could not aid you physically against Him, of course. I'm sure you've noticed a Sire's power over their Childe increases with proximity."

"I have," he replied with a wry smile. "I fully understand how you would be hampered in such a situation, perhaps even be used as a weapon."

She nodded gravely. "I sense you have done so, yourself."

"My eldest Childe destroyed the necromancer who cursed me to this fate. The old bitch thought she was going to use my Childe to destroy me. My power proved greater than hers."

Bendis raised an eyebrow. "I didn't know any true necromancers existed. This Childe, he is part of your crew?"

He shook his head. "She— was a whore I dallied with shortly before I was cursed. In fact, she was indirectly the reason I was cursed. A local boy was foolish enough to fall in love with her and challenged me in front of my crew for her. Naturally, I killed him, unaware he was a favorite of the necromancer. It wouldn't have changed my course of action that night, had I known. Later, she sent her zombies to capture me and bring me to her."

"Zombies?"

"Dead men animated by her magic. It turns out to be very difficult to defeat something which feels no pain, and whose parts reattach themselves if you cut them off."

"I can imagine. So, you turned the whore in revenge?"

"No. She was merely my first blood meal. I didn't understand the nature of what I'd just become and didn't realize what I'd done to her until well after I'd left that island."

"Unfortunately," he continued, "although I could sense the torment that bitch, Juma, put her through, I had to wait several years before I could return. I was warned that the necromancer would destroy me if I wasn't at full strength when I challenged her. I have since seen to my Childe's safety and proper training to control her powers and Hunger. She is thriving and bears me no ill for her fate, thankfully."

Bendis studied him for several minutes. "You sound as if you truly regret turning her."

"I do, even though it worked to my advantage in the end. I needed her blood, but I thought I'd only killed her. I've always been willing to kill for something I want or need, but I only inflict prolonged suffering on those who've earned it. She hadn't earned what Juma put her through."

Bendis sat and crossed her legs, head cocked to the side. "Do you think the witch tormented your Childe to make you suffer or to punish her for her unintentional part in the boy's death at your hand?"

"Both, I suspect. Juma was a vindictive bitch. She also used my Childe to spy on me. I used that to my advantage and let her think I feared her power."

"Clever."

She looked down at her hands and sighed, as if coming to a decision. Viktor waited patiently for her to speak.

"You deduced quite a bit about what Dragon did to me, and I've trusted you enough to give what vital information I can about him. In return, you've revealed enough about your own nature I feel I can trust you even further."

She looked up at him. "I've a feeling this existence would've been far more bearable for me had you been my

Sire rather than Him." She smiled wistfully. "I had enjoyed being human. I had no interest in taking a mate or carnal pleasure. I enjoyed being outdoors, and I earned a place in my village as one of their best hunters. Considering the subsequent cultures I've seen, I realize I was fortunate to not be forced into a role simply because of my gender; a role I would've been ill-suited for and would have hated."

"Indeed," he agreed. "I learned long ago not to underestimate women on any count. In fact, I've often found them to be more fierce, loyal, determined, and intelligent than many men I've dealt with. They are also quite cunning. I admire them for that."

"I can see and smell the sincerity of your words, Captain Brandewyne. The same cannot be said for my Sire. To Him, I am, at best, a tool to be used and an extension of His will. At worst, He sees me as something to be subjugated."

Viktor shook his head. "He did you, and himself by proxy, a great disservice with that mistake."

She smiled sadly in response. "Allow me to tell you how I became a Daughter of the Dragon."

Chapter 21

The smell of fresh deer spoor rose to the huntress' nostrils. She crouched to the ground and examined the leaf litter closely in the evening light. The pellets of dung still held warmth, and a large patch of leaves glistened with pungent urine. The animal had to be nearby.

She rose slowly and glanced around, looking for other sign. Ahead and to the left, a glimmer of white caught her eye. She padded over, nearly silent, to investigate.

The scent of pine sap greeted her; amber beads of the sticky fluid glistened around the edges where bark had been rubbed off a sapling, leaving the white flesh of the wood to gleam in the light of the dying sun. A small shred of antler felt, pink with blood, dangled from the bark at the edge of the rub.

"A stag!" The Fates smiled on her hunt after all. She allowed herself a quiet sigh of relief; she didn't want to risk spooking her prey this close to it.

Until that moment, she'd wondered if her village and hunt were cursed.

Going by the signs, a lone, rogue wolf had been ravaging her village for two cycles of the moon. At first, livestock had disappeared in small groups. Then, the occasional child began to vanish.

In both cases, the bodies were found torn and bloodless but not eaten.

The latter fact raised fears some god or demon had been angered, rather than a real wolf. The elders decided the three best hunters should try to track the marauding creature. Her lot had fallen to the north.

She'd snared countless conies and tied them out as bait but had yet to spot the creature. Instead, she'd found the small animals starved to death or missing a paw, bled out not far from where she'd staked them out. The wolf demon hadn't so much as sniffed at them, and the meat was no longer fit to take back to the village.

Coming across the stag's spoor, she merely faced the dilemma of using it for bait or taking it back to the village to be smoked for the coming winter. They no longer had enough livestock to see them through. Without meat, possibly several of the very old and very young would not survive the winter.

That decided her. She would take the deer and return to the village with it before continuing with the wolf hunt.

She readied her bow and proceeded in the direction the signs pointed.

Twilight took the land, and she paused to allow her eyes to adjust. She knew she was close enough to her quarry to probably take it before full dark ended her hunt for the night. The new moon would not provide enough light to safely hunt by.

Finally, the eerie half-glow and visual clarity rose in the forest. She continued her tracking with confidence but caution. How well she knew the half-light could play tricks, and she'd grown up with tales of strange creatures that came out at such times to torment or mislead the unwary.

Suddenly, she came upon sign of a great struggle. A large swath of fresh dirt lay exposed where something had knocked the stag to the ground. Gouges marked the raw earth from her prey's antlers and hooves. She also noted what appeared to be claw marks from a creature with five toes. This brought her brows together in a consternated frown.

Her first thought that the rogue wolf had finally put in an appearance, soon faded. A wolf paw, even the monstrously huge ones of the deep forest, only carried four claws, not five. This almost looked human, but what man could tackle a deer of this one's obvious size to the ground? Also, no tracks of this mysterious predator led to or away from the scene of the scuffle, only the stag's.

Blood spattered the exiting trail.

She found a spot where the creature stumbled and tracks which indicated it was lamed. That would make it easier to catch up.

A strangled, inhuman cry, abruptly cut off, reached her ears.

"No!" she thought. *"I can't lose that meat!"*

She quickened her pace, hoping to get there in time to keep whatever predators from ruining the meat, at least.

To her surprise, she saw the stag striding unharmed toward her in the clearing she approached. She didn't stop to think. She aimed her bow and let the arrow fly.

Just as the projectile entered the beast's breast, the stag dissolved into a puff of smoke. Before her now stood a handsome, naked man in full arousal and holding her arrow.

He smiled, a mixture of allure and arrogance, and held the arrow out to her. "I believe this is yours."

"Hello, Bendis," he said and walked toward her.

She took a step back and reached for a fresh arrow. "How do you know my name? Who are you?"

Before she could retrieve an arrow from the quiver at her side, the one formerly held by the stranger pierced the quiver through, pinned the arrow she touched in place. She glanced down in reflex then back up. The stranger stood close before her and placed two fingers under her chin as he smiled down at her.

"What are you?" She amended her question in a strained whisper.

"I am called Dragon, and I've traveled far to meet you, Bendis."

Before she could evade it, he leaned over and kissed her.

He gave her a puzzled frown, when he pulled back from the kiss. She stared coldly into his eyes.

"Do not do that again. My interests do not lay in that direction."

"I see," he said with a smirk and snapped his fingers.

A black wolf padded out of the shadows at the far side of the clearing. It dragged the carcass of the stag with it. She couldn't be sure, but Bendis thought it looked intact except for the torn-out throat. The wolf deposited her prey at their feet and vanished back into the gloom under the trees.

Dragon knelt and lifted the stag to his shoulders as if it weighed nothing. "I offer you this meat for your conversation."

Part of her wanted to spit on him and flee. Some instinct prevented it. Whatever his appearance, he was not human.

She remembered a tale from a traveler who'd passed through her village a few winters past. He'd told of gods traveling the earth in disguise and punishing the inhospitable people they'd encountered but rewarding those who graciously hosted them. Her village prided itself on hospitality to any and all, so the story struck enough of a chord with her to remember it.

"Come with me to my village. We will give you food, shelter for the night, and clothing to wear. There are also some maidens there who, unlike me, would be more than agreeable to your attentions."

His smile widened, an almost predatory expression, and he nodded. "I will accept your hospitality. Lead the way."

For a brief moment, some deep instinct screamed at her that she'd made a mistake. She ignored it. For better or worse, her lot was cast.

Bendis introduced Dragon to her "wife" Gatàki. The older woman greeted him warmly, not even blushing at his nudity. She did give him an appreciative smile, however, before she disappeared into another room.

Dragon gave his hostess a knowing look. "Ah, now I see where your interests lay."

Bendis laughed. "You are mistaken. Gatàki is my wife in name only. She is my brother's widow."

"This should fit, sir. You are of a size near that of my Andros," Gatàki said, returning with a chiton and brooches to pin it in place. "I see Bendis was telling you of our arrangement. It works out well for both of us. We both have some protection from unwanted suitors, and she no longer lives alone in what once resembled a stable."

"Domesticity was never my strong point," Bendis added with an affectionate smile. "I keep food supplied, and Gatàki takes care of everything else."

Dragon allowed Gatàki to dress him, then, he kissed her hand. "So, you are not lovers? Forgive my asking. It is rare to find two women sharing a household as husband and wife, in my experience."

"I admit it is rare in our land, but not unheard of," Bendis conceded. "I do love Gatàki, but we are not intimate. I do not wish to take a lover."

"I don't want any of the men in our village. Andros was the best. None of the others can compare," Gatàki added. She grew quiet for a while but shook it off. "You must be hungry. Let me fetch bread and cheese. I'm afraid I have only water to offer. This year has been poor, and our village had nothing acceptable to trade for wine."

"Thank you, but I cannot accept. I do not partake of mortal fare."

Gatàki blanched and quickly crouched to the floor before him. Bendis remained seated with a knowing look in her eyes.

"Forgive me, my lord. I had no idea we entertained a god. How may I be of service?"

He glanced at Bendis and raised an eyebrow. She bowed her head but raised it again. "I knew you were not a mere man when you first transformed from a stag and offered my arrow back, my lord."

"Yet you refused me."

Gatàki looked up at her in alarm. "Bendis, you didn't!"

Unfazed, she nodded. "I did. No disrespect was intended; I don't believe a god should have a partner who cannot fully appreciate their blessings. It is why I offered my hospitality instead and mentioned there were many in my village who would be glad to serve in that capacity."

"And what if I requested your lovely wife in my bed?"

"It is her decision to make, not mine. If she accepts, I will not forbid it."

Gatàki's face lit up with eagerness. "I would be honored, my lord."

Dragon inclined his head and took her hand. Without another word, he allowed her to lead him to the sleeping chamber.

Bendis silently wished her well and headed to the larder to fetch some of the bread and cheese they'd offered their guest. She knew Gatàki had needs she could never fulfill. She hoped their supernatural guest would more than sate her wife's appetites in that arena.

Tamara A. Lowery

Chapter 22

"Did he murder your wife?" Viktor asked when she paused. He'd found himself wrapped up in the story.

"No, He didn't kill her—." A note of pain colored her voice as she trailed off.

He waited patiently for her to continue.

Gatàki did not rise to prepare the morning meal. Bendis, who'd slept by the hearth, wasn't too surprised. The cries of passion coming from her wife and their guest had lasted most of the night.

Still, she felt it would only be hospitable to take some sort of breakfast in to them. She prepared a platter of cheese, bread, wild grapes, and fresh goat's milk, and carried it into the sleeping chamber.

Only Gatàki occupied the bed. She saw no sign of Dragon. Perhaps he was a night god? She first encountered him after sunset, after all.

She shrugged and set the food down next to the bed. Gently, she nudged her wife.

Gatàki didn't stir, although a faint moan escaped her lips. Her skin felt oddly cool and held an abnormally white translucence in the morning sunlight. Her breathing sounded labored.

Bendis frowned and fetched one of the bed furs from the corner. She covered the chilled woman and gently caressed her face.

"Gatàki? Can you hear me?"

"Hhn? B-bendis, is that you? Where did He go? Will He come back? I must have Him."

"I don't know, my love. I have not seen him since last night. Did he do this to you?"

"He was glorious." Gatàki sighed, her voice barely a whisper.

"I am glad he could satisfy you," she lied. She felt the beginnings of outrage at the condition their guest had left her wife in. It bordered on an abuse of hospitality, an offense even among the gods.

"I brought you some breakfast: cheese, bread, and fresh goat's milk. Can you sit up, or do you need help?"

Her wife flapped her hand. "Not hungry, thank you."

Bendis would have none of it. "Nevertheless, you need to eat something. You're as cold and pale as death, my love."

She put her hands under Gatàki's arms and lifted her to a sitting position, careful to keep the fur wrapped around her. The woman tried to resist but apparently lacked the strength. This also alarmed her.

"Here, at least have some milk." She held the clay cup to her wife's lips and managed to get her to swallow a little.

Gatàki let out a mewling cry right before she doubled over and vomited the milk and the remains of the previous day's meal all over the fur. Seconds later, she collapsed, unconscious, and the labored breathing returned.

Bendis felt like she'd swallowed a stone. Some deep instinct told her she'd soon be a widow.

She cleaned Gatàki's face and replaced the fur with a clean one. At least being a hunter afforded her the luxury of multiple furs and hides. Lacking the skill to tan them herself, she traded meat for the service.

The sun rode high before her wife regained consciousness.

Bendis stayed with Gatàki throughout the day. The woman refused any sort of food offered. Still, she kept trying and kept watch.

Bendis didn't know if she'd dozed or if Dragon simply materialized in front of her. He wore the chiton of her dead brother they'd gifted him. She gripped the long knife she held in her lap and gave him her deadliest stare. He'd put her wife in her current state; if he moved to bring more harm, god or no, she'd see if he bled.

"Greetings Bendis. You seem ill at ease."

"You are no god. You are some night demon. You've bewitched my wife and taken most of her life force. You have betrayed our hospitality. Restore her."

He smirked at her. "You are more perceptive than I gave you credit for. I am a skilled hunter, just as you are. Accompany me on my hunt tonight, and I will consider granting your demand."

"I dare not leave her side. She has done no sin worth dying alone for."

He cocked his head and gazed at his victim. "Very well, I give you my word she will not die this night. She has my protection for that time, and none will dare harm her. She will recover some of her strength as she rests."

Bendis rose and sheathed her blade. She took her bow down from the wall and strung it then tied it to her girdle. Some small voice in the back of her mind told her she should kill him now, but she feared it would doom poor Gatàki to a slow, wasting death.

"What is our prey?"

To her frustration, Dragon refused to name their quarry. She found herself forced to follow his lead blindly. She endured for her wife's sake only.

Obviously, he possessed better night vision than her. He soon picked up on a trail and led her deeper into the forest.

They passed through an open glade. Although the moon hid her face, the starlight provided ample illumination to see by. Next to a small stream which bisected the glade, she finally saw the tracks he followed. What she saw confused her.

Wolf tracks abruptly lost the forepaw prints, as if the beast stood on its hind legs only. Then the tracks changed shape over a few steps until replaced with human footprints. The size told her they belonged to either an older child or a woman.

Next the tracks told her this strange person had leapt, as if to cross the stream, but no tracks showed on the other side.

She looked up and saw a calculating smile on Dragon's face as he watched her. She narrowed her eyes and surveyed the area. Close to the trees on the other side of the glade, she spotted the footprints and sign of a single hand touching the earth. The drier soil provided less distinction to the tracks than the damp earth by the stream.

The renewed trail led into the trees. She took the lead on the hunt. Something told her this was the creature she'd been hunting when she'd encountered Dragon.

A nagging feeling kept eating at her about that encounter, but she couldn't call the memory clearly to mind. She knew some important detail escaped her, but every time she tried to think back on the incident she only saw an image of Dragon's dark eyes.

She shook her head to clear it and continued to follow the tracks. Just before reaching a second glade, they transformed back into those of a wolf. She paused and looked back at Dragon.

"What are we hunting?" Her words came out as barely a breath, so as not to alert their prey.

He laughed. "She can hear even that soft sound. There is no need for silence or stealth."

Bendis frowned, turned, and stepped cautiously into the glade. What she saw only puzzled her further. Not a single blade of grass seemed disturbed. No further track or sign could be seen, as if their prey had taken flight.

Movement caught her eye at the far side of the glade. A large she-wolf floated down from the treetops and alit close to the trees. Bendis nocked an arrow to her bow, but her companion stayed her hand before she could draw.

"Watch," Dragon whispered in her ear.

The wolf walked toward them. As it approached, it stood on its hind legs. Fur retracted into the skin of its rapidly shifting form. Soon, a pale-skinned petite woman with dark hair and eyes stood nude before them.

"What are you?" Bendis asked before she could stop herself. A flash of memory of a stag turning into Dragon, albeit at a much faster pace than this creature's transformation, told her what she needed to know. The woman and the man were of a kind.

"You see, my Lord? She shows great promise," the woman addressed Dragon.

"Indeed, she is a very skilled hunter to track you in this light with only human sight. Bendis, this is my Daughter, Carpathia. She is the reason I sought you out."

"I don't understand." She'd never seen this woman before, if woman she was.

Carpathia smiled at her, an action which chilled her to the bone. She knew a predator when she saw one.

"It has been my task to seek out those my Lord might deem worthy. You are one of the most skilled hunters I've observed in this part of the world."

Sudden realization hit. Bendis nocked her arrow and aimed at the nude female. "You are what stalked my village, destroyed livestock, and killed children. We will be lucky if half our people survive the coming winter. Murderer."

Before she could release the arrow, Dragon stood before her holding her weapons. She'd barely felt them taken from her hands.

"You are more than worthy. I shall make you a goddess."

Anger flashed in her eyes, but she reminded herself he'd promised to help Gatàki. She bowed her head. "I am honored, but I have no wish to be a goddess. I only seek the health of my wife and the peace and survival of my people."

He handed the bow and arrow to Carpathia, stepped forward, and raised Bendis' face to meet his gaze.

She felt control over her body slip away as she lost herself in those dark eyes which seemed to radiate a warm glow. Beneath the warmth, however, she sensed the cold cruelty of a predator.

"Twice, you have refused me. Know this, Bendis, I will not be denied. I will make you a goddess, but first, I will take my due. Afterwards, you shall learn the cost of your rebuffs."

He stripped her roughly. She stood naked but unembarrassed. She awaited the beating she felt sure to come for displeasing a being of such power.

What he put her through proved far more damaging than any beating could be.

Bendis, a woman possessed of no sexual desire or drive, found herself subjected to every violation of her virgin body imaginable. Her lack of physical response and failure to so much as utter any sound of passion seemed only to spur her assailant on. Even the shape-shifting female failed to arouse her in any way.

Finally, Dragon drove long, sharp fangs, like those of a beast, into the juncture of her throat and shoulder. As he continued to pound his flesh into hers, he drew the lifeblood from the fresh wound in great mouthfuls.

Her breath came in gasps, struggling for oxygen she now lacked sufficient blood to deliver. Her body convulsed in the first and only orgasm in her existence, as she felt the last bit of life slip away. She smiled, believing her torment had come to an end.

"Bendis rise."

Confused, she obeyed the summons of her master.

Her master? How was it she had a master? She'd died; or had she?

Yes, she had. She'd felt the warmth and life leave her body and peaceful numbness wash over her. This made no sense.

"As I promised, I made you a goddess. You now belong to me and are bound to my will, for I am your god and creator."

She wanted to argue that but found she could not speak the words. She did manage to shy away from His hand when He reached for her face.

"You defy me still." She could feel the ice in His tone; so cold it burned. "Know then the full extent of what burden our existence carries. I will shield you no more."

Bendis screamed as a crippling voracious Hunger swept through her. For how long she lay curled, screaming, and crying, she knew not.

Finally, Dragon had mercy and placed a calming hand on her shoulder. The Hunger pangs abated, though they still lurked in the back of her mind. His voice softened. "The Hunger will be with you always. I cannot change that. It is never satisfied. Only blood will quiet it for a time. Blood will give you strength and some small measure of peace. Come, let us feed."

This time, she took His hand. He raised her to her feet and led her toward her village. She only vaguely noticed the cruel smile on Carpathia's face.

"The three of us murdered the entire village; every man, woman, and child," Bendis told a rapt Viktor. "Dragon saved my wife for last. He wanted to punish me for not finding Him desirable."

She paused as a shadow of ancient sorrow passed over her face.

"You don't have to talk about it if you don't want to," he told her.

"No, I think I need to. In agreeing to aid you, if possible, against Him, I feel the need to purge the old demons."

He nodded, and she continued.

Bendis began to realize the full extent of Dragon's hold on her wife when they entered her home. The three vampires were naked and blood-soaked, yet Gatàki didn't seem to notice the gore.

She didn't even register the presence of Bendis or Carpathia, at first.

"You've returned, my love!" she cried, her face awash in delight. "I have craved your touch since you left."

He smiled and motioned toward Carpathia. "I have brought you a new pleasure, sweet Gatàki. My daughter, Carpathia, is to demonstrate to your Bendis how a woman may properly love a woman. It seems your wife has no true skill in that art."

"Do not judge her too harshly, my love. Ours is a marriage of mutual protection, as we told you before. I have never resented her lack of desire for physical pleasure. It is just how she is."

"All the same, Bendis is my daughter now. I have deigned to make her a goddess. These are things she must learn."

Gatàki looked at Carpathia with a touch of apprehension. "I have never had a woman as a lover. My skills are just as lacking as those of my wife."

The dark-haired, pallid beauty smiled. "Then I shall see to your pleasure first, so you may know how to give me mine later."

Bendis watched them at the silent command of her master. She caught Carpathia's glance for just a moment and fell to her new sister's power. The gore from their massacre of the villagers evaporated before her eyes, and Carpathia took on an ethereal beauty beyond any she'd ever seen.

She shook her head, and the illusion vanished. Once again, she saw the blood-soaked predator in human female form. At least now she understood her wife's lack of shock and horror at their appearance.

Carpathia stepped up to the only human in the room and cupped her face. She leaned in and kissed her skillfully. At the same time, she undid the brooches holding Gatàki's garment at the shoulders. She stepped back and gazed at her body, as the fabric slid down to the floor.

Stepping in for another kiss, she let her hands explore the curves and softness of her lover.

When they finally broke from the kiss, Gatàki's eyes glittered with lust. Carpathia snagged a seating cushion from the floor, laid her lover back on the low table, and placed the cushion under her head.

Gatàki emitted a satisfied hum, close to a purr, as Carpathia's hands worked their way down the front of her body, kneading along the way. The vampire leaned over and kissed her again briefly. She traced her tongue down the woman's throat, seeking out the pulse, as one hand teased a nipple erect. The other hand combed through the soft thatch of hair at the juncture of her legs.

For a moment, Bendis thought her new sister would drain her wife before her eyes. Dragon's voice put an end to that.

"She is not yours to feed on."

Carpathia turned to their master with a sly smile. "As you command."

She turned her attention back to the woman beneath her. She began diligently stroking the folds of Gatàki's pudenda. Her lover spread her legs wider and tilted her hips up to grant better access.

Carpathia worked her fingers between the soft folds until she found the sensitive nub. She started lightly flicking it, slowly at first, and gradually sped to a rhythm no human could match.

Gatàki gasped, moaned, and bucked beneath her, legs quivering as she lost control of her muscles. Bendis saw the folds of flesh grow moist and glisten with the juices of her orgasm.

Before her lover's body could relax again, Carpathia drew a gasp from the woman as she slid three fingers inside her. She kept them close together then spread them wide as she slowly withdrew. She repeated this process for a few minutes but kept the pace slow.

Gatàki moaned in pleasure. She thrust her hips up to encourage her to go faster.

Instead, she worked a fourth finger into the wet opening. Once certain her lover had loosened up enough, she added her thumb.

Rather than work in and out this time, she twisted her hand side to side until she'd worked it in past the knuckles.

She had to wait for Gatàki to buck her way through another orgasm. Using the added natural lubrication and her unnatural strength, she forced her hand past the cervix and into Gatàki's womb.

The woman gasped; her eyes wide in shock and pleasure mixed with pain. Her body grew rigid.

"What are you doing to her?" Bendis asked.

Carpathia glanced at Dragon, who nodded almost imperceptibly. She looked back at Bendis. "I'm stealing your wife's heart."

With that, she gave a short jab, eliciting a scream from Gatàki.

Bendis watched in fascinated horror as a hand-shaped lump appeared under the skin of her wife's abdomen. Gatàki moaned as her lover-turned-tormentor worked her hands slowly through her innards.

When Carpathia was in up to her elbow, she gave another forceful jab. Her victim could not scream this time. She couldn't even draw a breath.

Her hunting knowledge told Bendis the vampire had pierced the diaphragm of her prey.

A look of pleading filled Gatàki's eyes, and Bendis knew what she must do. She placed a gentle hand on either side of her wife's face and kissed her forehead.

"Forgive me," she whispered and snapped her neck, ending her suffering.

Or so she thought.

Gatàki's canines grew longer and sharper as she watched. The dead woman's gaze began to grow cognizant again, as well.

"End it, daughter."

Carpathia pouted but obeyed. Now with her arm in her victim's body almost fully, she grasped, twisted, and gave a sharp tug.

Though the fangs remained, life once again left Gatàki's eyes. Carpathia withdrew her arm, and blood pooled rapidly on the table between the dead woman's legs. The vampire had to give another tug to get her victim's heart past the cervix and out the birth canal.

Offal and ropes of intestines soon protruded like an obscene afterbirth.

Bendis retched and vomited blood.

"Dragon eventually grew so frustrated with my lack of sexual desire he placed a compulsion on me. I was to surround myself with every sort of debaucher until I learned to enjoy it."

She smiled and shook her head ruefully. "I still barely understand the fascination so many have with sex for anything other than procreation. Even that aspect eludes me, as I have another means of producing offspring."

Viktor thought about it for a while. "I must admit I can see why you would despise it, given what he put you through. You were like this before, though. It seems foreign to me. I truly enjoy having a woman. But I can see where the lack of desire could be liberating. Sex can be as addictive as opium and thus be used as a tool of manipulation."

"Yes, it can. I've often allowed my Children to use it to secure our safety and position. It used to puzzle me but now merely amuses me how many men in power love to indulge in various depravities. Yet, they don't wish for others to learn about their peccadilloes."

Viktor chuckled. "I imagine such knowledge can prove quite profitable, especially if the holder of it is powerful enough to be immune to the threat of being silenced permanently."

"True; I've also learned the threat of denying entry to my Court and its pleasures is a more effective weapon than the threat of revealing their indiscretions to their families or the public at large."

"As I said, it can be as addictive as opium."

Chapter 23

"I think it's time to rejoin the revels. I sense some of my followers have gotten carried away with your whore. I will compensate you if they've damaged her. I also grant you liberty to punish the ones who've defied my commands."

Viktor didn't blink at the sudden change of subject. He reached along his link with the siren and sensed she enjoyed whatever she was involved in with near total abandon

"I would be more worried she may have harmed some of your people than they her."

Bendis stopped and looked at him. "You share some bond with her, then. I thought I felt a ripple of power from you. Have you fed on her?"

He saw no point in denying it, so he nodded.

"You never truly intended to sell her."

"We've already established that. She is mine of her own volition. I do have a duty to protect her, however, and a duty as your guest to keep her controlled." He sighed resignedly. "Let's see what the damage is, if any."

The sight which greeted them caused Viktor to grow hard unexpectedly. Bendis' face only briefly registered annoyance, concern, and curiosity before her mask fell

back into place. Viktor only caught it because he immediately turned to watch her reaction.

He noted arousal was markedly absent from her expressions or scent.

Before them, Belladonna hung prone and naked, stretched out in the framework Bendis occasionally used to hold her meals spread-eagle. Before her, a nude man grasped her hair to keep her head at the proper angle, while he fucked her in the mouth. Between her outspread legs, a nude woman thrust her hips into Belle's crotch.

It took Viktor a moment to realize the woman wore some type of harness which supported a false phallus. He raised an eyebrow in curiosity. The action never occurred to him before.

"Well, at least she hasn't bitten anything off anyone—yet," he said with a wry chuckle.

"Karl, withdraw at once," Bendis ordered. "Beatrice, unstrap and step away. I don't want her damaged any more than you already have."

Both obeyed, the woman leaving the phallus embedded deep in the suspended siren.

Belle's head drooped forward a bit until she flung it back, flipping her hair over her shoulders and upper back. She looked over at the two vampires.

"I was enjoying myself. Why did you have them stop?" she said with a pout.

Bendis' eyebrows drew together in consternation. "How is this possible? I know that toy. It's usually reserved for torture, not pleasure. No human should be able to endure it used on them the way Beatrice was pumping it."

Viktor hid a frown before his hostess could notice it. He'd a feeling the siren's true nature just revealed itself.

Bendis strode over and gently grasped the protruding end of the phallus. The base seemed abnormally broad to Viktor. He surmised that might be to make it ride more comfortably against the pelvis of its wearer.

Bendis gave it a slow half twist to the right, and Belle moaned loudly in orgasm.

"What are you? You can't possibly be human, and you don't smell like vampire."

The siren only responded with a throaty plea. "Do it again— please! All the way around."

Bendis shrugged and fulfilled the request.

Belle growled in pleasure.

In response, the vampire drew the instrument out of the siren's body slowly. Her face registered genuine surprise. "Not the first drop of blood; intriguing."

Viktor easily understood her confusion. Now he saw the full device, he wondered how Belladonna sustained no injury from it. The shaft looked as thick as his forearm. Rounded nubs the size of a knuckle studded the fist-sized head.

As he watched, Bendis turned a small knob near the base which retracted the nubs. Until that moment, he'd wondered how they'd even inserted the thing.

She laid the device on a nearby table and rotated the framework until Belle hung vertically. The whole time, she peered intently at the bound female. She stopped by her left shoulder and brushed the crimson hair to drape over her right.

Bendis gasped audibly at the brand revealed on Belle's left shoulder blade: a scythe with a dragon twined about it.

"A siren," she breathed then turned her amazed gaze to Viktor. "How did you manage to snare a siren? And one who's encountered my Sisters— the only one that I know of."

"She was sent to help me with my previous quest. She took a bite out of me literally, and we've been bound together ever since," he replied.

"She is your master rather than you hers, then."

He shook his head. Belle chuckled.

"Viktor has no master. I pity anyone foolish enough to attempt to control him."

In a bid to turn the attention away from him, he pointed at the phallus. "You said that thing is usually reserved for torture."

Bendis nodded. "Dragon uses it on me when He visits. I refuse to give Him the pleasure of seeing my pain. Eventually, He gets bored and picks a random human female from among my followers. So far, none survive. The lucky ones lose consciousness early in the session."

"So, he definitely enjoys cruelty."

"He revels in it."

"Indeed, I do." The words came from Bendis' mouth, but they held a different timbre altogether.

Viktor saw her consciousness struggling against her Sire's invasion of her body. "I don't think she appreciates your presence, Dragon," he stated nonchalantly.

"Oh, I'm certain she doesn't. I always have her do things she claims she has no interest in, Viktor

Brandewyne. I could even make her fuck you, if you'd like."

"I find a willing lover much more enjoyable."

Bendis/Dragon laughed and stalked around to the other side of the bound siren, inspecting her as she/he went. "So I see. Yes, having a siren as a lover must be both a heady and a dangerously thrilling prospect."

She/he sniffed Belle's hair, savoring the scent. "Her magic nearly makes one drunk just smelling it." She/he traced a finger over the brand which matched the tattoo Bendis bore on her own back, the mark of a Daughter of the Dragon.

"That explains it. She is ancient indeed. Carpathia told me of the hunt which brought her and some of my other Daughters in contact with this luscious, wicked creature. She rid herself of her sister and inadvertently saved the hunt the trouble of disposing of a rebellious subject of mine."

"So she told me some years ago. She'd hoped removing her sister would persuade her sister's mate to leave her territory. It didn't work, of course. Only recently did I dispose of the sea dragon."

"Impressive, I'm sure. You seem to enjoy reckless behavior. Of course, you are young yet. Still, I imagine your youthful carelessness will cost you your life. I must say, I'm surprised you never lost control during sex and made the mistake of feeding on this creature."

Viktor just smiled. He realized Bendis was stronger than Dragon gave her credit for. She already knew he'd fed on Belle before. Even inhabiting her body, her sire hadn't gleaned that information from her.

Bendis/Dragon frowned. "That is not possible. Your very presence here puts the lie to that claim. No vampire could survive it."

"I am still alive," he stated simply.

"Yes, I can see that."

Viktor easily caught the irritation from the older vampire. Dragon already thought him reckless. He decided to play on that by figuratively tugging his tail.

"I mean I am not undead. Your puppet, Juma, cursed me. Mother also warned me against biting or allowing myself to be bitten by other vampires. I believe she neglected to give you a similar warning when she gifted you your powers." He waited and watched for his foe's response.

A glimmer of Bendis re-emerged in her/his eyes. So, Dragon was touchy about that subject. It also confirmed he still harbored a grudge against Celie.

"Why do you call that bitch 'mother'?" Dragon resumed control of the shared body.

Viktor refused to rise to the bait of the slur. He smiled and replied, "Twofold reasons: she raised me from an orphaned infant, and she now embodies the All-Mother. I accomplished the task she originally intended for you, and which you and your machinations had successfully thwarted for millennia."

She/he graced him with a cruel smile. "So, she's tasked you with my elimination now. There can only be two possible reasons for this. Either she sees me as proof of her fallibility, or I truly present a threat to her life." She/he shrugged. "Both prospects please me almost as much as ridding myself of you will."

"You wouldn't be the first to try." Viktor made sure his confidence and lack of fear rang true in his voice.

Bendis/Dragon didn't react to the taunt this time. Instead, she/he examined the other contents of the table the oversized phallus lay on. A short flogger, long needles both straight and curved, and an assortment of blades sat in orderly array.

"I've been told you captured my Carpathia like a genie in a bottle." She/he picked up a filet knife, examined it, and set it back down.

"Something like that. I take it Wormy found his way back to you."

"I assume you mean Captain Wormsloe. Yes, he relayed what you told him, including the claim you cannot free her from her prison."

Viktor nodded. "The spell which keeps her sealed away is beyond my power to break. I tricked her into the bottle, but I'm not the one who corked it." Regret colored his voice.

Bendis/Dragon raised an eyebrow and cocked her/his head. "You would free her if you could. I can see the truth of it. Why?"

"For what it's worth, I loved her. A part of me still does, even though she betrayed us both. Killing her outright would've been kinder than eternal imprisonment, starvation, and madness. I was counseled against it, though. It would've brought you into the game too early."

The debauchery around them seemed to intensify. Viktor felt the surge of power and knew his foe meant it for a distraction.

"You like games, do you?"

He shrugged. "It depends on the game and the stakes."

"You cost me one of my Daughters. I should take your pet in payment. This brand marks her as mine already." She/he pointed at the scar on Belle's shoulder then turned to face him fully. "I know Carpathia ensnared you. I felt it when she made the bond. How did you break free?"

"Sex and siren's blood."

In a flash, Bendis regained control of her body. She snatched a short, curved blade from the table and sliced a gash down Belle's forearm, drawing a startled gasp from the siren.

Blood sprayed briefly.

The wound closed almost immediately, testament to the sheer amount of sexual energy Belle had fed on. Viktor didn't hold it against her, even though they'd said they wouldn't. He hadn't been with her to help her maintain control.

The scent of raw power in the siren's blood drew the attention of the nearest vampires.

"One way or another, I will be free of you, my Master," Bendis said with a snarl. She licked the blood off the blade before anyone could stop her or even react.

She looked at Viktor and said, "Thank you." A split second later, her body collapsed into a pile of clothing, dust, and two shimmering fangs.

He caught Dragon's scent on a nearby vampire and knew his foe escaped Bendis' body probably a moment before her suicide.

"Scream," he silently instructed the siren.

Belladonna let loose with a hypersonic shriek which threatened to pierce his eardrums and made his head throb.

He snatched up a small sickle from the table, never questioning its presence.

Around them, nearly every human dropped to their knees grasping their heads and emitting screams of their own.

Viktor took to the air and began beheading every vampire as quickly as he could. With their mistress dead, they presented too great a danger to him and the siren to waste time trying to negotiate.

Not far from the framework holding the siren, hidden in one of the room's deliberate pools of shadow, Matthew Barnett defiled a goat, blissfully unaware of the drama unfolding behind him. A piercingly shrill noise brought him to a pause in mid-thrust. His eyes grew dull and lifeless, as a blood vessel burst in his brain.

A moment later, some semblance of life returned, but only with a rudimentary mind.

He resumed pumping away at the animal before him out of reflex and instinct. His new fangs formed, and he felt the first pangs of the Hunger. Lacking initial understanding, he increased his pumping hips to superhuman speed. This only gained marginal satisfaction.

The goat began to scream.

He reached for its throat and felt the pulse beneath his hands. Finally, his instinct knew how to direct his body. Never stopping his violation of the poor animal, he lifted it upright and tore its throat out with his new fangs.

He lapped greedily at the spurting blood until the flow ceased, thrusting in and out the whole time. When the creature grew limp and cool to the touch, he dropped it and scanned the room for fresh prey.

Sensing a newly minted vampire of his line, Dragon's essence swiftly inhabited Barnett's body. He found it mildly disorienting to find not only no resistance, but no mind present to resist with. It made the body graceless and difficult to operate.

Still, he managed to direct Barnett's body at Belladonna. The siren's alliance with his nemesis made her too great a risk to let her live. He knew the fledgling vampire would perish with the first taste of her blood, but he counted the sacrifice as the best use of the revenant.

Barnett only knew to follow his instincts to fuck and feed. Dragon's presence left him once he got close enough to catch the mingled aromas of blood and recent sex. He doubted the new vampire's death would take him with it, but why take the risk?

To her surprise, Belle found her bindings stronger than those required for a mere human. She wanted to help Viktor with the fight beyond incapacitating all the humans with her scream. The shackles and chains of the framework must've been forged to hold vampires, though.

She saw the naked male approaching her and thought him mortal at first. His vacant eyes indicated a mind she'd destroyed. Too late, she realized he moved too fast, and he was fully erect.

Barnett soon reached her and began fucking her vigorously. If it had been only that, she'd have endured it with mild annoyance; he wasn't particularly well endowed. To her horror, he also lunged and bit deep into her shoulder.

Thus ended the sordid life of Matthew Barnett; the disowned namesake uncle of one of the *Incubus'* crew of pirates. A pirate who'd met his own demise years prior in an encounter with a horde of venomous creatures controlled by Venoma Noir, one of the Sisters of Power.

Though the true death came to him instantaneously; his body remained perfectly intact. The weight, as he collapsed, caused his fangs to cut deep furrows from her shoulder to her nipple.

Belladonna gasped and felt unconscious creep over her. Unlike the knife wound earlier, her body could not heal fast enough from this vampire inflicted wound to prevent massive blood loss.

Chapter 24

Viktor dropped the head of the last vampire on the pile by Bendis' throne. Only he, Belladonna, and several brain-damaged humans remained. He planned to use the humans to haul the heads and bodies of the vampires out into the square before sunrise. Daylight would incinerate the corpses.

He turned to see Belle still bound. This puzzled him since he knew the siren possessed a physical strength at least the equal of his. Surely, she'd have broken free by now.

Then, he saw the corpse at her feet and a disturbingly large puddle of blood below her. He noticed her body seemed limp, and her head lolled forward.

"Belle? Pet?"

He got no response. A moment of panic hit him as he remembered a sudden burst of distress from her during his bloody rampage. Since it faded quickly, he thought she'd dealt with whoever caused it. He relaxed when his link with her told him she still lived.

He stepped around the frame, looked down at the corpse, and recognized it. Noticing the fangs, he surmised what manner of death took Barnett's uncle.

He turned to face Belle and felt a chill run through him. She hung unconscious with twin gashes running from her throat to her breast. Though slowed, blood still oozed from the horrific wounds. The smell of it and the magic it carried threatened his control over the Hunger.

He didn't understand fully why she hadn't healed at her normal, rapid rate. Dried blood on her arm was the only remaining mark of where Bendis cut her. Perhaps because the wounds were made by a vampire's bite? He did remember how, not long after she'd joined the crew, one of his cadre tried to feed on her. She'd healed slowly then, too, until he'd thrown her into the sea.

He looked around but didn't see her clothing or the flask of seawater she usually carried. Belatedly, he remembered the spare flask he'd brought, which hung from his belt. He untied the leather thong, bit the cork, and pulled it from the flask. He poured the briny liquid onto her wounds.

Her eyes flew open, and she jerked in her bonds. He watched the gashes close and vanish in mere seconds.

"Give!" she demanded.

He held the flask to her mouth and tilted it to allow her to drink.

"Thank you," she said after she finished the flask off. "I think the key is on the table. Get me out of this rig, please."

"I'm surprised you didn't just break free, pet." He rummaged about the knives and other instruments of torture for a few moments. Finally, he found the small key and quickly unlocked her shackles.

She stumbled a bit when her feet touched the floor. He steadied her and helped her over to the throne. He noticed her eyes shone amber rather than their grey-green human guise. He also felt the waves of hunger rolling off her.

"You need to eat, pet. It looks like you lost quite a bit of blood."

She nodded.

He fetched the closest human and brought them to her. He recognized the man as the one previously using her mouth to pleasure himself. "With Bendis dead, eating any of these should no longer pose a risk," he reasoned.

Belladonna grasped the man and pulled him to her. He didn't react until she opened her mouth nearly ear-to-ear and buried multiple rows of needle-sharp teeth in his throat. He opened his mouth as if to scream, but no sound emerged. His body bucked and struggled in her steel grip.

She held him that way until his struggling ceased, and he grew limp. With a snap of her jaws, she bit his entire throat out. His head lolled back on some thin strips of tissue and his bloody spine.

Before their eyes, the tissues of his neck began regenerating, and fangs grew within his open mouth.

She ripped his head off completely and tossed it on the pile of vampire heads Viktor started. She sniffed at the corpse and threw it away from her with a grimace.

"He already turned. The meat is no good to me now." She shrugged. "The blood did me some good, at least; time for a different tactic."

With that, she bounded from the throne and pounced on a nearby female. Within seconds, she extended her talons and used them to rip her victim's heart out. She watched the corpse twitch and grow still.

When enough time passed, and the dead woman didn't sprout fangs or show any signs of reanimation, the siren began to feed. She didn't finish until nothing remained of the corpse.

"Hold off on any more for now, pet. We need the others to get these dead vampires out to the square before dawn. The sunrise will finish the cleanup," Viktor declared.

She nodded her agreement.

Before long, they directed the remaining humans to lug body after body out. Viktor gutted one of the large pillows from an alcove and used it to collect the vampire heads.

It took two trips.

"It's still an hour or so until dawn," Belladonna pointed out. "What do you want to do with this lot?"

He surveyed the nearly mindless humans. They numbered around twenty with maybe half of those not diseased.

"Line up shoulder to shoulder," he ordered.

They shuffled around but gradually managed to form a line. He walked down it and used his vampire senses to pick out the healthy ones. These, he directed to stand on the other side of the pile of corpses and face away from it.

The remaining humans he placed next to the pile. Silently, he contacted the siren. *"Take their heads. Otherwise, they'll be like Barnett when they die and turn."*

"That would be very bad for this place," she agreed mentally.

She extended her talons their full, razor-sharp length and quickly beheaded the diseased. The bodies collapsed neatly, more or less, onto the pile of vampire corpses.

Both Viktor and Belle felt sure the conflagration the coming dawn would spark should prove sufficient to dispose of the less flammable human bodies. They knew how quickly and hot vampire flesh burned.

Satisfied with their preparations, they marched their remaining charges out of the city and down river. Once far enough away to avoid any early risers, Viktor called Jim and his cadre to him. Before long, the handful of vampires, crewmen he'd turned, alit before him.

Jim handed Belladonna a bundle of clothes, which she quickly changed into. He shamelessly ogled the siren the entire time.

"Lads, pick a human each and fly them back to the ship. Do not feed on them. They are mindless and will turn almost immediately. I want them placed in the larder hold until we can properly harvest their blood."

"Do you want us to come back for the others, Cap'n?" one of the vampires asked.

"No, I'll bring them in the boat. Jim, I've a special errand for you."

"Aye, Cap'n," his friend replied.

"You remember the scent of the vampire you encountered trying to spy on the ship?"

"I do; got a good look at him, too."

"Good because he might smell different. Depends on if Dragon is riding him or not. See if you can find him. He wasn't among the ones in the nest I just cleared out. He may try to find one of the other Daughters."

Jim smiled wryly. "So, find him and keep an eye on him. See where he goes. How long do you want me to spy?"

Viktor shrugged. "At this point, I don't know. I'll call you back to the ship if something important comes up."

"You can count on me, Vik." With that, Jim's dissolved into black smoke and reformed as the raven, Lazarus.

"Be careful, my friend. This one is nearly as powerful as his Dam was. I think she kept him blind to his own power to keep him from getting out of control."

The bird cawed and took to flight, headed back toward Antwerp.

Jacques had no idea how long he'd stood motionless. The death of his Mistress came as a shock. He felt unsure for the first time in his existence as a vampire, like a boat cut adrift on the tide.

On one hand, he mourned the loss of Bendis. Though he'd learned long ago she would never be his lover, he still felt loyalty and fondness for her. On the other hand, he felt a growing sense of freedom and betrayal. With the muzzle he'd never known she'd kept on his powers finally removed, his strength and magical virility blossomed.

It almost felt like being drunk, or so he imagined. He really couldn't remember what intoxication felt like anymore. He just knew he liked it!

Dragon's presence broke his reverie.

"Bendis is no more. She tried to betray me. Brandewyne and his pet siren destroyed her." Anger colored the draconic apparition's mental tone. *"She was always a disappointment, but she was MINE. If I'd wanted her destroyed, I'd have done it myself."*

Jacques merely bowed his head. Given his ultimate Master's mood, he didn't dare to think, let alone offer an opinion or try to defend the vampire who made him.

"You are the only Childe she should have been proud of. How many Children have you sired?"

The question caught him by surprise, but he recovered quickly. "Only three, my Lord."

"You are at least two centuries old. How is it you have not sired more? Did my Daughter forbid it?"

"She did not. Acceptable candidates have always been rare in the Court of Bendis, my Lord."

He felt more than saw Dragon's smile of approval. *"You are discriminating. Wise of you. It also explains why you are nearly as powerful as she was, despite her multitude of Children and millennia of existence. I will allow you to spare your Children. Starting next sunset, you are to hunt down the remainder of the bloodline of Bendis in Antwerp and destroy them."*

The command stunned Jacques so much he forgot himself for a moment. "Have they offended you, my Lord?"

"They are a liability. Without her will to keep them in check, they will run amok and draw attention. Part of the reason our kind has survived for so long is the doubt by our prey of our actual existence."

"It will be as you command, my Lord. However, sparing my Children is not an option. I felt their deaths shortly after my Lady's."

Only the rush of his full power finally being released to him mitigated the pain of that loss. It sharpened his sense of betrayal by Bendis. It also honed his desire for vengeance.

"My Lord, once my task is fulfilled I ask your leave to avenge my Children on Brandewyne. Your enemy is my enemy."

"Very well, Jacques, you may serve me in this. Once Antwerp is cleansed alert me. I will guide your vengeance. Given what I've observed, a direct assault would be ill-advised. He is far stronger than I expected and quite clever. We must find ways to weaken him and make him suffer in the process."

He gave his Master a grim smile. "I will be patient and savor his agony when it comes, my Lord."

Unnoticed in the shadows, a large black cat laid back his ears and narrowed his eyes.

Chapter 25

Dragon scanned his chambers the moment he returned to his body. He felt the weight of the daystar bearing down on him, though its light could not reach this room. Dawn came much earlier here than in Antwerp.

Two relatively young vampires, each less than a century old, lay naked and supine on the great bed, dead to the world until dusk. In a holding cell in one corner of the chamber, a few humans cowered against the wall when they saw him sit up.

He needed sustenance if he hoped to survive the daily death. He'd spent far more energy projecting his essence these past few nights than anticipated.

He rose and strode to the cage, opening the door on his arrival. The prey tried to cram themselves into the furthest corner; most already witnesses to the fate awaiting them.

A cruel smile crossed his lips as he spied an ideal meal. Exerting as much of his will as he felt safe with given his body's weakened state, he called a female huddled in the back to him.

One male tried to shield her and hold her back. Even this failed to hide the swell of her heavily pregnant belly. Dragon wondered if her would-be protector was her mate.

The man looked healthy and strong, an excellent choice for dessert.

"Come with her then. You may watch."

In answer, the fool lunged at him. Dragon caught him by the throat and lifted him off the ground with minimal effort.

In truth, it took more effort than he liked. He needed to feed soon. The fact it was daytime did not help. Even at his full strength, the presence of the daystar in the sky weakened him considerably.

He carried the man to the wall near the bed and shackled him there.

During the entire incident, the female did not move; held fully in his thrall. As he fastened a metal band around the man's throat to force his head up, the woman softly moaned.

A quick glance revealed this not to be in response to his actions but rather to the fact her water broke. His smile returned; this made his intentions easier to achieve.

Casually, he crushed the man's testes which rendered him momentarily unconscious. He turned his attention to his prey and led her to the bed. He then positioned her in a way to ease her beginning labor.

He dulled her pain to nearly nothing with his will and used a hand to help spread her dilation. Pressing gently on her abdomen, he willed her body to go into full labor.

Within minutes, she lay panting, drenched in sweat, and he held a healthy infant in his arms. He had her give one final push, and she expelled the placenta.

Rather than hand the newborn to its mother, he lifted the still attached umbilical to his mouth and pierced it with his fangs. He sucked on the cord until both it and the infant grew cold and pallid.

Although he'd found this method rarely resulted in an infant turning, he twisted its head off to be sure.

This feeding alone restored him to his full power. He decided to let the woman live. She could serve as a breeder. After all, a snack that nourishing was worth waiting for. What was a few months to him?

However, his Hunger still flared strongly. He knelt between her legs and methodically lapped until her bleeding stopped. He then crawled up to crouch over her.

"Where is my baby?" she managed to whisper.

"Dead."

She let out a heart-rending scream. He merely smiled and lowered his head to her breast. He took the nipple into his mouth and drove fangs into the areola.

He sucked while she wept.

At dusk, he allowed his vampiric companions to feed on the male. He instructed them to make it as painful as possible and to turn him. He wished to torture the man for daring to defy and attack him.

They accepted the assignment with relish. The chamber soon rang with the human's screams.

He sent the unconscious woman to his pet physician. He preferred his food healthy.

Once he fed again, Dragon reached out for one particular vampire of his siring. He finally located him aboard the *Altamaha* somewhere near the Canary Islands.

Jared Wormsloe stirred in his daytime hiding place aboard his brother's ship. He knew the touch of his Sire and Master's mind the moment it revived him. Dull pain washed through him as he realized the daystar still rode the sky in his location.

This must be important.

"What is thy bidding, my Lord?"

"Your prey is leaving Antwerp and very likely heading southwest. Instruct your brother to intercept him if possible and lure him to follow you. He knows the ship."

"It will be as you command, my Lord. Where do you want us to lead him?"

"You will lure him to Crete. Do not engage him directly if you can avoid it. I have observed him for some time now. He is too strong for you to overcome. I will see to it an appropriate reception awaits him."

"Bloody right the bastard's too powerful for us. I've seen him in action first-hand," Ethan Wormsloe confirmed when his brother relayed the message to him shortly after sunset.

"You sound as if you fear him."

"With good reason; he's every bit the ruthless pirate we remember from home, and he's already eliminated the oldest of the Daughters— and that's after they seduced each other."

Jared blinked at him in disbelief. "He seduced Lady Carpathia?"

"Aye; she became obsessed with him, and not just because of her mission to destroy him. I've never seen her act like she did with him; and I've witnessed her seducing her prey before several times. If I didn't know better, I'd say she was in love with him— as much as a heartless bitch like her could be."

"Do you think she would've betrayed our Lord to Brandee?"

Ethan thought on it in silence for a few moments before he answered.

"Aye, I think she would've." He shook as if possessed of a sudden chill. "I'll order the helmsman north. Maybe we can find the *Incubus* before she clears the Channel."

Fin

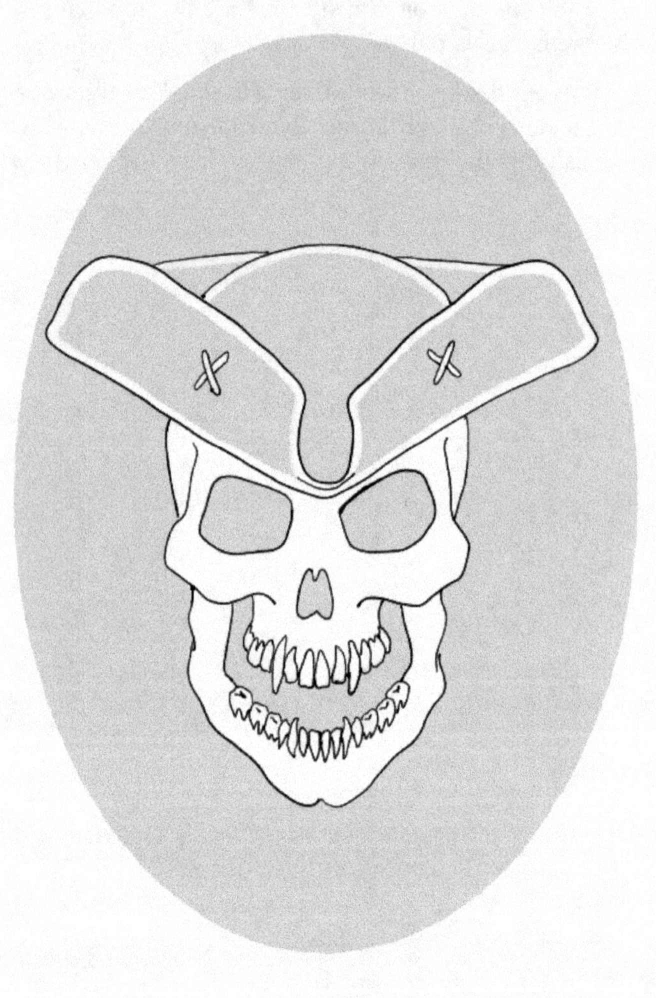

Here Be Spoilers

Blood Curse

After being shipwrecked by a British Navy ship and a killer hurricane, Bloody Vik Brandee and the survivors of his crew make shore in the fishing village of Terra Beau on the north coast of Hispañola. While waiting for a suitable ship to steal, he kills a local boy over a tavern wench, incurring the wrath of *Mamaan* Juma.

Juma sends her zombies to fetch the pirate. She curses him to become a living vampire. The tavern wench, Carmella, becomes his first victim.

Vik returns to his home port, Savannah, and learns from his foster mother Celie, aka the Thunderbolt Witch, just what has happened to him and how to break the curse before it destroys him. While there, Jim Rigger, his first mate, becomes his second victim. Celie resurrects Jim as a black cat which can take the form of a raven.

Celie sets Vik to find the seven Sisters of Power and sends him to Hell's Breath Island to Uncle Zeke, an ancient wizard of sorts. Zeke sends the siren/sea witch Belladonna with him to locate the Sisters using her visions.

She pinpoints *Madre* Dorada on the Isle of Youth. En route, Vik learns an old friend, Hezekiah Grimm aka the Grimm Reaper, has been taken by pirate hunters in Havana. He detours to rescue Grimm despite warnings from Zeke and Belladonna not to stray from his course.

Manages to find and rescue Grimm but arrives at the Isle of Youth only to find Dorada fled. With the aid of Paella, a local girl, he manages to track the Sister down and brokers a deal with her: one of her golden tears in exchange for an opal pendant called the Mermaid's Tear.

After some misunderstanding of what the Tear actually is, he finds it, helps Dorada regain her magic, and makes the exchange.

Demon Bayou

Viktor tracks the next Sister, Granny Glory, to the bayous north of New Orleans. When he finds her, she sets him to capture the demon Tulimanchulo, who possesses the body of a white alligator. He finds and captures the beast with a magic cast-net but is wounded in the process.

Glory slaughters the demon gator, collects its blood in a cauldron, and has Viktor remove all its teeth. She throws them in the blood and pulls them out as a necklace. Viktor must take it to Zeke. She warns him not to wear it at any time. She then has him toss her into the boiling blood. The hag emerges as a beautiful woman.

On Hell's Breath, Zeke burns the alligator teeth, releasing the demon's spirit. He fishes out a coal from his fire and puts it in a conch shell for Vik to return it to Glory with instructions no one else is to touch it and not to let it extinguish.

Vik returns to New Orleans and discovers a storm has altered the paths through the bayous.

While waiting for a guide back to Glory, he encounters true vampires for the first time. He ends up tangled in the local vampire politics because of attacks on two of his favorite brothels, one by agents of the Church, and the other by vampires curious about him. To get out of this predicament, he must kidnap the daughter of the Lord Mayor and make her vampire. This gives Jeorge, king of the local vampires, a means to spy on him.

On his final return to Glory, Belladonna begins to grow weak as the Sister's black water magic wars with the siren's salt water magic. She falls unconscious into the swamp but does not change into her true form. Vik must remove the coal and place it in his mouth to protect it before he can dive in after Belladonna. He knows she'll drown if she remains in human form. When he surfaces with her, the boat with his other companions is no longer in the area. He climbs out onto a hammock of land and Glory appears to him. He passes the coal to her via a kiss, returning the powers the demon stole from her ages earlier. She adds her spit to the golden tear of Dorada in the silver vial Vik carries for that purpose.

He returns Belladonna to the sea and sacrifices several of his crew to her appetite to restore her. He then abducts a couple of unwary sailors from port to swap for Grimm and Jon-Jon, rescuing them from Glory's amorous clutches, as he's learned she now has the nature of a succubus.

Silent Fathoms

The search for the third Sister, *Tia* Rosalia, takes Viktor to Mexico. He lands on the Gulf coast and must travel over the central mountains to the Pacific coast to reach her. She first tries to deceive and enslave him. Her spell manages to control his crewmen traveling with him, but his power proves stronger at the cost of one pirate's life. The Elder's Stone proves to her he is the One, and she gives him the quest of procuring Devil's Hoof, a key ingredient in her spells. She deliberately doesn't tell him where to look or what it actually is.

He follows rumors of a cave in the mountains where the Devil is said to live. Instead, he finds an old *brujo* (male witch) who was once Rosalia's lover. He tells him Devil's Hoof is an extremely hot pepper said to cause hallucinations with its spiciness. The pirates return to the ship. Navigator Zach Brumble tells Vik about such a pepper his father once dabbled in trading found in the northern part of the Bay of Bengal.

When he tries to contact Belladonna to sing up favorable winds to speed the voyage halfway around the world, he cannot reach her or even sense her presence. Unbeknownst to him, Zeke and Hell's Breath Island have sent her to hunt down the mermaid Alyssa, whom Viktor impregnated while seeking for the Mermaid's Tear. He'd also fed on the creature, and she began to turn while still alive. Belle must kill the mermaid but return the child to the island and Zeke's care. To prevent Viktor's interference, Zeke blocks them from any mental contact until her task is done.

The siren is finally able to rejoin Viktor as the ship is caught in the doldrums near the middle of the Indian Ocean. They make their way to a Bengali village near the Sundarbans, a salt swamp jungle. After warnings from a local elder not to anger the jungle goddess, Bonobibi, or the tiger god, Daskin Rey, they enter the swamps to find the pepper (known locally as the naga pepper). They must also harvest honey to safely transport the peppers in. One of their guides harvests more honey than they need, hoping to profit enough to laze away the wet season. This leads to an encounter with the local deities and the man's death.

With Devil's Hoof acquired, Viktor opts to cross the Pacific directly to Rosalia's home port.

Once back in Mexico, she tries her best to enslave him using fresh ingredients for her spell. He proves his power is stronger than hers, and she begrudgingly agrees to give him the portion of her magic he requires for his quest to break his curse.

After he returns to his ship, Hell's Breath manifests. Zeke introduces him to his son by Alyssa and orders him to get the child off the island. When the island vanishes again, Viktor finds the ship has been transported back to the Caribbean.

Black Venom

Viktor and his crew find themselves deposited close to Havana by the disappearance of Hell's Breath Island. Grateful for not having to sail around South America, they make for New Orleans. He must find a home and guardian for his merchild son, Robert, and wants to see if Gloribeau will take the boy on.

Glory agrees in exchange for Viktor in her bed for one night. The sheer magnitude of magic released by their climax alerts Jeorge, king of the New Orlean vampires, to the child's presence. He also becomes aware of Viktor's increasing powers, growing far faster than those of a truly undead vampire.

Jeorge "summons" Viktor to join him in a hunt. Because he needs to arrange protection of his son from the vampires, he agrees. They attend a reception at the Lord Mayor's for the new governor. Jeorge uses it as a fishing expedition to learn more about the boy and to put the new governor in his pocket.

Samantha Brumble and Captain Bainbridge arrive at the Islas de los Roques and encounter *Madre* Dorada. They learn that the lead which led them there is nearly three years old but gain valuable information about the nature of what Viktor now is and who sails with him.

After dealing with a small British blockade of the entrance to Lake Pontchartrain, Viktor heads for the Florida Strait. Belladonna rejoins the ship there and is given a victim to induce one of her visions to locate the next Sister of Power. *Mere* Venoma Noir directs a psychic attack back at the siren, revealing her power over all things venomous, even over Belladonna.

Jeorge's curiosity gets the better of him, and he sends a couple of his vampires to investigate Viktor's son. Gloribeau's dealing with this invasion of her bayou costs him both his minions and convinces him to leave it alone.

As the pirates near Venoma's territory, she uses her power to attack through the siren. Only the Elder's Stone and Viktor's blood can override the sister's magic. After landfall, she actively tries to kill him and the crew remaining aboard the *Incubus* with hordes of venomous creatures. Once he succeeds in reaching her, she relents and instructs him to retrieve an amulet imbued with her power which was stolen by a notorious slave trader, Quentin LaForte. They make for the west coast of Africa to search for him.

Commodore Critchfield encounters Lady Carpathia and Captain Wormsloe when they return Commander Turlington to the *HMS Quicksilver.* He has a dalliance with the vampire, never realizing what she truly is. They exchange information about Viktor, and she directs him to sail to Amherst in search of a vampire expert and hunter.

Venoma warns LaForte in a dream that Viktor is hunting him. He doesn't trust the old witch, but makes plans to protect himself nonetheless, especially since she alerted him to the possibility of using Belladonna against Viktor.

Close to the Azores, Viktor pirates a pirate which just took a packet ship. In a bid to thwart Viktor getting ransom for a promised bride taken prisoner, the other pirate kills the woman he believes to be her. The victim was actually the handmaid who'd changed places with her. The true bride, Brianna Belmont, stabs the pirate at the same time Viktor does. Grimm claims her as his share of the spoils and lets her know her intended husband was actually a pimp who specialized in well-bred virgins.

Samantha and Bainbridge arrive in Havana looking for fresher news of Viktor and Grimm. At the Crescent Inn, Luz passes a message to Sam from her brother Zach to abandon the hunt for her own safety. They learned the likely next port Viktor went to was New Orleans.

Lady Carpathia and Captain Wormsloe follow an old lead to the slaver, Delacroix. She learns about Samantha's hunt but nothing else of value. She kills the slaver and a priest looking to buy some new altar boys. The remaining children there, she takes for blood stock.

Viktor gets a lead on LaForte in Tenerife which sends him to Abidjan. They arrive in port and find the man in the process of exchanging a trader's hobbles for his own on a young female slave. She gets loose and provides enough distraction for LaForte to use his black magic to teleport away. They take the woman back to the *Incubus*.

Viktor learns she is called Nahila, and she is LaForte's daughter. She agrees to lead him to the slaver in exchange for her freedom. She leads them to a nearby river. As Viktor takes a small group upriver, LaForte teleports back to his shore camp. He uses the power of Venoma's amulet to ensnare Belladonna and sends her to kill the crew still on the ship.

Grimm's portion of the Elder's magic frees her from the spell. They stage the ship for the slaver and his crew.

Viktor gets word from the siren and flies back to the ship. LaForte falls for the trap. Nahila is brought back and kept captive for her part in helping her father try to trap Viktor.

Viktor nearly kills Grimm for keeping the Elder's magic a secret. Brianna's intervention saves the 1st mate.

They learn Nahila serves as a familiar for her father's black magic when the ship is mired midway across the Atlantic in a mass of jellyfish. Viktor has her drugged, and Belladonna creates a current to clear the obstacle and speed them back to South America.

Venoma requires Viktor and LaForte to fight to the death. Only the slaver's death can release the amulet's magic back to her. When Viktor is victorious, but the magic doesn't return, they tell her Nahila holds part of it. She makes the dead man's blood flow onto the slave and turns her into a scorpion. She gives Viktor a drop of the venom as her portion of magic.

The scorpion stings itself, turns back into Nahila, and dies, leaving Venoma forever magically crippled. For good measure and a bit of payback, Belladonna calls a lightning bolt and fuses the sand around Venoma's feet into glass, trapping the witch.

Hell's Dodo

The revelation that Brianna Bemont is pregnant with twins by Hezekiah Grimm temporarily interrupts Viktor's quest. The *Incubus* travels to Savannah to deliver her to Mother Celie's care. Grimm officially marries her and swears faithfulness to her alone. Celie pulls Viktor aside and warns him the unborn children carry part of the Elder's magic due to Grimm's connection with the old wizard. If he ever breaks his vow, the children will die, and that portion of magic will be forever lost to the world, possibly destroying it in the process.

Viktor tries to release Grimm from his service and the crew, but the first mate won't hear of it. As they clear Tybee Island, heading back to sea, they encounter and take the *Georgia Belle* and her captain, Chadwick Harris. One of the prisoners manages to shoot Viktor in the neck, rendering him mute temporarily. He gives the man to Belladonna to torture and eventually eat.

The vision she has as a result confuses her with its vagueness. After describing it to Viktor and his officers, Zach Brumble realizes she's seen the kitchen at a tavern in Salem, Massachusetts, called The Dragon and the Dodo.

Commodore Critchfield finds Britt Westin in Amherst and proceeds to learn as much as he can about vampire hunting. During the voyage back across the Atlantic to Caribbean waters, the younger man tells him of his quest to hunt down Lady Carpathia and exact revenge for the murder of his family. Britt remembers his father accidentally killing his mother over believed unfaithfulness and abandoning his little brother, Jim. However, he thinks these were false memories implanted by the vampire who later turned his father.

Viktor and crew make use of a newly acquired Colonial Navy flag to get into Salem's harbor. They learn the Sister fled months earlier by turning into a bird and flying away. Instead, they find an excellent cook in Nathan Trundle, the owner of the tavern who uses a trick she taught him to addict customers to his egg pies: add a drop of blood to the custard before cooking it.

Samantha Brumble and Captain Bainbridge arrive in New Orleans looking for news of Viktor Brandewyne. The revelation of her last name, but not her true gender, lands them in custody of the *gendarmerie*. The Lord Mayor has them released when he sees she is not male and learns her brother Thomas is innocent of the kidnap of his daughter, Melanie. Later, Jeorge has one of his vampires abduct Sam and questions her about why she seeks Viktor. He erases the memory of his interaction with her and returns her to her ship.

Back in the Caribbean, Viktor and crew take a Brumble & Sons convoy. In the process, they acquire an old salt by the name of Leland Stoud who once sailed with Billy Black, Viktor's former mentor.

In Cartagena, Viktor encounters Lady Carpathia for the first time. He finds himself unusually attracted to her, much to Belladonna's consternation. The siren warns him this is the vampire sent to hunt him. During the encounter, however, he leaves a few drops of his blood on Carpathia's blade. Neither vampire thinks much of it at the time.

Britt Westin inadvertently discovers his bunk mate aboard the *HMS Quicksilver*, Commander Turlington has been bitten by Carpathia. He tries to warn Commodore Critchfield. Not long after, Britt is cudgeled and set adrift. Critchfield has the information he needed from him and sees him as a liability now.

Having no luck on finding Auntie Clarissa, Viktor sacrifices two crewmen to the siren for a clear vision. She returns to the ship just in time to keep him from killing Grimm when the vampire's Hunger takes control. The truly blessed emerald cross brings Viktor back to his senses, but Belle has to seal herself in the cabin with him to protect Grimm and the crew before the power drains from the cross.

She directs Grimm to make a course to Tierra del Fuego, south of the Magellan Strait. Days later, Viktor and

Belle both wake from the sleep spell she used to dampen his Hunger.

The *Shining Star* came across Britt Westin adrift in a small boat. Sam is struck by his close resemblance to the dream man who ravaged her and left her severely weakened. She nurses him back to health. They bond over their hatred of Commodore Critchfield and compare notes in their respective hunts for Carpathia and Brandewyne.

Viktor reaches the previously uncharted Tierra del Fuego. He, Grimm, and Zach Brumble go ashore to seek Clarissa, while Belladonna goes hunting and takes a leopard seal as prey. The pirates find the Sister. She names three different prices she'll accept in exchange for the portion of her magic Viktor needs. The first two, he recognizes as traps. He has no choice but to agree to the third: the eggs of a dodo and a dragon, and a drop of blood from the Daughter of the Dragon. She then turns into a hummingbird and flies away.

Not knowing what a dodo is but remembering Jeorge's extensive library of ancient texts, Viktor decides to make for New Orleans. It takes much of Belle's weather magic to race the ship north ahead of the southern hemisphere's winter and sea ice.

During the voyage, Stoud tells of once bedding the siren when he was a young man. Jon-Jon refuses to believe until Belladonna confirms it and reveals she is a few millennia older than she looks. The old salt regales the crew with tales of encountering a kraken and even of the existence of dragons. This last draws Viktor's attention, and he finds out he needs to hunt that egg in the islands between Asia and Australia.

Lack of ships to pirate forces Viktor to put in at Port-of-Spain, Trinidad to hunt. He again encounters Carpathia. They hunt together, then she has him as a guest in one of the local vampire kiss' safehouses. During their tryst, he spots her tattoo of a dragon twined around a scythe and learns she is the leader of the Daughters of the Dragon. When she dies for the day, he steals some of her blood and places it in the vial Clarissa provided him. He returns to the ship and sets sail for New Orleans.

Carpathia pursues the next night aboard the *Lorelei*. Belladonna becalms her ship and delays the pursuit to the point that many of the crew fall prey to the vampiress before the wind returns. Still, she knows where he's headed.

Critchfield arrives in Savannah and heads to the Black Flag looking for news of Brandewyne. A drunken Chadwick Harris gripes about his treatment by Brandewyne. Maggie, now owner of the Flag, bars him from her establishment and has him abducted and shipped from Savannah to protect him from both the Navy and Viktor. Critchfield has Turlington take Harris' ship, the *Georgia Belle*, to act as bait for the pirate-turned-vampire, since Viktor seems to bear Harris some grudge.

Critchfield seeks out the Thunderbolt Witch to verify rumors of the pirates delivering a pregnant girl, supposedly the reaper's bride. Celie keeps Brianna hidden. She proves to the Navy man he has no power to truly threaten or harm her. After he leaves, Brianna goes into premature labor from the stress.

Viktor learns from Jeorge only what a dodo is and where it was discovered. The vampire king of New Orleans does not try to prolong the visit this time, catching Carpathia's scent on the pirate.

En route from New Orleans to Savannah, the *Incubus* encounters the *Quicksilver.* When sent to spy on the Navy man, Lazarus finds himself instead transported to Mother Celie. She shows him the twins and sends him back to

Viktor with the message to avoid Savannah until he finishes with Clarissa. Having escaped the pursuer in a fog of Belle's making, Viktor takes the advice and sets course for Africa.

Carpathia arrives in New Orleans and proceeds to make Jeorge's unlife miserable. When she learns Viktor delivered his merman son into the old swamp witch's keeping, she sends men in to find the child. Gloribeau uses her succubus powers to deal with them but leaves one man alive to carry her warning back.

Carpathia finds dried blood on one of her blades from her first encounter with Viktor months earlier. She consumes it and forms a bond with him instantly but tries to hide her presence. He picks up on it and gets Belladonna to help him distract the vampiress. The build-up of pure power from his and Belle's passion proves enough to force Carpathia to vomit up the blood and break the bond.

In Mauritius, Viktor learns from a local teacher and historian, Jean Beaujolais, that the dodo has been extinct for over a century. He continues to the East Indies to try to acquire a dragon egg. The encounter with a Komodo dragon costs one crewman a leg. The siren, well fed from a mermaid hunt, uses her healing magic to regrow it.

Hell's Breath Island intercepts them on their trip back to Clarissa. Viktor is grateful for the encounter after learning that dodos still exist on the travelling island. Zeke agrees to give him an egg in exchange for the vial of Carpathia's blood. The old man then reveals that the siren is branded by the Daughters of the Dragon and that, as a siren, she is the daughter of a sea dragon. Her blood will fulfill the Sister's requirement.

Viktor completes his journey to Clarissa. She uses the ingredients to make a pie, which she then consumes. She transforms into a bird and lays an egg. This, she breaks and crushes into the vial with the magical tokens from the other Sisters of Power. Too late, she realizes her plan to gain control over Viktor with the blood in the pie has actually enslaved her to the source of the blood. Zeke knew what a disaster it would've been to give control of one of the Sisters to the second oldest vampire in the world. Belladonna has no desire or need to control her.

As a parting gift, Viktor leaves Nathan Trundle with Clarissa, since she acquired some of the siren's sexual appetite, and the cook was prone to seasickness.

The Daedalus Enigma

Viktor and crew spot the *Georgia Belle* near Sapelo Island and give chase, thinking to have some fun at Chadwick Harris' expense. He soon realizes his favorite target no longer sails the ship. Instead, the pirate captures Joseph Turlington, who'd been set to catch the pirate by Commodore Critchfield. Viktor takes Turlington to his cabin, where Lady Carpathia takes possession of her pet's body and ensnares Viktor.

Belladonna kills the human and uses her blood to prevent him from rising as a vampire of Carpathia's line. She initiates a passionate round of lovemaking with Viktor in an effort to free him from the Daughter of the Dragon's trap. During this, he feeds on the siren and almost dies from it. Her toxic blood frees him from Carpathia's power, though.

They make port in Savannah. Grimm goes to Mother Celie's to reunite with his wife, Brianna, and to meet their twin offspring. Viktor heads to the Black Flag tavern and brothel to learn from Maggie what really happened to Harris and what events had happened in his absence.

When Viktor goes to Celie's, Lazarus and Belladonna join the assemblage. The siren tells him of a vision about the next Sister of Power he has to deal with. She is located somewhere in the Aegean region of the Mediterranean. He gives Grimm the option to remain with his family. The first mate chooses to remain part of the crew. They engage in a subterfuge to get the twins christened without revealing Grimm's family is staying with Celie. They then sail north to hide their true destination across the Atlantic from any possible British spies.

On the crossing, Belladonna reveals she would be in danger of being claimed by a male siren as mate if she returns to the Mediterranean. Viktor gives her a couple of men as sacrifice for a clearer vision of where to hunt the Sister. This results in learning he must deal with Circe, the witch from Homer's *Odyssey,* who can turn men into animals. Belle insists on staying with him to aid in passing the navigational hazards surrounding the witch's island.

The siren guides them through a reef, a watery maze of rocks, a series of whirlpools, and a fog-shrouded ship graveyard to get to Circe's island. Only Viktor, Grimm, and Belladonna go ashore. Lazarus remains undetected in his raven form.

Circe tries to get them to eat something, but they politely refuse. She does confirm she is the same Circe who dealt with Odysseus. She tries to seduce first Viktor, then Grimm with no success. The power Zeke the Elder shared with Grimm frightens her and convinces her to stop with her games. She directs Viktor to a labyrinth beyond her dwelling on the island. He is set to retrieve a puzzle box which lies at its center. Lazarus surreptitiously helps guide him through and avoid any traps.

He finds the box, but several portions are missing from the puzzle. He learns he must revisit the other Sisters of

Power to retrieve the missing pieces, which the Elder disbursed among them.

After Viktor's departure, Circe summons Xandricus, the sea dragon/male siren. Other than the ship graveyard, all the island's outer defenses magically disappeared with Viktor's arrival. She wants the dragon to restore the enveloping fog. He agrees after discovering Belladonna has been there and will return. He plans to await her return and claim her as his mate.

Viktor decides to visit Venoma *Noir* first, thus getting the most unpleasant of the Sisters out of the way. She sends him into the depths of the cave she dwells in to find the portion of the puzzle box in her possession. He encounters Arachne, a giant spider-like creature that can take on human form. He ends up killing the creature and cutting a red crystal from its forehead, the puzzle piece he sought.

Next, he visits *Madre* Dorada. Paella now bears the title and power of the Sister, Carina having passed menopause thus unable to control or use the power. He meets his daughter, Viktoria Auna. Dorada agrees to give him her portion of the puzzle, a piece of moss agate, in exchange for siring a son on her. While he is fulfilling the price with great relish, carina tries to kill Viktoria and reclaim the power. Both Dorada's and the child's magic combine to call the golden vines and destroy Carina and heal Viktoria.

On his way to New Orleans and Gloribeau, Viktor and crew take a packet ship carrying Jean Beaujoulais. He decides to take the old tutor to New Orleans himself, knowing the man is in search of Jeorge's library. He also takes three young women being sent to escape the brewing war in the colonies and several bolts of valuable silk from his prey.

In New Orleans, he finds Carpathia in residence. She destroys two of Jeorge's vampires as punishment for him not informing her or her sire about Viktor's frequent visits to the port. When she threatens to use Melanie to track and control him, he proves he is more powerful than her by mentally holding her motionless and sending his Childe to the safety of his ship.

At Gloribeau's, he encounters his son, Robert, now a gangly youth. The boy should only be a toddler, but he is half merman. Glory's price for her portion of the puzzle is two-fold: deal with Carpathia and take Robert to find a mate among his own kind. Her powers are very similar to those of a succubus, and she is a danger to the young mer, who is rapidly approaching sexual maturity.

Belladonna tells him how to trap Carpathia. He manages to trick the vampire and captures her in a silver-lined bottle in her amorphous form, as she is one of a very limited number of vampires that can change forms. Gloribeau uses her magic to seal the bottle so that only Grimm, who corked it, can ever open it. Later, Robert is introduced to a pod of mermaids to mate and live his now adult life.

On the way to Tierra del Fuego and Clarissa, Lazarus spots and visits the *Shining Star,* hoping for the luck of taking his human form as Jim Rigger and having some sport with Samantha Brumble. Instead, he finds her with Britt Westin and learns they are long-lost brothers. He'd only been a small child when their father accidentally killed their mother then abandoned him, taking Britt away with him. Those painful memories had long ago been suppressed. While there as Lazarus the cat, he witnesses Sam and Britt marry. He bites his brother as the newlyweds sleep, ensuring he will never lose his family again.

By the time Viktor reaches Clarissa, his Hunger is trying to get out of control. He takes a crewman with him as a potential meal when he goes ashore. He attacks and almost bites the Sister when she shows herself. Her power brings him back to his senses. She does not have a piece of the puzzle for him, as she and Circe never got along. She sends Mr. Trundle back with Viktor in exchange for the man he had planned to drain.

Sailing north along the Pacific coast of south America, headed for Mexico and Rosalia, Viktor's Hunger gets back under control. Belladonna, however, seems to lose much of her power and eventually goes into a sort of coma. When Viktor forcibly revives her, she miscarries the child he unknowingly had sired on her.

Rosalia makes herself difficult to get to and places traps to hopefully enslave Viktor to her, she fears him that much. She agrees to give him her portion of the puzzle, a black opal, in exchange for his promise to never enter her territory again.

Viktor sails south, hoping to pass back through the Straits of Magellan before turning back north toward the Caribbean. He seeks to face *Mamaan* Juma to get the final puzzle piece. It quickly becomes clear they'll never make it before winter and sea ice close the passage, so he has the ship turn back north.

Hell's Breath Island intercepts the ship. Viktor, Belladonna, and Grimm start ashore, but the island separates them. Grimm is returned to the ship. Viktor is allowed to continue on to find Zeke. Belladonna is transported to a submerged cavern within the island and a crystalline entity known as the heart of Hell's Breath, an embodiment of the All-Mother. She explains something of Viktor's nature to the siren and gives her a contraceptive spell to preserve her magic in the future. She then sends the siren to rejoin Viktor.

Zeke tells Viktor he's not ready to face Juma yet and reminds him there is another Sister of Power he knows, Mother Celie. The island transports them to just off the Bahamas. From there, Viktor sails on to Savannah.

Celie no longer possesses the final puzzle piece, a sardonyx ring with the carved face of the god Janus, but she knows who has it and roughly where they are. She directs Viktor to sail to western Ireland to seek out Darcy O'Malley, a descendant of Grace O'Malley the pirate queen. She also gives him a box of moly, a magical herb which will protect him from Circe's transformative powers and instructs him on the dosage and that he must finish all of it before returning to the witch's island.

During the crossing, Viktor grows to hate the headaches and temporary weakening of his powers associated with using the moly. Finally, he sees there is only about one dose left after doctoring his food. He decides to just finish it off and be done with it. He gets no headache this time but grows strangely detached. He accidentally cuts himself and doesn't immediately heal as he's used to. Lazarus appears and licks the blood off his arm, convulses, transforms into Jim, and promptly dies for the day. Viktor blacks out.

Belladonna and Grimm have a couple of hapless crewmen apply peppermint oil to revive Viktor. He attacks and feeds on the man chosen, calling Jim back to awareness to feed on the other sailor. His moly-rich blood gives Jim the ability to take and keep human form at will.

In Ireland, Viktor, Grimm, and Zach Brumble visit Harlowe, a smuggling contact known to young Brumble as well as a former fence the two pirates used to do business with. He informs them of the recent widowing of

Darcy, and the political plotting of her suitor/kidnapper, Lord Brookston. Harlowe gives this information in exchange for Viktor taking about twenty young hotheaded Irishmen who want to go to the colonies to fight the English off his hands. He'd contracted transport for them, but the captain had gotten conscripted by the Royal Navy. Having the lads still about would be bad for business if the Navy came calling.

The pirates go to the village Harlowe indicates. They make contact with one of the women who help smuggle messages in and out of the O'Malley keep. They then have a satisfying brush-up with a group of Brookston's thugs behind the village tavern. Viktor experiments and learns the moly has given him the ability to take the form of any creature he's ever eaten. He takes a small amount of blood and some hair from Darcy's dog, the message carrier, and takes on its form to get into the keep.

He flies Darcy out then helps her entrap Brookston into admitting to her husband's murder. This gains him the ring piece of the puzzle box. Assembled, it reveals a lock. He surmises Circe has the key.

Hell's Breath intercepts them again shortly before they reach Gibraltar. Zeke informs Belladonna she has earned a pardon and is no longer barred from entering the Mediterranean. He revokes Xandricus' claim to her. Of course, he points out that won't stop the sea dragon from trying anyway.

Near Circe's island, the sea dragon boards the ship and demands Belladonna come with him. Viktor challenges him. When Grimm moves to protect his captain, Xandricus stabs him with his talons and throws him overboard. Battle between the pirates and sea dragon ensues. Viktor eventually defeats him by flying down the dragon's maw and cutting his head off from the inside. He is nearly crushed in half as the corpse shrinks back to human proportions. Belladonna heals him.

Grimm's body cannot be found afterward.

When Viktor takes the puzzle box back to Circe, he learns of her collusion with the sea dragon and decides to torment her for her part in the loss of his first mate. She lies to him about having to wait until dawn to retrieve the keystone and key and offers him a bed and a meal. Knowing it for the trap it is meant to be, he accepts her hospitality.

Sensing her strong desire, he pretends to seduce her, working her up even more. She grows extremely agitated when he eats some of the pork she'd cooked. He knows of the transformative spell on the meat, but the moly protects him. He continues to eat until she cracks and begs him to stop. She tells him she can save him if he'll make love to her. He refuses. She finally admits she doesn't have to wait until dawn to get the keystone and key to open the box. When she leaves to retrieve it, he disrobes and deliberately turns into a hog, then a dog, a hog again, back to human and gets dressed again. He hides the box.

She arrives with the items and panics over the missing puzzle box. When she leaves to try to find it, he puts it back on the table and disrobes again. She returns and desperately opens the box, mixes the contents with her wine, and drinks the solution to restore her full power. Viktor picks that moment to transform back into a hog.

She tries to turn him human again. He resists her powers completely and turns into a dog, just to rub it in. Finally, he turns human when she tries to turn him back into a pig in her ire. He refuses to tell her how he escaped her spells.

Jim arrives with Jon-Jon to collect Circe's portion of magic. She transforms into a sow, and Jon-Jon gets a single drop of milk from her to add to the vial of the Sisters' combined magic. When she returns to human form, she begs Viktor to make love to her. He refuses and denies her the use of either of his companions. He lets her know he killed Xandricus and holds her partially responsible for Grimm's death. He reminds her that Grimm carried a portion of the Elder's magic and she may have to answer to the Elder for the loss. The pirates leave.

Maelstrom of Fate

Mourning the loss of Hezekiah Grimm and traumatized by his own near-death encounter with a male siren in sea dragon form, Viktor Brandewyne sails from the eastern Mediterranean headed to Savannah. He needs to break the news to Grimm's widow, Brianna.

The pirates encounter a Royal Navy patrol near Gibraltar. They take all three ships. Viktor turns Captain Kendridge and sets him adrift in his ship with no crew, only rats to feed on.

When they reach Savannah, Brianna Grimm and her children are missing. Not even Mother Celie remembers them or that Grimm had served as first mate for the past six years or so.

Celie offers the theory that the world and time reset to preserve the bit of the Elder's magic Grimm carried. Viktor sets out to see how widespread this erasure of his friend and his family is. He and his crew remember Grimm clearly.

Viktor and Belladonna learn the priest who officiated Hezekiah's and Brianna's wedding and christened their twins died in a rectory fire which also destroyed the records. The fire took place about the same time as Grimm's death.

They find Maggie, madam of the Black Flag, in a coma from a head injury that happened about the same time. Belle heals the physical damage, but Maggie has lost two decades of her memory. Cord McVarish *does* remember the Reaper's family because of overhearing Harris tell Commodore Critchfield about them.

Viktor tries to summon Hell's Breath Island in the hope Zeke can tell him what happened. Instead, he ends up catching a very young mermaid, Naia, a granddaughter via his son Robert.

They sail the *Incubus* up the Altamaha River to hide it from both the Royal and Colonial navies. Vik, Jim, and Belle sail a small ketch up the coast to Charleston. They investigate the brothel Brianna's father had unwittingly sold her to on the chance Percival Worthing had managed to find and abduct her. She isn't there, but Vik kills the pimp and johns. He takes the girls and women working there back to Maggie for her to hire or free them.

Viktor's control over his Hunger begins to erode during the voyage from the Colonies heading to Hispañola. Feeding directly brings him the emotional oblivion he's been longing for ever since Grimm's loss.

Wormsloe arrives back in New Orleans to find Carpathia no longer there. This explains Nolan Westin's loss of control over his Hunger. Jeorge had no warning of Wormsloe's arrival. He tells him Thia supposedly left with Viktor. Jeorge also helps him get Westin under control before he leaves port again.

Wormsloe stops a loaded slave ship with an offer of news. This gives Westin a chance to feed without decimating the *Lorelei*'s crew again. They'd been en route to Savannah at Westin's insistence. Viktor spots this on his way to Hispañola. He takes the cargo and gives the slave ship and its crew to Wormsloe as a replacement for the boat Vik stole from him and his brother when the three of them were still boys. Jim kills Westin, his father, for the murder of his mother.

When Viktor demonstrates to Wormsloe how Carpathia could be imprisoned in a bott, the man tosses said bottle into the sea to prevent her from ever being freed. Belladonna secretly retrieves it for Viktor to use as leverage in the future.

Samantha and Britt Westin wake from a shared nightmare about the fight between Jim and his and Britt's father. Jim told them in the dream to look in Tortuga. They convince Captain Bainbridge to take them there.

Jim asks Vik to put in at Tortuga to wait for Sam and Britt. Belle argues against it, but Vik doesn't want Jim distracted during the upcoming encounter with Juma. He sends the siren to intercept the *Shining Star* near Cartagena and speed them on their way.

Jim notices Vik barely used alcohol on the latest batch of blood-brandy. Vik refuses to feed on the captured slaves directly. He realizes his Hunger has become too much like the opium addiction Grimm struggled with many years ago. He doesn't want to risk losing control.

Jim figures out why Vik seems to fear confronting Juma. He likes being a vampire and worries that breaking his curse might strip him of his powers or destroy the vampires he's made.

Critchfield intercepts the *Shining Star.* Britt and Sam try to hide below decks. They are found. He lets them go but has the ship followed. Bainbridge suspects this but believes they will finish their business in Tortuga before the Navy arrives in force, since any spies would have to report back first.

When they reach Tortuga, Bainbridge anchors the ship pointing out of the harbor to give them a head start if they have to flee. He knows it would take some time to turn the *Incubus* to pursue them. Britt outfits his wife and the captain with crucifixes to protect from vampires.

Zachary Brumble, Anvil, and Jon-Jon fetch Sam, Britt, and Bainbridge to the pirate ship for a dinner invitation from Viktor. The vampire quickly proves the holy items are useless against him. Jim, as Lazarus, turns from raven to cat, a form Sam recognizes.

Viktor feels some relief when Bainbridge makes mention of Grimm, gratified someone else outside his crew remembers the man having sailed with him.

When Jim takes human form in the safety of the windowless cabin, Sam slugs him and tries to stomp his privates. Later Jim lets Britt know what really happened after their mother's death.

Belladonna tries to warn the humans to flee just moments before Viktor's Hunger takes him. He attacks Samantha. Jim retrieves the emerald cross and puts it on Viktor, quelling the captain's Hunger. This leaves Jim with holy burns on his hand. Belladonna heals Sam.

Jim manages to convince Viktor to leave the ship and hunt. He plans to join him after sunset. Belladonna has to cut the damaged tissue from his hand and make it regenerate. She consumes the bodies of the victims he takes to replenish his energy. They then begin to track Viktor.

While recruiting a few extra men to the crew in an effort to hide how many kills he and Jim made that night, Viktor encounters one of the Navy spies. Belladonna dispatches the man. Jim finds the other spy later and deals with him accordingly.

Viktor gives Thia's bottle to Britt for safekeeping. Jim and Viktor both agree to release their claims to Sam and Britt. Jim sends them to a priest he knows in port for cleansing from their vampire bites.

Critchfield receives a message from his erstwhile spies and heads for Tortuga with his small armada.

The Westins delay their departure from Tortuga until a few days after the pirates in order to set out with a convoy bound for Havana. They spot the *Quicksilver* entering the harbor just before the island dips below the horizon behind them. After a few more days with no sign of pursuit, they break from the convoy and make for New Orleans.

Critchfield is frustrated that he missed Brandee by under a week. He orders the small launches to patrol the harbor mouth and stop and search every vessel entering or leaving. He dresses as a merchant captain and goes ashore on a personal fact finding mission. He learns what happened to one of his spies by sexually torturing a whore.

He has his crew round up every whore on the island and interrogates them in a similar manner. Over the course of several days of this he only learns that the *Shining Star* left with a convoy a few days after the *Incubus*. He dispatches a ketch to find the ship.

Viktor arrives in Terra Beau in Hispañola. Initially, Belladonna is angry when she learns he intends to kill Juma. He explains he is supposed to kill Juma to restore balance not disrupt it.

Juma sends a zombie to fetch him. He makes sure Jim and Belle stick close. He doesn't want to risk Juma's necromancy ensnaring Jim like Venoma's power did Belladonna. The Elder's Stone prevents the zombie from being able to touch them.

Juma surrounds them with zombies until they can no longer push through. She means to hold them in place long enough that they turn on each other in desperation to survive. If Jim leaves the stone's protection, she will control him. She doesn't know he can turn into Lazarus and survive the sunrise. She also hopes Belle will turn on Viktor to secure a return to the sea.

Viktor, carrying Belle, and Jim fly up and out of the trap. They spot Juma's fire the next hill over. They land and wait for her to arrive. She tries to unnerve them with magic and keeps the fire between them. She lets them know she plans to kill Vik, take the magic he's collected from the other Sisters of Power, and become more powerful than the Elder.

Silently, Vik instructs Jim and Belle to play along with Juma. She orders Jim to hold the siren. She then summons Carmella, Viktor's first victim and Childe. She intends for Carmella to either kill Vik or turn him into a true vampire. In a moment of distraction, the vampire beheads the witch instead.

They burn Juma. Vik sends Jim with Belle back to the ship. She urges him through their link to get rid of Carmella. He learns that his first Childe has never tasted human blood. They collect Juma's ashes and return to the ship.

Viktor contacts Jeorge via Melanie to arrange safe haven and training for Carmella.

Critchfield heads for New Providence in the Bahamas. He encounters a derelict which carries Vik's Childe, Kendridge. A few men are lost during retrieval of the ship's logs. Critchfield keeps the fact they're dealing with a vampire from his crew. He declares the derelict to be a plague ship and orders it burned to the waterline along with the murdered men and the "madman" still aboard. He then studies the logs to learn what happened to the former Navy captain.

He changes course for the Gulf of Mexico via the Florida Strait. There, he finally encounters the *Incubus* again.

Viktor has Belle use her weather magic to keep the *Quicksilver's* lead escorts grouped too close together to try to flank the pirate ship. Lazarus is sent to spy out the central ship of the three escorts to locate the forward powder magazine. Viktor uses a harpoon with three lit grenades lashed to it to set off the powder and destroy all three vessels at once.

He has the siren create sea ice to trap the *Quicksilver* and her two remaining escorts. She crushes the hulls of the escorts and allows them to sink.

Vik flies over to the Navy flagship. Critchfield offers to remove him from the lists and give him a Letter of Marque provided he swears fealty to the King of England and makes the Commodore a vampire.

Viktor arrives in New Orleans to deliver Carmella. He tells Jeorge how he left Critchfield tied to the ship wheel and took or killed the entire five hundred plus man crew. He let the Commodore *think* he'd left some of the lowest ranks to rise as potential vampires, and they could turn him, making sure he understood that a vampire must answer to its Sire. He then had Belle set the *Quicksilver* in its ice flow adrift and aimed towards Tortuga.

On his way to Savannah to deliver the magic and ashes, Viktor's Hunger grows increasingly worse. Sex with the siren helps distract him for a while, but it's not enough. She also lets him know she redirected Critchfield towards Nassau to let the current help conserve magical energy.

Viktor feeds on Jon-Jon. Belladonna saves the man by putting the emerald cross on Vik. She merges her consciousness with Viktor's to give him the control he needs to subdue the Hunger.

The closer they get to Savannah, the more his body begins to waste away. When Vik and Belle finally get to Celie's, he gives her the vial holding the magic of the Sisters of Power. When he hands over the bag of Juma's ashes, she notices that the drawstring has come partially undone. It is the source of his deterioration.

He lets her know he knows she's been manipulating him for years.

She combines the ashes and the magic in a wooden bowl. She has Vik stir it with the Elder's Stone. The stone transforms into a crystal dagger as it absorbs the concoction. She orders him to stab her. It breaks his heart, and he refuses until she tells him his Hunger will soon make him kill her anyway and remove any chance of freeing him from his curse.

Celie rises, rejuvenated, as the All-Mother.

As she explains why Gloribeau had been stripped of the mantle, allowing it to eventually pass to her, Viktor begins to die. She gives him a taste of her blood. It revives him and breaks his curse. He retains all his vampiric abilities but is no longer controlled by the Hunger. He can even make his fangs vanished or manifest attack will.

She tells him to go back to Hell's Breath Island to learn from Zeke what his new, ultimate task will be.

Zeke sends Vik to the island's interior in search of a stone with a notch carved to hold the Elder's Stone. He tells him he will meet a guide.

Vik finds Hezekiah Grimm and his family safe on Hell's Breath. Vik and the Grimms are both shocked by the encounter. They'd thought Viktor was dead.

Hezekiah shares how he came to the island after being stabbed and flung into the sea by the male siren. Viktor tells them of their erasure from memory in the world and his theory of why. He also points out their daughter, Celeste, is a potential heir to the All-Mother should Celie ever have to surrender the mantle. Celie had used part of her own life-force to keep Brianna and the children alive after their premature birth

Vik tells Grimm what happened with the sea dragon. Grimm leads him to an ancient cemetery full of stones too old to read surrounding a large, black granite marker. On it is Viktor's name. In front of it grows a cluster of blood red irises.

When Vik touches the flowers, they blacken and crumble to dust. The marker ages before their eyes, and a date,1619-1641 appears. The dash is carved in the exact shape of the Elder's Stone. Vik inserts it. When the magical glow subsides, the inscription has vanished. A small wooden chest pushes its way to the surface of the earth. In it, he finds an obsidian cross wrapped in silver wire filigree with a clear crystal mounted on it.

Viktor accidentally slices his finger on the edge of the obsidian. The blood fuses with the crystal, turning it red.

The All-Mother appears and tells him it is the different type of magic he will need for his next quest.

About the Author

Tamara A. Lowery, who once considered herself close to becoming a Crazy Cat Lady is now down to two cats. She lives with them and her husband in Tennessee and builds cars to pay the bills when not writing. She's been writing since the early 1980s but only published since 2011.

In addition to the Waves of Darkness series, she is the author of a steampunk episodic serial, The Adventures of Pigg & Woolfe.

She hopes to release a short story collection sometime in the near future, as well.

Website: talowery.wordpress.com

Facebook: facebook.com/Waves.of.Darkness

Instagram: Instagram.com/talowery_author

Plurk: plurk.com/Viksbelle

YouTube: youtube.com/user/Viksbelle

Waves of Darkness

Sisters of Power arc
Blood Curse

Demon Bayou

Silent Fathoms

Black Venom

Hell's Dodo

The Daedalus Enigma

Maelstrom of Fate

Daughters of the Dragon arc

Hunting the Dragon

Facing the Hounds *2026*

The Adventures of Pigg & Woolfe

Season 1

The Girl Who Fell from the Sky (S.1 omnibus)

Episodes

A Chance Encounter

The Truce

In the Woolfe's Den

Chase the Lightning

Peril in the Philippines

Rendezvous in Hong Kong

Double Jeopardy

Chance and Fortune

The Italian Connection

Rescue at Sea

Ghost Riders in the Sky

Castle in the Clouds

Season 2

Turmoil in Tunilia (S.2 Omnibus)

Episodes

Airborne Alliance

Under the Mountain

Reversal of Fortune

Frustrations

Going Underground

Evade and Elude

Escape

Sanctuary

Message in a Bottle

Strange Bedfellows

Family Reunion

Berthing Assignments

Season 3

Pathway to Downfall (S.3 Omnibus)

Episodes

The Canary Has Flown

Truth and Consequences

Forces Reunited

The Canary's Eye Conundrum

Season 5 *(TBD)*